The Age of Anxiety

The Age
of Anxiety

Pete Townshend

CORONET

First published in Great Britain in 2019 by Coronet
An Imprint of Hodder & Stoughton
An Hachette UK company

This paperback edition published in 2020

1

A CIP catalogue record for this title is available from the British Library

Paperback ISBN 9781473622951
Trade Paperback ISBN 9781473622944
eBook ISBN 9781473622920

Typeset in Sabon MT by Hewer Text UK Ltd, Edinburgh
Printed and bound in Great Britain by Clays Ltd, Elcograf S.p.A.

Hodder & Stoughton policy is to use papers that are natural, renewable
and recyclable products and made from wood grown in sustainable
forests. The logging and manufacturing processes are expected to
conform to the environmental regulations of the country of origin.

Hodder & Stoughton Ltd
Carmelite House
50 Victoria Embankment
London EC4Y 0DZ

www.hodder.co.uk

For Rachel

Book One

Chapter 1

Light. Blinding white light. A man is standing with his back to us, arms outstretched. He is naked to the waist. His hair is golden, curling, shoulder length. We cannot see his face. As we slowly approach the man from behind, he begins to block the light. The sun is setting. His hair creates a halo. Suddenly the man leaps forward and we fly with him, sailing through the sky, over the blue-green landscape towards the sunset.

It is with trepidation that I sit here in my eyrie this evening in June, a few days before my sixty-seventh birthday in 2012. I am Louis Doxtader, and this is my story. I am in the topmost room in a house already squatting high on a hill beside a busy road just outside the scruffy southern French hill town of Magagnosc. This house is rented and run by a rather lovely, but eccentric psychic woman who invited me to stay with her here this summer. I pay all the bills, and she looks after me so that I can write.

Only she knows why I am driven to relate this story. She knows my secret because she was a witness to it, and understands how important it is for me to demonstrate the way wonderful events have transpired as the result of something I once did that I greatly regret. I don't want to be forgiven; I want to sense some balance. I can't change the past, but neither can I allow a misunderstanding of the past to change the future. After you've heard my story, you will be able to make up your own mind.

From this lofty position where I sit at my little desk I can see the Mediterranean Sea and the distant Bay of Cannes, the port of La Napoule. Down in the valley is the nearby town of Grasse, famous for its perfume factories. Very few of the fragrances they produce reach me here, but the pine-scented air from the mountains that separate the valley from the pistes drifts down sometimes.

Doxtader, my surname, is probably Dutch in origin, but my great-grandfather was originally from Norway and I have lived in Britain all my life. My father Edvard – known as Ted – had been named after Edvard Munch who painted *The Scream*. A dark, presaging idea when I was a child, and possibly one that helped shape me, as will become clear I hope.

Munch was still alive when my father was born, and my grandparents had met the great man and been impressed. My father Edvard had moved to Britain between the wars, and remained here after the Second World War broke out. My mother always told me he had worked as a spy for the War Office during the war, Norway having capitulated to Germany. He was based near RAF Northolt Airport, west of London, from where he went on a number of flight missions to Norway. He met and married my English-Jewish mother Claire during the last years of the hostilities and I was born just as Germany was forced to give up on *Lebensraum*.

I first came to spend long periods of time with my godson Walter when he became friends with my daughter Rain. They were at the same schools together from childhood, and had been born respectively in December and August of 1966.

Walter is a musician. Even at the age of eight he was always blowing and sucking on a mouth-organ, often with his head inside a plastic bucket in order to amplify the sound and shut out the world. I was close friends with Walter's parents and in awe of the orchestra in which his father performed.

You might be interested to know how Walter Karel Watts got his middle name. Walter's father Harry was a superbly gifted classically trained musician, but also a science fiction enthusiast. Karel Capek was a Czech playwright who wrote *R.U.R.: Rossum's Universal Robots*. It was Capek's brother who came up with the word 'robot' which in Czech means 'drudge'. Harry had great things planned for Walter, which is why he gave his son a middle name inspired by Karel Capek's percipient play of 1920 about intelligent machines taking over the world. In his father's eyes Walter was destined for scientific greatness. Instead Walter chose playing the mouth-organ.

In their late teens Rain became a journalist and Walter went to horticultural school. But Walter ended up concentrating on the music of the mouth and its associated organs. Playing in pubs and clubs, he began to earn a good living even while he and Rain were still students. Walter became part of what has been called the Fourth Wave of rock, the one that happened in the nineties – bands like Nirvana, Pearl Jam and Smashing Pumpkins – but Walter's own music was a throwback to the post-punk years of the late seventies: the pub rock of Dr Feelgood, the Stray Cats, the Fabulous Thunderbirds and the Dave Edmunds Band. This was the simple, honest music Walter wished to revive and honour. Whatever wave he surfed in on, in my eyes Walter K. Watts was and always would be a twenty-first-century fifties pub rocker. That is an addled statement. I am prone to them.

I'm sad to say that as a middle-aged father in the early eighties I succumbed to drugs. I scrambled my brain, and but for a miracle would probably have died penniless. My wife Pamela left me, telling me she was taking herself off to a nunnery and for many years I didn't know where she was. Incredibly perhaps, she left me with Rain to look after. That turned out to be a clever move, at least for me. The responsibility of looking after Rain, who was still at school with Walter, probably saved my life. I have gone on to do as well in my field as Walter has done in his. For today – while Walter is a famous rock star – I am now a well-known and respected art dealer in what is known as Outsider Art. It is also known by slightly snobbish New York gallery owners – and of course by the French, who invented it – as *Art Brut*. It is drawing, painting, sculpture, carving and writing by artists who think differently, indeed they live differently. Sometimes their work is naive, sometimes it is obsessive, and sometimes it is extraordinarily fine or detailed. Behind such work there is usually a single idea, a single system. There is, sometimes, a revelation, a vision or a mental explosion underlying the work, and they feel haunted or even possessed. They may hear voices, like a schizophrenic, and believe they are being directed. Some believe God is guiding them.

The miracle of which I speak, the one that really saved my life, was that – perhaps because of what I had done to my brain – I was able to see the value in the work of such mentally complicated artists. I became one of the first dealers in Europe to specialise in Outsider Art. I was certainly the first outside France and New York. Wealthy collectors and even some of the best international galleries acquire this stuff now. Indeed, it was through my work as a dealer that I came across Nikolai Andréevich.

One day in the spring of 1996, sixteen years ago, a woman telephoned me at my home in London. As I have no gallery, I work from home.

'I hope I am not bothering you, Mr Doxtader, but I have been informed that you are the leading dealer in this country for Outsider Art.' The woman's voice was rather husky, with what I would call a rather posh accent, tweaked by a soft northern lilt.

'That's correct,' I replied.

'My name is Maud Jackson. I am the wife of Paul Jackson of the rock band Hero Ground Zero. Perhaps you remember them?'

6

'Yes I do,' I answered. But I was racking my brain, trying to remember one of their songs. 'How can I help you?'

She explained that she had something to show me that might be of interest.

Paul Jackson, I now recalled, had been a sixties rock star turned movie actor in the mid-seventies who had been the founder of Hero Ground Zero. The band's name had been meant to echo the kind of anger and frustration of his young audience in the language Salinger had used in *The Catcher in the Rye*. A critic described Holden Caulfield as a 'hero ground-zero'.

'What is it exactly you wish to show me? Are you an artist?' At the time my roster of artists was full, every one of my clients a difficult creature in one way or another. I was anxious not to over-burden myself.

'Oh no,' she responded quickly. 'I am not the artist in this instance. Can I come and see you?'

A few days later Maud Jackson came to my apartment-cum-gallery in Richmond in west London. As I opened the door to her I smiled involuntarily.

'Mrs Jackson.' I hesitated. 'Do come in. I was expecting someone—'

She cut in. 'Younger? Older?'

'Not at all!' Indeed, her age was immaterial at this precise moment. Assessing her quickly, as you do when someone new arrives at your door and you must invite them in and make them feel comfortable, I experienced a small but perceptible flutter in the region of my heart. Her face seemed familiar.

Maud Jackson walked past me into my apartment with an elegance and dignity that – as I watched her from behind – made me feel lascivious. I quickly checked myself. But there was something intriguing about the way she moved. The tilt of her head as she turned and held out her hand to me made me feel I had met her before. The shade of her greying hair suggested that she had once been a natural blonde. Her skin was starting to loosen a little, and to discolour slightly and its tone was uneven, but her strong cheekbones pointed to a striking beauty, or at least a diverting prettiness, that she must have enjoyed when she was younger. She was not tall, but had a strong and upright posture that gave her presence. Her shoulders were square; she might have once been a competitive swimmer. Her eyes were a pale blue, her unsettling gaze hinting at a more vibrant past; she had a frank and direct way of looking at you. I estimated her age at between forty-five and fifty. It was hard to tell.

I ushered Maud into my living room, decorated with the work of many of the artists I represent. I have kept a lot of the finest pieces for myself, and that has been the investment that makes me Walter's equal, financially speaking. Maud immediately walked across to an intriguing piece given to me by its creator: a calendar painting covered in dates and numbers.

'I love this,' she exclaimed. 'Who is it by?'

'Simeon Blake. He has an extraordinary memory for dates and historical events, and the progression in this painting revolves around my date of birth, and leads both back and forward several thousand years.'

'He uses a computer or something to establish that your birthday fell on a Wednesday in 1945?'

'He makes that computation mentally, and all the progressions involved, in microseconds. In this painting he has selected only my birthdays on June 20th if they happen to fall on a Wednesday. Not only that, but he can attach significant events, happenings and facts to every day he selects.'

'Remarkable!' Maud leaned closer to the painting as if in doing so she might unlock the mystery of Simeon's gift. 'I see that he hasn't attached any significant world events here on your birthday.'

'My birthday fell close to the end of the Second World War—'

'As did mine,' she interjected, giving me the opportunity to say that she looked younger than her years. Thank heavens I avoided doing that; it would have been corny. She was the same age as me, then, fifty?

'Ah! So . . .' I bumbled along, increasingly drawn to this attractive middle-aged woman.

'A few months,' she said, 'before the news of the gas chambers was published.'

'Ah yes,' I replied. 'My mother Claire was Jewish.'

'And so – you?' she asked.

'My father was not Jewish, and my mother's family were all killed in the war. Anyway, I live a secular life. I'm not sure about God. Are you?'

'Once I would have agreed with you. But recent events have made me revise what I grew up believing, or rather not believing.'

I offered tea, which she accepted, and I went to the kitchen and poured boiling water over the leaves in the pretty blue china pot I only brought out for visitors. Her voice carried from the living room, and again my heart bumped. Did she sound like my long-lost wife? I couldn't place what was giving me that pain in my heart.

I carried in the tea and set it down.

'So,' I urged. 'Please tell me what you have to show me.'

As she gathered herself I sensed she had something of a tale to tell. 'My husband grew old in his band. His bandmates were younger than he was and always wanted to do more touring than he felt comfortable with. In the early seventies there was no sign of the touring slowing down.'

'My godson Walter is a musician,' I said, interrupting her. 'He was a huge fan of your husband's band when he was a kid.'

9

I immediately felt I'd said the wrong thing, casting Maud Jackson's husband as a has-been from years gone by. I tried some redress: 'But of course Hero Ground Zero continued to enjoy lots of hits, didn't they?'

She shook her head. 'Their last big hit was in the early seventies. But by 1975, despite the lack of hits they'd enjoyed at the start, audience demand for their live shows was still growing around the world. I saw less and less of my husband Paul as the years went on.'

At this moment Maud became real for me. She was a good-looking woman married to a hugely successful rock star who had probably spent much of her life overshadowed by him, and perhaps alone and lonely.

I knew Jackson had acted in a movie. Walter had always been a big fan of Hero Ground Zero before becoming an R&B purist. Later, I did some research and got the whole story. At forty-three years old, worn down by commercial success with no creative expression, Jackson had broken up his band at the height of its success in 1979 in order to become an actor. The film – *The Curious Life of Nikolai Andréevich* – was written and directed by John Boyd, an eminent British cinematographer with Jackson in the role of Andréevich, a charismatic musician who starts a religious cult.

'Paul found acting extremely tough,' Maud continued. 'Rising before dawn and working until after midnight every day for several months was very different to the kind of intense but sporadic work he'd done in the band. Also, in the band he had been the boss. He'd had control of the schedule and the workload. He'd become a very heavy drinker but he stopped in order to cope with what he knew would be a punishing filming schedule. To his credit, John Boyd never pretended the filming would be easy for my husband. But he was a famously hard-driving and meticulous director. Paul reached a kind of pinnacle of anxiety as the filming of the last scene approached. He knew that soon he was going to have to fend for himself again, freed from the discipline of filming that had helped him stay sober.'

Maud wondered if I had ever seen the film.

'I did see it, yes,' I replied.

'Do you remember the final scene?'

I tried to summon up the iconic image; I remembered it had been absurd in a way, and rather overblown. Maud saved me the trouble; she rustled through the contents of her bag and produced a dog-eared page torn from the shooting script of the film. She handed it to me.

Light. Blinding white light. A man is standing with his back to us, arms outstretched. He is naked to the waist. His hair is golden, curling, shoulder length. We cannot see his face. As we slowly approach the man from behind, he begins to block the light. The sun is setting. His hair creates a halo. Suddenly the man leaps forward and we fly with him, sailing through the sky, over the blue-green landscape towards the sunset.

'So this is the last scene in the film?' I was confused. 'It seems like a grand beginning, an opening scene to an adventure.'

Maud laughed. 'It should have been. It was the beginning of a new phase for my husband, and for me too. But it was the end of the film.

'My husband had been standing on the summit of Skiddaw in the Lake District.' She sounded to be on the edge of tears. 'He looked down at the glory of Derwentwater and the blue-green hills; it is the most extraordinary spot. The cameras were rolling, and an enormous Klieg lamp behind him was singeing his hair. He was exhausted from two months of solid work. All these extraordinary images and events have since been handed down like folklore among the local people.'

She described the scene beautifully. I realised that at the time, her husband still lost to her, she had probably been trying to make something poetic out of her loss, as well as open up.

'So what happened then?' I asked.

'My husband lost his marbles.'

Maud went on to explain that the scene in question was to run under the credits to the film. This was itself unusual, as films are rarely shot in chronological order. It was – as they say – *a wrap*. Shooting over, the crew congratulated each other.

'One of the crew said that after flying down the mountain in the hang-glider, right over the second unit waiting down near the lake in order to shoot him flying low overhead, he was supposed to land and return to the unit in the second unit jeep. The helicopter chasing him could not follow as the light was fading. He disappeared into the gloom.'

'Where did he land?' I asked. I was becoming increasingly curious to know more. 'What did the film crew say?'

'None of them seemed to know,' Maud said. 'They said he would probably have found an updraught and would be flying low, although by this time it was more or less pitch dark. They said he was an expert by then. He had been practising of course, but . . .

'Naturally there was a boozy celebration-gathering held that evening by the film crew in the nearby White Horse Inn at the foot of the hills.'

Maud quickly looked away.

'I had arranged to meet him there but he didn't show up. I quickly realised something was wrong and set off alone to find him.' At that she fell silent, gazing out at the sky for a few moments.

'Do you believe in coincidences, Mr Doxtader?' Maud asked as she turned to look at me, searching my face for any sign that I might be an unbeliever.

'I don't think they are significant in the way some people do.'

'Neither do I,' she agreed. She looked down into her lap. 'It did seem to me that Paul's disappearance must have been planned in advance. I suspect the film producers recognised it would make a story that would greatly help the film. I felt no one was taking Paul's disappearance very seriously and thought they probably knew very well where he was.'

'But he might have been killed!' I was shocked at the idea that Jackson had been subjected to some kind of stunt. 'Surely they would have let you in on this?'

'Exactly,' agreed Maud. 'But one of the crew mentioned that the movie's insurance was still valid. They seemed rather callous.'

'Paul was their star,' I said. 'They would have needed him for all the publicity surrounding the release, surely?'

'I'm afraid I thought the worst of them all, but I also had a bad feeling about Paul.'

'That he had crashed?'

'Yes, but not in his hang-glider. I feared he had crashed emotionally at some point during the filming. He could be a very difficult man. As I say, he was used to being the leader, and making all the decisions in his life and career. He was also used to drinking hard whenever he felt under pressure. It had always been an effective medicine for him.'

'What are you saying? That he had screwed up the filming in some way?'

'Not exactly,' she said. 'My fear was that he had lost the affection of the team around him. Maybe he had started to drink again and they had become tired of him, and were probably all glad to get rid of him.'

'They surely knew they were getting a tricky old rock star when they hired him?'

'What do you know about the behaviour of the artist who drinks too much? Do you have any alcoholics on your own roster?'

'Very few of my clients drink. They are intoxicated enough.'

Maud smiled at this.

I wanted to talk about myself, to engage her in my story, to draw her into my life and feelings. 'I drank and used drugs myself,' I confessed. 'I know what happens.'

Maud did not seem surprised. She smiled once more.

'I climbed Skiddaw myself to search for my husband.'

How much she had loved her man, however foolish he was. I was envious of him.

'I don't want to make you do another interview' – I smiled, hoping to reassure her – 'but what happened next?'

'Well, I took a room in the White Horse Inn. But I hardly slept. So in the early hours of the next day, as soon as there was enough light, I got up and dressed and visited the local policeman who lived in a nearby cottage. To my great relief he arranged a search party. In contrast to the indifference of the film people, the locals treated it all very seriously. Apparently any soul lost on the fells gets the same response. After two days of searching – the team was getting increasingly worried – Paul was found.'

'Where? How was he?' What an extraordinary story she told.

She put up both her hands, and seemed to wave them in mid-air, as though impatient with me. 'I'm sorry, this is always hard to tell.' She went on: 'He had managed to fly about fifteen miles, as the wind was strong, and the hills indeed created lots of updraughts that kept him soaring. When he finally landed, he was alone in the dark. The search party who eventually discovered him were shocked at his condition.'

'Were you there?' I cut in. 'With the team who found him?'

'I was nearby,' she explained. 'I was there shortly after they found him.

'He was still stripped to the waist as he had been in the film. He was shivering, and at first appeared to be delusional. He'd been sheltering in a shallow cave halfway up one of the mountains. He was a pathetic sight,' Maud went on sadly.

Her eyes were now moist, but then she cheered up and began to smile.

'He was also quite impressive!' She grinned. 'He looked like a castaway on an island who is rescued after years of living on coconuts.'

She paused for what seemed like an embarrassingly long time. At first, I didn't stir, but our meeting was taking up a lot of my day.

'Would you like some more tea?' I offered.

Maud shook her head. She used her right hand to make sideways circles, like someone describing a 'movie' in charades.

'This is the amazing part,' she said. 'He told me he had experienced a divine revelation. Triggered by the heat and light from the film lights, and the sheer magnificence of the vista across Derwentwater, he had seen what he described as the "Harvest".'

My attention was sparked anew.

Maud went on with her story: 'He was extremely specific and very coherent about what he had seen, but he would not be talked down from the mountain.'

'What did he mean by the "Harvest"?'

'All very strange, but I knew my husband; he had definitely seen what he described. He saw a hundred angels, all in the shadow of one massive angel with wings that stretched from one side of the valley to the other, all flying low over a seething mass of several thousand human souls waiting for guidance and transport to wherever they were destined.'

'Destined?' I interjected. 'Where?'

'I assumed he meant to some other place: heaven, hell, the Astral Plane. I don't really know.'

I had endured my own awful visions as a result of drug withdrawal, but I had never myself experienced anything quite like what Paul Jackson had felt and seen.

Maud took out a small handkerchief and dabbed her eyes.

'I asked him where this flood of human souls were supposed to go, but he said he didn't know. When I allowed some scepticism to show, he said angrily that he had seen what he had seen, and he could never be the same again. But I believed him.' She turned to me, almost in an appeal.

Maud had stayed in her small room above the noisy bar of the White Horse for several months, sometimes spending a morning climbing to her husband's little cave. It was really more like a cutting in a hillside protected by a tree. On these occasions she took him various items he told her he needed: maps, a tent, a small shovel, a compass, a knife, pencil and paper, a waterproof jacket, a drinking water-bottle, a huge supply of small plastic gas-lighters of the kind used by smokers, blankets and a walker's backpack. He planned to kill small animals to eat, but she also took him food.

'I sometimes tried to give him money,' she explained. 'But he would never accept it.' Perhaps remembering the pain she had felt back then, the impotence and frustration, her face hardened and she suddenly looked older, her lips tight and lined like a smoker's.

'I thought he might have begged for money from fell walkers he came across on his walks.' At this memory, she smiled again.

'Why did you think that?'

'He sometimes had things in his cave that I knew had not come from me,' she explained. 'And in the second week of the second month I gave him a complete collection of Wainwright's *Guides to the Lakeland Fells*, and that he did accept. Do you know about Wainwright?'

I nodded my assent. It is often said that it would take a lifetime to cover all the ground that Wainwright himself had explored in order to produce his famous guides to the entire

Lake District; it seemed Maud's husband had dedicated what remained of the rest of his own life to the task.

'From the time I gave him the guidebooks,' she declared, 'he became much harder to track down.' Maud explained that her eccentric husband lived like a tramp-cum-hermit very successfully for a number of years on the hillside near Keswick.

'I'd almost given up hope of ever being able to have a normal life with him again.' As Maud spoke of all this her eyes filled with real tears, and I took the opportunity to move to console her, putting my hand on her arm. She dismissed my action, not kindly, with a series of impatient nods, dried her eyes and continued.

'Of course I called him Paul, his given name, the name of the man I'd married, but he told me firmly that he was now Nikolai Andréevich. He was living out the character he had brought to life in the film. I must – he said – call him Nik. He insisted that one day the world would understand that the revelation he had experienced had come about as a direct result of his work on the film. He said he had become a new man in those last moments of filming.'

'Does he still call himself Nik?'

She nodded. 'And I have accepted it, I call him that too.'

'How did you manage? Did you have anyone to help you?' I tried to imagine how she must have felt alone up in Cumbria, trying to keep communication with her husband open, desperately concerned for him.

'Three months after the final scene of the film was shot,' she said, 'the completed feature was released with the usual publicity fanfares. It was then I realised that even if it had not been planned by the producers, my husband's wild adventure, his absence, and the story of his mental condition were going to make useful and controversial publicity material.'

Boyd's film had been a success. The riddle around the leading actor's disappearance in the mountains of the Lake District, his visions, and finally his adoption of the elaborated name of the character he had played in the film, all added to the mystique of the project. The PR company spun the story to great effect but after a successful release the wheel eventually wobbled and stopped, and Paul Jackson was forgotten.

Eventually Maud returned to London and visited her husband less frequently. Sometimes she would drive all the way to Cumbria only to spend several days wandering the fells herself, never coming across him. Finally, she simply sent packages for him to a policeman she had come to trust, and he would march up to Nik's cave on his day off and leave them under a pile of rocks.

'Old Nik,' said Maud. 'Like the name of the devil!'

She was laughing again. Her husband Paul had re-christened himself Nikolai, and the locals and the fell walkers shortened it to the new nickname. He was rarely sighted in the area, but he was seen often enough for Maud to know he was still alive, still holding up his arms to the rising sun at dawn, and again as it set in the evening.

'I wondered,' said Maud, 'if he was still seeing the hosts of angels he had spoken about. Were they still ushering legions of lost souls? Was he seeing souls passing on to the next life?'

'The next life?' I couldn't hide the incredulity from my voice. Whatever each one of us believes, when we speak of such things in the modern world it is unwise to betray too much metaphysical faith.

I found Maud attractive and intriguing, but she seemed oblivious to my interest in her and I'm afraid my patience was really starting to grow thin. Our meeting was overrunning the time I had allowed for it.

'Interesting. But how,' I asked, I feared quite rudely when I looked back later, 'how does any of this concern me?'

Maud explained that having lived rough for fifteen years, a

few weeks prior to calling me, her husband had walked into the public bar of the White Horse Inn in the Derwentwater valley.

'He announced that he had come down from the mountain for good.'

The first thing Maud knew about her husband's return to the normal world had been a message that he was in a police cell in Keswick. The local people had become fond of Maud, and by reputation and gossip of Old Nik as well.

'The story was that one afternoon Nik appeared in the doorway of the inn. His hair was long and curling, afire with the light behind him.'

The Lake District in Keswick had been enjoying the quiet part of its season, spring was slow to set in and it should have been cold and rainy. That afternoon was an exception. The bar was populated by a few locals, a number of professional-looking walkers with the usual thick socks tucked into their boots, and a group of rather trendy-looking teenagers surrounding a gaudy, noisy, electronic gambling machine.

'My husband was lucky.' Maud glanced around my living room, her eyes flitting along the carefully hung paintings. She shook her head sadly, and turned back to me, looking me in the eye again. 'From the point of view of the people in the bar he must have appeared to be a strange old man. But one of a group of young farmers standing around the buzzing and burbling machine had recognised him from his days as a rock star, and as Nik roared that he was thirsty, they bought him a pint – really strong local beer – and he drank it down in a single throw.

'By the time the local policeman arrived to calm him down he was preaching hell and damnation.' Maud laughed. 'He hadn't had a drink for years, and was accusing the young farmers of trying to poison him. He was shouting that he would fly away; fly away back from whence he had come.'

I summoned the memory of insanities of my own for a moment. No doubt, in the ramblings of the freshly re-pickled alcoholic, Old Nik saw stars, frogs, goblins and probably fire-breathing devils with pitchforks.

Maud travelled north to rescue her old man the same evening, and after a brief appearance in court for disturbing the peace he was released. Then, following a brief round-up of his possessions, spread all over a dozen hiding places in the Lake District, she brought him home to their house in Chiswick. The one item she left behind was his hang-glider.

Despite his latest vision, it seemed that – at last – he had remembered who he really was, and had been all along.

'I still wanted to call him Paul of course,' Maud recalled. 'But even our close friends started to call him Old Nik, despite his youthful-seeming suntanned body and his lovely, long curly hair, which was still almost golden.'

Maud caught my eye as she said this. I must have looked sceptical again, for she looked down at the floor shyly and seemed slightly ashamed.

'I've had visions,' I said suddenly, wanting to bring her back to the present. 'I think I understand what Nik saw, or thought he saw. My visions were induced by drugs, but I saw extraordinary things.' I wanted to tell her about screaming faces I had seen in an old bedhead, while I was still married to Pamela. It was a long story. I took a breath to begin, but as if by this confession of sympathy I had qualified myself to be worthy of the moment, Maud unrolled the waterproof tent groundsheet she had brought with her, and I gazed at the first of her husband's magnificent drawings. I was astounded.

I greedily flipped through the sheets: there were at least twenty, and Maud said there were dozens more. Each one portrayed with breathtaking precision a single freeze-frame of Old Nik's vision of the angelic Final Harvest.

'This work is extraordinary,' I spluttered. 'It's stunning stuff. Imagine – if he could really see what he's depicted here – what that means!'

She told me that Old Nik had spent a number of his years while living rough making the drawings; that they were rolled up and stored in the cave where he had often sheltered. 'They were a complete surprise to me,' she continued. 'Paul had always been a competent artist. Ex art school like so many of his rock-star peers, but he'd never drawn more than a few simple portraits for family birthday cards in the past.'

I was gratified that none of the sheets was signed, because I knew immediately and instinctively that Nikolai Andréevich was a better moniker for an Outsider Artist than Paul Jackson. *Nikolai Andréevich*, I mused silently. Born while filming the story of his own rise and fall. Everyone in the world of Outsider Art should be gratified he had gone mad in the process.

It is a cliché to say it – and I am ashamed that such a bald notion passed through my mind as I surveyed the exquisite pencil and charcoal drawings before me – but I heard myself whisper. 'Maud,' I said, my voice barely audible, and quavering a little with excitement. 'You and I are probably going to make a lot of money!'

For the first time since she arrived in my apartment Maud looked happy, with a happiness I felt I knew. Again, my heart fluttered.

Chapter 2

By the time Maud came to visit me in 1996 Walter was already established in a successful career. His eponymous pub rock band was known as Big Walter and His Stand, later known simply as the Stand. He called himself Big Walter in homage to Little Walter, his mouth-organ-playing R&B hero from Memphis, Tennessee. Walter's band's name, the *Stand*, was in fact a reference to a way of standing. At certain points in his performance he would position himself like a statue, his mouth-organ in his right hand ready to play, held in what appeared to be an attempt to keep light from his eyes. His left hand was stretched out as though he were balancing on an imaginary surf-board, his knees slightly bent, and turned a little to the right, his body twisted slightly at the waist. When he took this pose, the audience knew they could soon expect a powerfully explosive mouth-organ solo, and the girls began to scream and the boys to shout.

After one such exciting night in 1995, Walter showed up at my flat. As I opened the door to him I was reminded of how good-looking he was, with his high cheekbones, but also that by some measures of good looks he was flawed. His eyes were rather small, and a somewhat indistinct colour, and for a man of just twenty-eight years old he looked weather-beaten, like someone who had worked for years on the deck of a fishing boat, or thrown ropes from a horse to lasso cattle. His hair was black, and thick, worn long.

Now he looked anxious, but didn't speak immediately.

It was late, and I was ready for bed, but he knew I took my role as his godfather seriously, and my door was always open to him. I had always been his mentor. I had long wondered if Walter thought I understood him in ways his parents didn't. Harry and Sally had been confused when he completed his horticulture degree and picked up his mouth-organ again. Had they expected he would become a sort of gentleman landscape gardener?

'Uncle Louis,' he said. (He'd always called me Uncle Louis.) 'I need some help.'

'OK,' I replied, worrying he'd turned to drugs or got into trouble with one of his fans. 'What's up?'

'It's hard to talk about this. I'm not going mad, but I know when I start to speak about what's happening to me you might think . . .' Walter seemed to lose momentum.

'Walter,' I said gently, 'of course you're not going mad. What is happening to you?'

'I've been hearing shit,' he said. 'Usually after gigs; I can't sleep.'

'Hearing shit,' I teased. 'Mmm. That's intriguing.'

'Uncle Louis.' He sounded rattled. 'I'm frightened.'

'Tell me what happens,' I said, serious now.

'Our shows have been amazing recently. Intense. I've been singing well, but my harp solos have been getting better and better.'

'That's good.'

'Yeah, it's cool, and the audiences have been going completely nuts.'

'That *is* cool,' I agreed 'So what's the problem?'

'I can't work out quite what's going on, or why it's happening, but I think I am making some kind of deep connection with the people down the front.'

Frankly I had no idea what Walter was on about and was trying not to look blank.

He continued earnestly. 'I know you deal with artists who have mental trouble, but they kind of fold it into their creative work.'

'Walter, just tell me what's going on.'

'You know, I've spoken to you about this in the past; some of our fans are there every single night, often right in the same position.'

'That irritates you? I think I remember you saying as much.'

'I fucking hate it, but I hate it that I hate it: they are fans. They pay the rent after all. But I feel I don't have to win them over, they're in the bag already. They don't offer a challenge. They know what I'm going to do next, what I will say between songs. I find myself some nights actually following their emotional lead rather than driving my own journey.'

'I see, but you said you were hearing stuff,' I said. 'What is it you're hearing? Is this to do with these loyal fans?'

'When the music finishes, when the applause dies down, there is music in my head that carries on – and sometimes it feels very dark.'

'Your ears are ringing?'

Walter laughed. He had a rhythmic laugh that rattled like a machine gun. For a moment the concern left his face, and he looked young again. 'Yes of course they are! But this is different. This is music, sound, and it's more than something in my ear. It's in my head and I can feel it as well. It's like I'm having attacks: sound attacks. It sounds crazy. I knew it would sound crazy.'

'No,' I tried to reassure him. He was getting terribly upset. 'It doesn't sound crazy, and it's obviously very serious, to you at least.'

He didn't reply.

'Walter?' I reached out to him gently; I had not seen my godson looking so vulnerable since he'd been a small boy. He sat with his hands in his lap, like a boy outside the headmaster's study awaiting a punishment of some kind. He looked up into the air, at the ceiling, then to his left and right.

'I can hear it *now*, Uncle Louis,' he said, his voice almost breaking into a sob. 'It feels like a kind of mental attack. I feel like calling this a *sound attack*. When I talk about it, or think about it, it comes back, I hear it again and I think it comes from the fans at the front.'

'Who else have you spoken to about this?' Walter was married to a beautiful Irish girl a year or two older than he was, called Siobhan Collins. 'What about Siobhan?'

'I've spoken to her about it.'

'What does she say?'

'She isn't wild about anything to do with the band, to be honest. All those pretty girls down the front. Anything to do with my band work is hard for her. She thinks I need to do more serious work, to take myself more seriously.'

'You mean she wants you to leave the band?' If I sounded surprised then, I also wondered where Siobhan was coming from – although I thought I probably shared some of her worries. Walter's manager Frank Lovelace was particularly hard-driving, with a large stable of artists. He always had an eye on the big deal, keen to make commission. Walter was pivotal to the band's success and Frank Lovelace had an overly controlling personality where Walter was concerned.

'I don't know. She's never said as much. But she's Irish!' He laughed again, that musical laughter bringing him back to life for a moment. 'She wants me to be the new Seamus Heaney or something.' He shook his head.

Siobhan worked for the BBC in the central newsroom in London. She was in charge of a group of foreign correspondents; one of her team was my daughter Rain.

'Have you spoken to Rain?' It was a silly question. Rain had been away in Afghanistan for a few months.

'Not about all this; listen, Uncle Louis, this has never happened to me before. I feel I'm jacking into thoughts that are coming from the crowd.'

'But it's what you're good at, Walter.' I was right, Walter often seemed to hold the audience in the palm of his hand.

'No, this feels very negative. Like I'm hearing their fears, magnifying them.'

'Tuning in to your audience, anticipating them is what you do. Especially well. It's what all good artists do. Surely Siobhan is proud of you?'

'She is, but it's not just the band she feels is beneath me. She thinks clubs like Dingwalls pretend to be better than they are.'

'They pretend to be like an Irish pub with fiddles and pipes and Murphy's fresh from the brewery?'

Walter laughed. 'I've been with her to a few of those back in Waterford. They're pretty wild.'

'I have no doubt they're full of pretty girls too,' I added.

For just a moment Walter seemed more like his old self. He had always been self-assured and determined, but I could see something had changed in him. We talked for another half an hour. I thought that listening, just listening, was probably better than trying to come up with ideas or grappling for a solution.

He had always told me that whenever he played music he had to listen. In fact, he claimed that good musicians were divided between those who listened and those who simply played. Great musicians did both: played and listened. Walter aspired to that greatness, and lately – when he listened – he had begun to hear these strange sounds that were both unexpected and unwelcome. So he was becoming afraid of this listening; he was terrified he would be unable to continue as a musician working with others.

A police car siren jolted me from my thoughts. I realised I hadn't asked Walter a very obvious question.

'So haven't you spoken to Harry?' Walter's father, my old friend. Harry had been a good father, if rather a distant one. He was, as I say, a successful musician, toured a lot, and seemed to live in an elevated world. Classical organ; Messiaen and Bach. Harry's wife, Walter's mother Sally, was also a confidante of mine, telling me about some of their difficulties as a couple.

'I don't want to worry my dad,' said Walter quietly. 'Not yet at least.'

'So you will speak to him?'

When there was something he didn't want to explain, or reveal, Walter simply said nothing. Now and then he would send a signal that he was considering whether to speak out or not: he would rub the side of his nose while wearing a slightly mischievous expression. Sometimes this would lead to him saying something. Sometimes it would just preface silence.

On this occasion he did speak at last but I got the feeling he was not saying what he had intended to express. 'I think I should probably see a doctor first.' Walter explained that he knew that if he talked to his father, his first response would be to ask if he had seen a doctor.

'Write down your experiences,' I suggested. 'It will help if you do see a doctor.'

'What, describe it? Or score it?'

Walter's technical abilities as a musician were not equal to his father's. He couldn't read or write music.

'You know I deal in Outsider Art, Walter.' I laughed. 'If you write it down, if you could enable others to get a sense of what you are hearing, you could join the fabulous artists on my roster. As a poet!' I laughed again, forcefully, trying to bring Walter into the present, to lighten what he was feeling.

He sat back and looked away.

'I can describe what I hear,' he said, looking up at me with a sad look. 'But I would find it very hard to turn it into music that people could hear.'

I'd known Walter since he was a child. But I knew the way he was perceived by others, by his bandmates, by his fans, by the band's manager. They saw him as someone who was 'merely' handsome, rugged and cool. He looked like a man who could do pretty well in a fight, but I don't think many people had any idea of his inner depths.

I'd seen signs of it even when he was a child. He had studied gardening and his dream was to create a maze one day, he said. He told Rain that it might take twenty-five years for a maze to grow thick enough to get lost in – even longer in some cases. Every maze could become a real labyrinth, given enough time and care.

He struck me as a young man who – unlike most of his friends who wanted their desires fulfilled as quickly as possible – understood the joy of waiting for nature to take its course.

'Was there anything else?' I enquired. Walter was holding something back.

Either I'd said the wrong thing, or I'd touched a nerve. Walter shook his head and picked up his coat and bag. A shaft of light caught his face and I found myself musing that this new vulnerability would make him even more irresistible to the women he allowed close to him. My daughter Rain had always loved him. The childhood crush had become an unspoken passion. Siobhan had sensed she might be a rival, and as her boss at the BBC always seemed to be packing Rain off to faraway trouble hotspots.

Walter hugged me and smiled his goodbye.

In the winter of that year 1995, my daughter Rain came to see me at my apartment – I thought for afternoon tea – and, using the door key I had given her, let herself in, crashed her journalist's attaché case to the floor, slammed the front door and threw her coat to the ground in the lobby. She strode into my living room, slumped on to the sofa and with a disgusted look, and without any preamble, announced that Walter was married.

'I arrived back in London, went to the office, saw the ring on Siobhan's finger, and asked a friend who was the unlucky man. She told me, "Siobhan married her boyfriend. Your friend Walter."'

Rain had been away in Afghanistan with a BBC unit travelling with a US-supported Mujahidin patrol on and off for two years, documenting the anticipated end of hostilities in the region.

Of course I on the other hand knew Walter was married and had been at the wedding on 25 June 1994.

'Why didn't you let me know, Dad?' Rain had tears in her eyes. 'I should have been there, at Walter's wedding. He was like my brother.'

I knew that what she really meant was that Walter was her passion; she should have been his wife. She must have known it would not have been feasible for me to contact her while she was on patrol with the Mujahadin. I had been completely smashed at the wedding. I remember almost nothing. I had woken up the next day feeling like death, and quickly tried to forget all about it.

As Rain sat, miserable – she had good reason to be upset – I stopped what I had been doing, poring over some accounts. I regarded my offspring intently as if for the first time. She was quite beautiful at that distraught moment. Her hair – cut short – was strawberry blond. Her skin was slightly freckled, pale and always sensitive to the sun. She had very little of my mother Claire's beautiful Jewish colouring, but she had inherited her maternal grandmother's strong bone structure. Rain was not the image of her mother; neither was she the image of me – lucky for her, as I am no oil painting. Rain's mother, my long-lost wife Pamela, had been pretty enough, and extremely ginger. I don't use that word pejoratively, I can assure you. I was a sucker for the look. It would be absurd to call her a redhead; Pamela was ginger, and delightfully so when she was young. Her appearance matched her personality. She was excitable, unpredictable and capricious. Spicy.

So it was a shock to me that, when Rain was born, Pamela suddenly decided to become celibate. Oh, and also to become a Catholic. Up until that time she had been, to put it as politely as I can, almost a nymphomaniac. She had been legendarily ginger: hot. As a young husband prior to Rain's birth I sometimes felt as if I had landed in paradise. No man could have wanted more from his wife sexually speaking.

I need you to know that women found me attractive. Some women still do. I'm a strange-looking man in some ways, a mix of racial stereotypes, the Aryan with the Jew. But it's worked well for me. I am middle height, with brown eyes, jet-black hair that I usually wear long, and although I'm getting thin on top, I have enough up there to pass for a man a little younger than my years. Not bad, for I've never looked after my body or my face. The one thing I find that occasionally causes some women to shrink away from me is my beard. It isn't long, and I don't always sport it, but I prefer wearing a beard – I feel my chin is a little weak. When I look in the mirror I don't often shout, *you hand-some devil, go get 'em*, as I splash on the cologne, but it has happened a few times. My face has the appearance of being wider at my forehead than it should be, but that's because my chin is small. I've painted a strange picture of myself, but Pamela often used to call me cute or gorgeous. When we made love, and our faces were close together in the half-light, I would call her beautiful – because that was how she looked then. She would call me handsome. I assumed she was telling the truth. But we

31

were never a family who exalted the notion of high self-esteem, and Rain didn't think of herself as the beautiful woman she had become. Men fell for her – but Walter always treated her like a sister.

Suddenly, as Rain sat – clearly seething, and the air buzzing with her beauty, the room sizzling with her abruptly evident but frustrated sexual energy – I saw her mother in her.

'Come on, Rain,' I said. 'My godson has married a fan, that's what she was.' I tried to laugh, but I was winging it.

This caused an even wilder display of irritation from her. 'Siobhan is super-smart, Dad. If she was a fan, she was also being secretive with me. They must have decided to get married on a whim. How could you have been at the wedding and not let me know?' She exploded, jumping to her feet, banging her palms on to her thighs so hard they probably bruised.

I didn't want to face the fact that I really didn't remember very much at all about the wedding. I had a dim recollection of giving some drugs to Siobhan's younger sister Selena who was there with her pretty friend Floss.

'Siobhan is actually older than me, Dad! Walter has married my fucking boss!' She had started to pace the floor, then stopped and, whirling around, slapped her hand on her forehead. 'Jesus! I reckon Siobhan packed me off to Afghanistan for two years while she did the dirty deed.'

Then Rain slumped again, and there were real tears.

Of course I did have influence in Walter's life and career. Rain knew this very well. I was Walter's chief mentor, his guiding light. Perhaps partly because he had seen me at my worst, and seen me recover, he listened to me. I could have helped him to see that my daughter was in love with him – if only I myself had noticed.

But I hadn't spotted Walter and Rain as potential lovers. I had missed a beat. To me they would always be a couple of kids playing in the garden in a paddling pool, or digging in the sand on the beach at Clacton. Being a single father is difficult for many obvious reasons, but I made it all even harder for myself by being an addict. The drugs didn't stop me functioning. They numbed some pain, but also my senses; I hadn't been entirely alert to what was happening between these two lovely kids right under my nose. They loved each other, but Rain had gone further and fallen in love romantically.

Rain would have been about ten or eleven when Pamela and I were attempting to hold our marriage together. I was using heroin as a way to survive my unrequited sex-drive for the ginger-fuck-fest-wife I had once enjoyed. One day in a very strange period in which I was trying to get off the smack, we decided – the ginger-fuck-fest-wife and I – that we needed a larger, wider bed.

'You want to sleep further away from me,' I mumbled pathetically, adding something I didn't mean. 'But I want to sleep further away from you too.'

'Ha!' exclaimed Pamela. 'You think this is a game.'

'No,' I corrected her. 'I do think a bigger bed would be a good idea for us. We've been married for a long time now. I know women get bored with their husbands. Maybe even find them irritating. Do I keep you awake?'

'You don't snore, if that's what you mean.' Pamela laughed. 'You don't fart; you don't say other women's names in your dreams. Truly, Louis, why do you think I want a bigger bed? So I don't have to have sex with you? Don't you think I can fend you off if you come too close to me? You're such a dope. I'll always love you, Louis. I want to give you what you need, but something has changed in me. It's massive, Louis. I wish this hadn't happened, but it has.'

It didn't occur to me to try to process what Pam signalled by her use of the adjective 'massive', but then heroin tends to dull

33

anxiety. I simply hovered between smacked-out insouciance and self-obsessed withdrawal. For Pam it must have been like living with a cuddly sheepdog that occasionally wakes up to chase a mosquito.

We found a sort of warehouse in Hampshire that sold old French beds, and drove out there to select one that suited us.

We agreed on a hugely overbuilt and oversize double bed that had a high walnut headboard and footboard. The headboard was richly grained, and in the rather dim light in the corner of the warehouse where the bed had been positioned, it seemed quite attractive. It was when the deliverymen assembled the bed in our sunny bedroom that I noticed something quite strange. The wood grain on one side of the headboard seemed to be more richly incised than on the other. It was as though one side had been persistently polished by some obsessive soul throughout the hundred and fifty years of its life in a grand farmhouse somewhere in France.

'You know what those marks are, Pam,' I pointed out. 'The darker grain is because someone's head has rested there, night after night, greasy hair – like wax – bringing out the images suggested by the natural whorls in the timber.'

'Yes, and those smudges are from a man's head,' said Pamela, grimacing with distaste. 'That's the man's side of the bed.'

'My side!' I managed a laugh, but I felt degraded by the exchange, and it didn't feel fair. I hadn't stained the damned headboard. I didn't wear any kind of gel in my hair.

My side. Smudges. Greasy hair. On my side.

I was an addict before I met Pam. When she eventually realised I was using the drug regularly, I think she really thought she could change me. In part, her failure to get me clean made my addiction worse. Shame was ladled on to discomfort when I tried to withdraw, and Pam was impatient. She was such a potent woman, so powerful and dominant. Was she a mother figure to me? No, I worshipped her like a goddess and I think that infuriated her. She wanted passionate and hearty sex, companionship and excitement. At first I think I intrigued her and, stoned as I often was, our languorous and lengthy sex sessions suited her. Then suddenly everything that was good about our marriage was slipping away. I had become a self-obsessed bore. Perhaps I'm being hard on myself. She had her part to play, but listening to me revel in my drug-induced hallucinations must have been infuriating.

At that moment, in the welling delirium of withdrawal and the feeling of Pamela's absolute disdain for me, and possibly – at that moment – for all greasy men, the whirls and shapes in the grain took on a psychedelic nature, and a dozen screaming ghost-like faces appeared, like those created by my father's namesake Edvard Munch. Somehow this image penetrated so deeply into my vulnerable psyche that for several months I became completely obsessed with figuring out who had once leaned his head in that spot on the bed night after night, and what had been in his mind – what nightmares, what visions, what horrors? I remember Rain, poor kid, trying to console me over and over again, promising she would help me somehow.

By the time I recovered, a week later, Pamela was gone, never to return, never to make any claim on me, never to make any claim on Rain. Pamela simply disappeared. I had no way of tracking her down. Of course my drug use got worse for a while. The hallucinations evolved into full-blown conversations with erotic nymphlike angels and diabolical gargoyles that I could touch and even smell if I wished. I was fearless, and therefore very dangerous to myself and my daughter. Pamela had no idea, I felt sure of that. Walter's parents, Harry and Sally, helped me greatly in that difficult time. They took Rain in for months on end, and let me stay in their guest room so I could be close to her.

They were both expert riders and because Walter had taken against horses as a child for some reason, they jumped at the chance to teach Rain to ride. It took her mind off my particular troubles that were of course really no worse than her own, and she adored their two horses. I often wondered then at how well Rain handled being without a mother. I remember Walter and Rain, barely twelve years old, both sitting in tense rapture as I described some of the peculiar things I was seeing in my head. Rain stopped trying to convince me she could help me back to sanity when she saw that Walter – who she worshipped – thought that what I was talking about was really very cool.

'Artists maybe see things differently to you and me.' I was sitting with them both before a blazing log fire, hot chocolate for them, cognac for me on top of a heroin and cocaine speedball. 'Or perhaps the difference is that they try to let us share what they see by transforming it into drawings, music or story. I wish I could be an artist. What I often see and hear when I'm not feeling all that great is as interesting and enthralling as what I feel when I'm joyful and happy.'

I wished I could tell them about the nymphs and gargoyles.

'When we feel pain, we know we are human, that we are alive. For me physical pain is not always something to be numbed, but what I do need to dampen down is what goes on in my head. I need to be able to see and hear it clearly, to have some distance, to be able to express it.'

The kids wanted to know exactly what it was I could hear and see. I didn't want to frighten them, but I wanted to explain myself, why I was the way I was.

'You're old enough to know about drugs. I bet the older kids at school are experimenting. But the chemicals in our own bodies and brain are far more powerful. If I stop for a moment, and look intensely at something – like the flames and smoke in the fire there – my mind can go either way. Like now I see nude women dancing. Nothing naughty, it's like a ballet. But now they turn into writhing golden snakes. Now the smoke looks like heavy fabric, and the embers hide a glowing animal beneath. Something like a whale, on fire.

'What an artist can do is take such images and turn them into something tangible. When one of my clients, the painters or sculptors that I represent, shows me their work, they know I appreciate that there isn't always a clear logic behind what they do. They might simply be trying to tap into what normal people might call madness.'

Harry and Sally Watts were part of the same set as Pam and me. We were arty-farty types who tolerated each other's eccentricities and self-indulgences, and could often be overheard saying to one another things like: *Your work ethic is what makes you who you are*, or *If you hadn't been a junkie you wouldn't be able to appreciate the kind of artists you work with*. We were all overly liberal and I think Harry and Sally thought my addiction was a kind of badge of honour. But we all made money, enough to live a decent and comfortable life. Harry and Sally lived with Walter in a pleasant road that ran along the quiet side of Ealing Common. Unusually, their large Edwardian house had never been divided into flats, and they enjoyed a huge rambling garden as well as the three guest bedrooms on the second floor that had rarely been used until my arrival with Rain. We were never made to feel we were in the way. I'm not a bad cook, so I was able to contribute to the running of the house, shopping and making many evening meals. Harry was often working in the evening, performing at concerts, sometimes away for days at a time. Sally seemed to genuinely enjoy my company, rather than merely tolerate it. She was a very successful painter of modern equestrian scenes, and of racing events and famous meetings like the Grand National. The fact that I dealt in art gave us some common ground.

Harry and Sally kept their horses at a large establishment in Harefield, a green belt village in Middlesex, about thirty-five minutes' drive from Ealing. Harefield's compact main street boasted a few antique shops and a post office, and the village was surrounded by fairly flat woodland and fields perfect for hacking and jumping. Rain quickly became an eager horse-woman, despite Walter's reluctance to get involved. Harry and Sally were regarded as experts, and although they didn't compete, they were keen on attending all the gymkhanas and dressage events in the area. Without the passion for horses and riding, that fire, that explosive exhaustion that his mother in particular felt after a gallop, Walter would never have been born. She told me that it was only after a gallop that she and Harry could make love.

In this upper-middle-class world, caught between town and country, art, music and the meadow, Harry and Sally managed to make this a relatively happy time for Rain and me. One distinction in parenting protocol that arose awkwardly in our time at the Watts household was that Walter and I seemed rather to follow our noses in our chosen pursuits, while Harry, Sally and Rain believed that intense and long practice sessions were what led to success.

I understood perfectly that without her old-school training in fine art Sally would never have become the excellent draughts-woman she was. She had churned out nearly five hundred paint-ings and drawings before she made her first profitable sale at the age of thirty-one. Her style was refined and perfected by that time, and yet still evolving. She had never stopped training: she sketched constantly, taking advice and lessons from other paint-ers, and analysing the work of the great equestrian painters who had gone before, or were her contemporary competitors.

For his part, Harry practised incessantly on his large home organ. It was an old-fashioned console with three keyboard manuals, two ranks of stops and a full pedal-board, but it was entirely electronic, and he often practised late into the night wearing earphones. It was as if he became part of the machine; he could play almost any organ music placed before him. His sight-reading was unconscious and perfect. And yet his performances were highly regarded for his ability to bring emotion and new life to the well-known organ classics.

Rain, riding as often as she could, jumping like a champion, wanted to be a writer. She read constantly, but also wrote stories and poems and was soon contributing almost fifty per cent of the content of the magazine published monthly by the Harefield Equestrian Centre they used.

I ran against the grain. The paintings I preferred were mainly by untrained artists. The music I liked best tended to be by the renegades of serious music. So I introduced Walter to a lot of wild jazz and primitive folk music as well as some of the less conventional orchestral composers of the period. Walter seemed to lean this way too: he learned harmonica, piano and guitar without lessons of any kind. His practice was self-indulgent; he played what he wanted to hear, or he tried to play what would most delight him. So he was constantly aspiring to do better, but never thought to have lessons. Harry couldn't really help Walter musically; his own world was too traditional and conservative. Sally often complimented Walter if she heard him play something she liked, but she too had taken the academic road and wished that Walter would work with a real music teacher rather than hang out with me listening to my old vinyl albums of Fats Waller, Louis Armstrong, Sun Ra, John Fahey, Bert Jansch, Davey Graham, Archie Shepp and Stockhausen.

We were all surprised, pleasantly, when Walter suddenly took an interest in the neglected garden at the house in Ealing, and began to work it, almost intuitively as well as skilfully, into a semblance of order and dignity. It seemed natural then that he should be attracted to nearby Kew Gardens, and to the lectures and tours there, and after his GCSE exams he enrolled as a student at the Royal Agricultural University near Cirencester. Harry's sister and Walter's favourite aunt, Harriet, lived in nearby Tetbury, so the location was perfect. Walter studied for two years, and passed his finals with honours.

Then, to Harry and Sally's chagrin, he joined Crow Williams's band. Crow was already doing very well at Dingwalls at the time, but he accepted that Walter's charisma and talent would be a boost. Crow also wanted not to be a front man, and it was he who christened the reoriented band 'Walter and His Famous Stand'.

For a time while sharing the Watts' home, I became increasingly unhinged. Stopping using heroin isn't the hardest thing, at least not for me. It's dealing with the creative itch that is tricky.

As I say, I had explained to the kids the extraordinary things I could see, but now this became an uninvited part of my everyday life. I wanted to be clean, to live with who God made me, as it were. So one day, I can't really remember exactly when, I committed to getting straight, and it was then that I realised why so many addicts don't manage to stay clean. It isn't the misery of withdrawal that propels you to pick up again, it's the enormous magnitude of what it feels like to be merely a normal human being, passing through a regular day. The bedhead visions that had so irritated Pamela began to flood into everything that I looked at intently. I started to see, in every piece of wood grain, what I took to be the faces of various incarnations of gods, messiahs and other divine messengers.

This didn't feel like madness to me. It felt like revelation. I felt as though I were being given clues, signals and signs that I was on the right track, that I was in contact with a spiritual mechanism that would free my soul. These 'found' images were the basis of a new code for me. I was becoming increasingly obsessive as the months passed. Then I diversified, seeing the very same kind of beatific or screaming faces in the pattern on the linoleum on the floor of my GP's waiting room, in the clouds in the sky, in smoke rising from a fire or in the ripples in running water.

I would like to try to explain what transpired, how I found my way back to sanity, but it is really, truly, another story. In a way, Walter and Rain, even as the little kids they both were, really did help me. As I say, they listened. I worried that I might have frightened them, planted terrible seeds of fear about what might happen to the human mind given enough stress, trauma and ginger-fucking-headed-nympho-disloyalty. In my case after several years I 'relapsed', as addicts call their return to drugs.

Even now, as I write about those times, my anger returns. Those kids helped me. My own story is tightly interwoven with Walter's.

Let's just say that after a while, I got well. By the summer of 1995 I was clean. As a result of what I had seen, and suffered, I began to look for the aberrations in art, the distortions and the nightmares. What I had experienced, and the visions I'd had, would have enriched my life had I been a painter like Munch, or Van Gogh, or Dali. But I am not an artist, and yet I had seen ghosts, and then found a new language in every aspect of nature, that spoke to me of good and evil and all the shades in between. Best of all, soon after, I discovered the Outsiders, the *Artistes Bruts,* and in the end I felt that it was probably all predestined.

Chapter 3

In the summer of 1996 the time came when I had to speak to Andréevich formally about our business affairs. He, the artist. Me, his dealer. Maud brought him to my apartment, and it quickly became clear that despite her great love for Nik he was starting to irritate and annoy her terribly. He was fidgety, and uneasy, but smiling all the time, in a dreamy, unengaged way. He had begun to look so much older than Maud. His long curly hair that she had once described as 'golden' now looked dirty. His skin was wizened by the sun; he was still handsome, but looked smaller than I imagined he would be, but that is often how the pop stars of our youth appear when we confront them for the first time face to face. They are often smaller, or taller, uglier or better looking. Photographs, movies and television all deceive in different ways. I'd never seen him perform, but knew his records. He was growing old, shrinking into himself. He seemed to be at the absolute centre of his own world.

'You like my paintings?' He picked up one of his own charcoal drawings that was now beautifully framed, already sold to a collector who happened also to be a retired rock star (one of Nik's peers in fact).

'Very much, Nikolai,' I said. 'What you saw up in the Lakes was extraordinary, but even if you had simply drawn things you imagined your work would be stunning.'

'I saw it all right,' he barked, but not aggressively. Rather he almost shouted gleefully. 'A huge angel that filled the sky.'

'Yes, dear,' soothed Maud. 'There is no question about what you saw.'

'My godson Walter would send his respects, I know.' I wanted to distract them both. 'He has all your albums.'

'Our first album sold forty-five thousand copies in the first six months, but in ten years it had sold close to one million: nine hundred and seventy-seven thousand, six hundred and forty-nine copies.'

'Amazing that you can remember!'

'Our second was much more successful. We sold two million, seven hundred thousand—'

Maud interrupted him: 'Please, Nikolai . . .'

'You can't stop me now,' he shouted. His head was high in the air, rocking from side to side. Indeed, she could not stop him, and he listed the precise sales of every one of the twelve albums his band released prior to his appearance in John Boyd's film. It took nearly ten minutes.

'Last,' he said, coming to the end, 'was the album we called *Hero Ground Zero* which contained the song "Hero Ground Zero" that was written for John Boyd's film, in which I appeared as Nikolai Andréevich. That sold quite poorly because I had left the band before the filming, and we didn't tour. Just eight hundred and fifty-two thousand copies – it's the only one I don't have precise figures for.'

'Precise enough!' I laughed.

'No!' He turned on me, very serious. 'Not precise enough at all; I wish I had exact figures.'

'The film changed things for you,' I said, a simple statement of fact that seemed to divert him and bring him back into the present.

'I saw these wonderful things,' he said, smiling happily. 'And I was able to draw them. Now I paint them. You sell them. Maud gets money. This is all very good indeed. I am very happy about it.'

'Good!' I agreed, watching Maud who appeared to be terribly uneasy, perhaps embarrassed at what a simpleton her husband had seemed.

Nik noticed Maud's anxiety and startled both of us when he spoke again. 'Louis likes you, Maud,' he said. 'I can see that. I'm not jealous.'

This unsettled me. How did he know I was so attracted to Maud? I supposed he had an eye for it, or sixth sense.

He turned to his wife. 'I neglected you, Maud, when the band was on the road all the time. But darling, I never cheated on you. All the other rock guys were cheating, but I loved you so much. We should have had children, Maud. But how could we have a family when I was away all the time? Life is better now. Don't you think, Maud? Don't you agree that life is better for us now?'

Maud nodded, looking shyly at me. It was clear that Nik was a good-hearted man, a sweet, kind man. What he had seen, and his representations in charcoal and paint obviously delighted him; he felt special. He felt chosen. He was proud of himself.

'Life is good, Nik,' she agreed. 'Better now, yes.'

But I sometimes wondered if Nik's dependence on her was hard for her to accept. Now she looked at me awkwardly, as if to say: 'I will never have any peace now.'

It occurred to me while we were talking that Nik might be able to give Walter some advice. Despite Maud's discomfort I decided to take a chance. Walter was frightened, troubled and on the edge of depression. Nik by contrast was happy.

'Maud, Nik, can I prevail on you for some advice?'

They both nodded.

'I told you about my godson Walter,' I continued. 'He has been experiencing some strange things himself. Not visions, but sounds, like music, and it is rarely pleasant.'

'You think Nik could help?' Maud looked quizzical.

'You know, yes, I do think he might be able to help,' I confessed. 'Nik seems to bear what happened to him, the massive breakdown he suffered, with such equanimity, and he has steered it to such a wonderful outcome with his art.'

'Nik was a working musician once, just like your godson.' She was ready to agree. 'I can't see any harm in trying.'

I described what Walter had been experiencing, without embellishment; my godson was hearing daunting sounds that he believed might be emanating from the people in his audience. Nik and Maud listened carefully. Then Nik seemed to make a decision.

'There is no question,' he interjected firmly. 'I can help your godson. I know exactly how to help.'

After they left, I considered whether I should call Walter, and when.

I hadn't spoken to him for some time. His manager Frank Lovelace was, as I say, an extremely hard-driving and high-achieving man, and I'd heard that Walter was becoming uneasy about where his band were headed under Lovelace's guidance.

Lovelace was good-looking in a slightly battered east London way with a good head of dark hair. He was mid-height, about five foot nine, and carried himself lightly, in a manner that suggested he would be fast-moving in a fight. He was always suited up, in a kind of shiny mohair that looked cheap but was actually very expensive. He was not always without a tie, but he preferred expensive dark shirts in equally expensive-looking material, often with gold or silver thread at the seams, two top buttons left open. His hands were calloused because he spent a fair bit of time boxing for a hobby as his slightly battered nose betrayed. His eyes were a vivid blue, his teeth rather wolverine, but they were shiny white. Even so, his breath wasn't always good. One felt challenged not to grimace and look away when he came close in order to say something intimate or secret.

To make deals in the music business it was not unusual for managers to be tough guys, and to intimidate the record company people into favouring the artists they represented, but also to bully the artists in order to make good careless promises they had made to record companies or show promoters.

'He'll do what I fucking say,' Lovelace would tell the business people he dealt with, the show promoters and record company bosses. 'Just give us the advance we need and leave him to me.'

If there were any qualifications or reservations he might sink into personal attacks.

'Listen,' he would hiss, his face inches from his adversary. 'You fucking little twat. I was in this business when you were at school lusting over Debbie Harry.'

Despite my conviction that he was potentially an artist destined for more than Dingwalls, and that Lovelace's efforts could almost certainly make him richer, Walter seemed to be entirely comfortable in the old dive, and in other modest venues like it. He appeared to love the smoky pubs and clubs packed to the roof with fans who could reach out and touch him, punch him or even spit at him in the Fourth Wave manner if they wished. The band was selling a lot of albums and CDs, and he and Siobhan had a good little flat in South Ealing. She had also inherited her father's cottage in Duncannon close to the sea near Waterford in Ireland. They retreated there sometimes when Walter wanted to write new songs. Walter's band line-up was simple: singer with a mouth-organ, guitar, bass, drums.

I'd often been to see them at Dingwalls – rehearsals and live performances. I'd station myself at the bar at the back. On guitar was Crow Williams. Crow was a purist. He played a Fender Telecaster with heavy strings through a small, but loud, vintage Fender Deluxe amplifier.

'For fuck's sake,' he would shout in rehearsal. 'I can't fucking hear myself. And when I can hear, we sound like a bad imitation of the fucking Shadows.' His Telecaster would bounce off the wooden floor and there would be another scar on its pale cream body. The band members just looked on, impassive. Crow never hit anyone, but he was scary.

He used no effects. No pedals, no echo, no compression. He got his name from his black hair that he wore long like Ronnie Wood of the Stones; or it could have been from his grim expression and slightly hooked nose. He was striking-looking, and attractive to women – his blonde wife Agneta was a stunning and voluptuous Swedish businesswoman who looked like a glamour model. Crow had met Walter in their college days. He had been at a nearby college studying art, while Rain was at the same place studying journalism, so he knew her pretty well. Rain told me that Crow was really the leader of the band, even though he never wrote songs and never spoke about the band in public. In group interviews with the press he would never utter a single word, and rarely even nod to support what the other band members said. But he was the one who decided what they would play, how they would play it, and even how long they would perform. He was against on-stage showing off of any kind, except by Walter, who was permitted a few lairy moments simply because he was the front man. Crow never seemed jealous of Walter's status or reputation. Whenever creative matters came up for discussion, for example prior to recording sessions, he would simply pull out the same six vinyl albums.

'Let me remind you lot what our mantra is here – what it is we do.' Then he would yank his shabby army-surplus bag open and lift out several old vinyl albums. 'This is the pinnacle. This is the White Cliffs of Dover we jump from. This is where we start. We are a pub rock band; we do not play fucking jazz.'

The albums were *Booker T and the MG's Greatest Hits*, *Jimmy Reed at Carnegie Hall*, *The Everly Brothers Greatest Hits* (two albums), a white label collection of Johnny Kidd and the Pirates' singles, *The Best of Little Walter* on Chess Records, and Bob Dylan's *Nashville Skyline*. Crow wanted to control where they were supposed to be heading with their music, not merely to exert influence. Somehow, after sitting for several hours in moody silence while Crow made the band members, and anyone else who was creatively involved, listen to each album or set in turn, the band would knuckle down. As soon as they began to play one got the impression of a large old American car with a V8 engine always spitting nearly a quarter of a gallon of wasted gasoline from its exhaust pipes on to the tarmac before it finally got rolling ruthlessly towards you blowing out blue smoke.

On bass guitar was Steve Hanson. Hanson, as he liked to be called, was the exception to the pub rock rule in Walter and His Stand.

'We get it, Crow,' he would say. 'No jazz.' He would rub the side of his nose slowly and deliberately, aping Walter's quirk, both teasing him and getting a conspiratorial smile from him in return: Crow was too serious, that was their message to each other.

Hanson was tall and very heavily built and possibly even a little overweight. But he was regarded by everyone as a gentle giant. The truth is he could have been a fighter if he'd wished, but was too laid-back to bother. His grey-blond hair was long, and slightly thin on top, often pulled back in a ponytail. He usually wore light-coloured clothes, safari jackets, and sometimes even those Australian hats that seem too big, and should come with corks hanging down, like Crocodile Dundee. In winter he always wore a raincoat that nearly touched the ground. He didn't care if he looked unfashionable.

If he had not been on bass, more of his extraordinary musicianship might have been manifested. Indeed, it was a measure of his musicianship that he was both able and content to serve as bass player, and to do so without any ostentation whatsoever. He never played an unnecessary or superfluous note. And yet he was a gifted pianist and classical organist, and when Crow allowed, Hanson would move to the Hammond organ (always played straight, without the whirling Leslie speaker sound so loved by most rock keyboardists) and covered the simple bass patterns required for Walter's music with his feet and the organ pedals.

'When you play a Hammond solo can you just play the fucking notes and not twiddle that underwater thingie,' Crow would command, and grin menacingly, but Hanson understood. No whirling Leslie speaker.

'Keep your effing wig on.' Hanson held his own with Crow, never raising his voice. 'I get it. We need to be more *Green Onions*, more early Booker T than Billy Preston. But fuck it, Crow, both those guys are geniuses.'

'But you're not,' Crow would retort. 'Keep your Grade Seven shit out of this band.'

Hanson often quietly took Walter aside and made him sit and listen to the experimental orchestral recordings of György Ligeti and the advanced and anarchic piano jazz of Bud Powell. The intention was never to try to broaden what they did in the band, nor to challenge it, merely to acknowledge that crazy music was out there, and that what they were doing was providing a kind of deeply rooted backbone, a link to the very guts of popular radio music most appropriate to listen to while driving down a long straight road.

On drums was Hanson's wife Patty. Patty was – like her husband – a musical dark horse. She too had studied at the Royal Academy, and could play viola, most of the instruments in the baroque viol family and she could do OK on cello. She could play double bass too if the band ever wanted to take their music down a tone, and evoke the early Nashville Hank Williams Trio sound that Crow occasionally permitted. Patty also had an extraordinary and versatile voice that was mostly wasted in the band. She could read music, of course, and could sing opera if she wished. She could also emulate and imitate almost any female singer under the sun. She did wonderful, funny impressions of Dolly Parton, Tammy Wynette, Nina Simone and even singers with quite unique voices like Ella Fitzgerald. What made her so great as a pub rock drummer was that it sometimes seemed she could barely play. Despite her extraordinary body, statuesque and curvaceous, but also graceful and strong – a body that had already passed into legend among her fans – she didn't appear to have the strength or coordination to be a powerful rock drummer, and so she played very little, but very well, and very tightly. This was precisely what made the sound of the band so distinctive. Because they were so tight they seemed louder than in fact they were.

It might be useful here to speak about Walter strictly with respect to his work and role in the band. As a musician Walter was disciplined and devoted. He felt supremely lucky to do what he did, and not to have to follow the career path laid out for him after college, slaving in some commercial garden-centre-cum-blue-rinse-lady's day out like Wisley, pruning roses all day. His song writing was always impulsive, he rarely thought deeply about what he would put down on paper, and usually left the music to Crow to polish off. Walter could play both the guitar and the piano pretty well, and did so on the demo recordings he made in his little home studio, but unlike Crow he was not averse to experimenting with effects boxes on his mouth-organs to create new rhythms and complex and interesting sounds.

Walter's wife Siobhan, like me, had great ambitions for him, but of a different nature. As Walter had told me that night when he suddenly turned up at my flat, she felt he could be a poet. In my view, had he not chosen Dingwalls as his primary performance venue, Walter might have made a half-decent poet. The fact is, few people know what a poet really is, or what a good poem should be, whether it should be spoken or sung, or rapped out in street slang. Walter had a fairly good way with words. It was his immense good fortune that Crow had absolutely no interest in taking any credit for helping Walter to complete his very basic home demo recordings. The fact that Crow helped Walter tighten up his songs but wanted no share in the writing royalties meant that neither of the other two members felt they could demand a share. Walter didn't think about this very much; he made about three times as much money as the rest of the band members, but they sold plenty of CDs, the proceeds of which they all shared, and they all lived well enough.

It must be said that, although Crow felt sure neither he nor Walter would ever leave pub rock behind, Steve and Patty Hanson wanted to be famous and rich. This was not about amassing money. It was because they knew that sooner or later they would begin to feel trapped by the sheer simplicity of what they played in the band. Being rich would allow them to diversify, and maybe to do so in a medium less commercially safe than pub rock. They saw Big Walter and His Stand and their residency at Dingwalls as a stepping-stone. Walter and Crow were both aware of the Hansons' ambitions, but it was also very clear that Crow for one had no conception of what they might have in mind. Crow had deliberately confined and limited his musical language in order to give it nozzle power. He might have understood that the Hansons might want to write symphonies, but he would have had great difficulty allowing the idea to stay in his mind long enough for him to start worrying about it as a reality. It would be like someone sitting down to enjoy a meal consisting of a perfect steak, salad and fries longing instead for *foie gras* and mixed olives. It simply wasn't conceivable; it was not in his vocabulary.

The Stand wasn't exactly a straitjacket for Walter. There were subtle differences in the band and musical influences beyond the basic pub rock, but I knew none of them could help him with the strange sounds he was hearing. He too seemed to sense that. The politics in the band were set in stone. Whoever he turned to, he would upset or distract the others. Crow might understand, might even be sympathetic to Walter's dilemma, but he would want him to 'man up'. The Hansons would start prattling on about Stockhausen and the mysticism of sound, and Crow would flip. Crow was the boss. He represented the end-stop to all and any musical diversions.

Many months later, after some time worrying and fretting about how I might help my godson, a new possibility had presented itself.

I phoned Walter on a warm, sunny morning in August. 'Walter! I met with Paul Jackson, Nikolai Andréevich now of course. I'm selling his paintings for him.'

'Aha, terrific,' breathed Walter. 'How did that come about?'

I explained about the visit from Maud, Andréevich's wife.

Walter had loved *The Curious Life of Nikolai Andréevich*, returning to the cinema to see it over a dozen times when he was between the ages of eight and thirteen. It had become something of a cult classic, shown regularly at the Electric Cinema in Portobello Road.

'He's a painter now?'

'Extraordinary drawings and paintings made while he was living rough up in the Lakes.'

'Does he still make music?'

'I think he experienced a really enormous trauma of some kind, while he was working on the film. He just produces art now. I say that, although he hasn't done anything new since he returned to his wife, but I'm hopeful. I'm just organising the first exhibition of the works he did while he was up the mountain. There are lots of them, and they're all good.'

'So how is he? Is he OK?' said Walter.

'He is very clear about what happened. He speaks of a revelation.'

'Not mad then?'

'Not mad,' I confirmed. 'Neither are you mad, Walter.'

'I'm hearing some really strange stuff; you know that. A psychiatrist might regard me as mad. A little bit.'

'You told me about the "sound attacks". Isn't that what you called them?'

'Yeah,' he slurred. 'And I've been getting more of them. And there's something new: I am starting to see lights now too, and they usually combine to form a single very bright light. You know I don't do drugs.'

'That sounds like Nik's final moments in the movie,' I said. 'His revelation began that way, with the intense light from the lamps used to backlight him. Is it like that?'

'Not quite,' said Walter. 'I do see a light, almost like a star in the sky, but it's explosive. Inside that starburst is a child.'

'Like in the movie *2001*?'

'Classic film!' Walter laughed. 'It's similar in a way; what I can see is a baby girl I think. It's like a black hole in reverse. A kind of birth in the cosmos.'

Walter really did need to speak to someone. I decided to press him. 'Listen, Walter, Nik would be happy to speak to you. I think he could help you. What he experienced is not precisely the same as you, but he found a way to . . . to survive.'

'Survive,' repeated Walter.

Mere survival didn't seem like a great offer, I realised. 'He is also happy. Very much so.'

I didn't add that he seemed to have become almost autistic in his behaviour. Walter would find that out for himself if he met with him.

I went on: 'He will make as much money selling art as he ever made selling records.' By then I had sold at least ten of Old Nik's pictures for between twenty and two hundred thousand pounds. I knew Walter didn't care that much for money, but I was making a practical point. Nik would make a good living working as an artist, despite his afflictions. 'You should meet him. He will help you, I'm sure of it.'

'Can I come to your place and see his work?'

'Of course you can,' I replied. I felt I'd made a start.

Walter arrived at my flat two weeks later; the summer of 1996 was drawing to an end. When I saw him face to face, I thought he looked different. Usually so self-consciously cool – like one of those carelessly handsome young male models-actors in a perfume commercial – he was now uncharacteristically eager, and seemed younger. I was reminded of how he had been as a kid when I described my hallucinogenic adventures. Whatever was going on had shaken him.

Walter looked at a few of Old Nik's paintings and drawings at my flat. There was one in particular that caught his eye. A huge angel filled almost the entire canvas, and unusually this particular painting was almost mono-tonal; there was no colour, no relief from the apocalyptic vision. But what caught Walter's eye was the face of a child, neither male nor female – a kind of cherub-seraphim – who seemed to live within the flowing robes of the huge angel. He drew my attention to it.

'This face,' he said with restrained excitement. 'This is very much like the face I see in the starburst when I get my sound attacks. It's a familiar face. It's half child, half angel.'

'Are you sure you're not seeing your own 2001 star-child, yet to be born?' I laughed. 'Have you and Siobhan been discussing plans to have a family?'

Walter smiled and looked at me. He looked down and shook his head almost shyly.

Poor me. Poor Louis Doxtader. As the moment approaches when Walter Karel Watts meets his hero Nikolai Andréevich I can feel myself, and my great secret, fading inevitably into the background of this story. I sit in my eyrie to write. In the last few days of my writing here in the south of France the weather has been sunny and the view clear all the way to the sea. My Collie dog Bingo, rescued by Siobhan from a rather cruel farmer in Ireland, sits at my feet, breathing deeply, staying cool in a shady corner, but the window is wide open and a breeze is blowing. This morning we walked together in the small botanical reservation behind the hilltop village of Châteauneuf, and tried to avoid crushing the exquisite purple, yellow and blue wild flowers growing there. Already shimmering, they were set sparkling further with the fluttering of pale blue, brown-red and white butterflies of various sizes. As I threw a stick high in the air for Bingo, I spotted what looked like yet more butterflies hanging in the sky in the distance above the mountains behind the Château and Monastery of Gourdon, thirteen hundred metres above the sea and about fifteen kilometres away. There were a dozen or more hang-gliders, some swooping, some as still as humming birds, working the vortex rising along the ridge of the mountain.

That was one of the things Walter had loved most about Old Nik's film when he was a young teenager: it was the first time he had seen a hang-glider. In the movie, as Maud had described when she came to visit me, he leaps from a mountain top in a hang-glider and soars above a huge lake. This was set up to illustrate how Nikolai Andréevich had been spiritually liberated by the abusive privations he had to undergo in the story.

So I fixed a meeting and in September Maud and Nik turned up at the flat where Walter got to meet his childhood hero.

'My husband, Nikolai.' Maud ushered Old Nik into the light-filled living room that served as my gallery. His once golden hair was now completely grey, white in places but now long, curly and luxurious. I guessed that Maud had persuaded him to start washing it. He had a scruffy beard. As he looked around the room, and saw some of his own work displayed, his eyes widened in surprise and he was suddenly very attentive. His expression was wary; he was on alert, it seemed.

'I am glad to see you again,' I said. We shook hands, and his grip was weak. I turned to Maud. 'Thanks for this, Maud. Walter will be here soon.'

When Walter arrived he sensed Nik was frail, and took charge, taking his arm and standing with him to look at the paintings. They spoke quietly together, but I overheard some snatches of their conversation. It seemed Old Nik had become something of a pedant. He was correcting almost every reminiscence Walter brought up.

'No no no,' I heard Nik say firmly. 'It was May 27th. That's when we did Batley Variety Club.'

'That was recorded at De Lane Lea, not Olympic.'

'No, we never played in Hungary or Czechoslovakia.'

'We were managed by Carlton Entertainments. Our production manager was a little snot called Frank.'

'Maud's work? You must ask her.'

At this I turned to Maud. 'Yes, what was your work? Do you still work?'

'I looked after my husband's affairs at home, his studio, his clothes, his archive and so on. Frank Lovelace looked after the road work.'

Walter looked over to me and grinned. It was fun to imagine Frank as a young runner, fetching cups of tea for Old Nik, and hailing taxis for him.

'You two can stay here and talk if you like,' I offered. 'I'll take Maud to Richmond Park, it's a pleasant day.'

'No.' Walter turned to Nik, tilting his head to invite an answer. 'Will we go to the park? It will be good to get some air.'

As Walter guided Old Nik out to the lobby and stood by the lift, Maud and I caught each other's eye. There were two generations of rock star, both regarded by their fans as inviolable, powerful, arrogant, successful and potent. We knew that both of them shared the same difficulties with fame. As the lift doors closed on the two musicians, Walter raising his hand to wave, they looked for a moment like father and son.

It was a weird moment for me. I felt a little jealous. I had wanted to be the one who unlocked the box for Walter. I knew that Andréevich would help, and I had introduced them. But I felt I might be losing Walter.

What would happen between them? Maud and I chatted about all kinds of things, but we both knew that in our minds we were asking the same questions.

What was Old Nik saying to Walter?

What was Walter saying to his hero, what was he asking him? How were they getting on?

What useful advice could the old rock star turned film star possibly pass on to the young, deeply rooted, humble and practical pub rock artist who was my Rain's dear old school friend Walter?

What had Old Nik learned from his visions?

Would anything that passed between them break the link between Walter and Siobhan that I prayed was loose enough already to fail, opening a way for Rain to tell the fool she loved him, and always had? That might be too much to ask for.

One thing was certain with the benefit of hindsight: from the day of his meeting with Andréevich, Walter began to turn his back on his old life.

Chapter 4

As I awoke this morning, sixty-seven years old, I asked myself what I most wanted for my birthday present.

What first came into my mind was so absurd that I find it hard to share it here. I wanted to change one thing in my past, something I had done of which I was terribly ashamed. Yet if I had been able to grant myself that wish this story would have no ending. Indeed, there would be no story to tell.

But let me give away a single picture here. It is a wedding. A pub rock wedding. *The* wedding. This was the wedding that, because Harry was really not well-off, was paid for entirely by me. Godfather me, in godfather role. So in a sense this was my wedding as much as it was the joining of Walter and Siobhan. There were flowers, there was good food, but the crowd was small. The solemnities were over and we were in a garden somewhere. There was music and Walter was on the stage with the Stand. There were pretty girls. Two in particular come to mind. Selena and her old school friend, Floss. Floss, the one with a blackened front tooth? There were other very pretty girls. Crow's wife Agneta was one of them and her posse of gorgeous blonde buddies from Gothenberg became a blur of feminine intoxication.

'Make sure you bring some decent gear, Lou,' Crow had instructed. 'Agneta likes that Bomber gear.'

Crow meant the horse tranquilliser, ketamine. I was the presiding tranquilliser-in-chief at the wedding of Walter and

Siobhan, so it isn't surprising I don't remember much about it. But I have been told by my host here in France that I did something very, very bad. Something she alone witnessed. She urged me to come clean. And so I agreed to write, to try to explain, to try to unravel it all. That's why I'm here. For myself as much as anything else. I wish my life was as simple as Bingo's. I ruffle his head. Waiting his entire life to catch a rolled-up ball of paper, he is the exact opposite of tranquillised: sharp, alert, growing older like his new master, but never ready to give up.

As I looked from the window of my eyrie, it was as if the entire world were bathed in cloud or mist. I could barely see the road that runs past this house down to the valley. In such gloom I could not write a word. Bingo ate his breakfast eagerly, and tried to cheer me up, but as I walked him around the garden I began to feel damp. Damp and incomplete.

Happily, a little later, the sun broke through and I sat at my desk. Bingo seemed thrilled that I was in motion, albeit merely with my pen and paper.

Does it matter that the tale I recount is now all about me when in fact I promised it would be about my young hero Walter, and his hero Old Nik? Today I turned sixty-seven! Laugh. Cry. A billion souls have passed this way before. Hence, Old Nik's hosts of harvesting angels perhaps? For this is the one-way traffic of being alive; at the end of this road is death, sweet or agonising, welcomed or dreaded, it is inevitable.

To understand the tragic and transcendent events that followed you need to understand the Irish dimension to this story. So let me take you back to Waterford where Siobhan and her little sister Selena grew up in the care of their father Michael.

Selena was the most beautiful girl at that wedding. She went to the wedding with eyes only for Walter, but now she waits for me upstairs.

She has told me all about their childhood. Michael's wife, her mother, mother to the two girls, had died when Selena was born and Siobhan had been just ten years old. Her father Michael was too worn out to be a single parent. He was a drinker and a bully, a man with a great and grand heart. But he had no understanding that a punch from him – one that might propel an adversary from one end of the public bar to the other, and where that adversary might crash laughing, ready to bounce back with an equal blow of his own – such a punch might kill a young child. He did not know his own strength; neither did he know when drunk that his elder daughter was not his wife.

In even more unhappy times, having run with their father from Waterford to West Acton in west London to impose on kindly relatives and attend better free schools (free of priests at least), tragedy struck. One evening in 1984 eighteen-year-old Siobhan wiped the blood from her lips, sucked on a tooth that had been temporarily loosened, and glared fearlessly at her father. I picture him standing swaying slightly, holding his bruised right fist still clenched, his temper – having risen – now wavering before him. And, as I imagine it, he saw and felt it as though it were a sheet of shimmering ice or glass stretching out across the small, neat sitting room. He could hardly see his elder daughter standing defiantly before him.

Little Selena stabbed Michael Collins in the back, and he died. Siobhan was now a mother as a result of murder, and it would be several years before she felt sure enough of herself, and of her strength to survive in a world of predatory men with flying fists, to let Selena find her own way.

One evening in the spring of 1994 Siobhan, in her late twenties, felt free at last to drink and dance, and as Rain's guest found herself standing at the bar in Dingwalls, slightly tipsy, watching Walter blowing his mouth-organ, adopting his famous 'stand', driving the girls wild. Realising that this handsome young pub rock star had a way with words that was redolent in some endearing way of all she could recall of the gentle south-west of Ireland she had known before her father lost his wife, her mother, and then lost his mind, Siobhan decided she would marry Walter. She was older than her new man by one year.

Chapter 5

Here on the hills of Grasse, Selena and I usually sit mid-morning in the shade of three huge palm trees to drink coffee, scoff a *pain au chocolat* and gaze at the distant, shining sea. She asks how my writing is going, and where my memories are misty she fills in the gaps. I knew that she had been one of those Dingwalls girls at the bar who had set their hearts on being Walter's lover, or even wife. In a way it had been best that her beloved older sister had married him, and not one of Agneta's spectacular Nordic blondes. She never betrayed any ill feeling towards Siobhan.

The older sister had found a good kind-hearted man in Walter, one who might have poetry in his soul. She married him and planned to shape him soon into the poetic kind of genius she deep down knew he surely could become. I suppose Siobhan and I were united in this belief in Walter's endless potential, but we never spoke of it. It might be possible that from the dark and vile reality of all she suffered as a girl she had taken up with dreams, and fantasies and schemes. We'll soon find out how far her great ambitions took her; indeed, how far they took her man.

And so the opera can begin, with voices, singing and speaking, and music made from every kind of noise that man and nature ever generated, here combined. There will be an opera.

You will imagine this evocative sound, and this music, just as I heard it for the first time. In fact, I make the claim that my aberrations may have played a part. As Walter's godfather, let me play God Himself and make a bridge between you and him, allowing me to let you right inside Walter's mind. Just for a while we float above the chronology, the passing years, months and hours of the story I have told so far, and occupy the timeless space inside a man's creative soul. We hear the deep vibrations of his still young mind as he begins to search inside the universe of childhood, its noise and chaos, in some hope of order, and some meaning for us all, his audience of the future, past and here and now.

A three-year-old boy. A terrifying storm. Wind, waves, blowing gravel, trees bending and cracking, occasional small crashes as debris is blown through the air and lands nearby. After a minute or two the storm subsides. We are left with the sound of the sea, or rather the seaside on a quiet afternoon. A beach somewhere. A few children playing. Distant calls, parent to child, child to child. Seagulls of course, but also a distant radio. The sound of galloping hooves on soft sand. Thudding rhythmically, two horses, breathing hard. Jumps. The whip. Faster. Faster. Then splashing through shallow water. The horses arrive, whinny, rise on two legs, then thud down again, blow air, turn and ride away.

For a long time, I think, I was the only person Walter trusted to see his first 'soundscape' description. It evoked poignant, but powerful images from his infancy. It revealed the fear of horses he had felt, and the sadness too, aroused by his childish notion that his parents might love their horses more than him. It's possible of course he might have shared it with Siobhan, but I saw no evidence that she knew about Walter's mental aberrations. I wondered if Andréevich would have been able to break out of his self-obsession long enough to read them. Probably not. But I did believe he would help Walter carry the burden of an over-active imagination, or even the psychic connections with the people around him; acting as a kind of counsellor, based on his own experience, he might help Walter to feel less afraid.

Chapter 6

Some godparents merely send modest presents to their charges at Christmas, and on birthdays. I may have taken my obligation to Walter too far, but I did feel it to be a spiritual imperative. Andréevich was no more meant to be a replacement father than I was. I merely felt the opportunity for Walter and the old man to meet had been placed in front of me.

Harry tried to be a good father to Walter, but musicians seem lost on several fronts when it comes to parenting. Harry had fans! No one could play the Preludium in E Major the way he could. Many organists shifted on the bench as though they had a carrot up their arse. But from behind Harry was elegant. He seemed strong. He was a performer.

'My dad did try,' Walter told once me. 'But he practised for hours in his studio. Then he would be in and out, in a dress suit. Gone. He was rarely out of bed before I set off for school.'

There was a silence then. But Walter did not appear resentful. He was not a neglected child. Harry had charged me, not to be surrogate, but to double up, as it were.

'He was not a snob about music,' Walter continued. 'He just couldn't accept that we loved what had come out of Memphis and New Orleans. I love him, Louis.'

Walter looked at me and for a moment I saw the boy I had once coached in the art of manly absurdity while Harry was away on tour. We played awful football, clumsy tennis, swam like dogs, then he'd be as properly shattered as I was when I got him home.

Walter is handsome. He has the ruggedness of the instigator of trouble, but none of the swagger. He doesn't normally talk much.

'Did you believe I'd done it with Rain?' he said.

'It's possible?'

He shook his head.

'You were late to it though,' I said. 'Like Rain?'

'You know more about your child's sex life than my parents know about mine.'

'But the girls do put out to you.'

'Put out.' He laughed. 'That sounds old-fashioned.'

'I am that.'

'Working in a club where we have no stage to speak of, just a raised platform, it's the boyfriends I have to watch. They wait until I'm taking a drink between songs and walk right up to me and poke their finger in my face. It's my bird's birthday, they say. And she wants to hear "Satisfaction". If I hesitate they speak more quietly. Fucking play it, you cunt. *Satis-fucking-faction*. Play it yourself, you little shithead, I say. And before it can go any further we deafen him and he will slink away.'

'Don't they get you later?'

'Crow sorts me out if they try. They have knives these days. Crow carries a fucking Beretta.'

A shining star vibrates with the sound of a vast, shimmering and dissonant choir. A newborn baby cries. Shattering glass. A thousand million cathedral windows in a building as high as the sky, shaken by the rumbling of an earthquake, every pane of leaded glass, every lantern, loosened, falling, at first crackling, then as the amount of glass that falls increases into an almost constant shower the noise gets louder but also softens, losing its edge. Instead a sound almost like falling water fills the air. The building itself is of glass, so when the earthquake hits it eventually takes down not just the panes of glass, but also the building, until all that is left is the occasional tinkling of another last drop of silica rain. Out of the last few small echoes of glass shards slipping – one leaning against another, and sliding, breaking again – comes a long, throaty moan. It is the sound of some kind of creature perhaps, or air being forced through some sort of narrow pipe or slit. This sound transmogrifies into the blast of exhaust from an engine, revving up, then taking off. A massive tractor engine of the kind used in American trucks: noisy, throaty, hearty, off and away.

As this grand operatic spectacle now unfolds – I have started speaking in iambic beats of seven. The correct name (I have looked it up) is 'heptameter'. As soon as there is music I become rhythmic, like someone who – here comes the beat of seven – *has had a few too many and begins to swing and sway*. It's pathetic. I can't dance. I can't sing. But I am powerless. It must be clear by now that in this story something strange was going on inside young Walter's mind and I am tempted to evoke it.

It just so happened that I was present at his last performance with the band, invited by their manager Frank Lovelace. It was clear to me that Frank wanted to show off. A week before he had negotiated a huge financial deal for Walter's latest song, 'Freedom on the Road', about the joys of life out on the road behind the wheel of a smoking, fiery rod. He'd sold it to Ford in the USA, who were bringing out a new version of their huge four-wheel-drive utility pickup truck and the song would feature in a fifteen-million-dollar advertising campaign. It would soon be on every TV screen in the USA, and Frank expected that in years to come the song would become a staple of a long-drawn-out campaign. With each new phase of that campaign Frank would deal again, and make more money for Walter and himself.

The agency making the television commercial loved some of the cheesy erotic lines, which Walter managed to make seem genuinely sexy when he sang them on stage.

> *Your turn to drive, you gotta shift the stick*
> *Your turn to drive, we gotta get there quick.*

This wasn't Walter's finest work, but it had suddenly made him a lot of money.

> *Freedom on the road, I always wanna ride,*
> *I warn you, I'll explode,*
> *If ever I'm denied.*

Politically incorrect and chauvinistic, and accepted tongue-in-cheek by the worldly R&B-loving crowd at Dingwalls, it targeted the kind of hard-working American men who used the big pickup trucks for their work. In Britain such men have white vans; equally over-powered, but more discreet.

Walter played a great show; it seemed the usual thing, no strings, no strange vibrations on the surface that I could detect. You've glimpsed a description of the strange sounds and music Walter himself had started hearing in the darkness of the night, but up on stage that final evening, he signalled the imminent close of the first half of their show with one splendid frozen 'stand'.

The girls went crazy, and he played a killer mouth-organ solo that rocked old Dingwalls so damned hard the bottles up behind the bar began to rattle, leak and fall.

My godson. I felt so proud. My rich godson.

I celebrated whatever it was that Old Nik had passed to Walter when they met a few days before.

As Walter left the stage, announcing a short break, the crowd went wild; the applause in Dingwalls usually faded quickly, but on this occasion something very special seemed to hang in the smoky air. He pushed through the appreciative cheering crowd towards the bar where Frank and I were leaning. As he slowly approached, he looked around him, and pulled out a small red silk scarf from his pocket and wiped the sweat from his face. He seemed to tower above the crowd as they parted to allow a narrow way through.

He was, I was reminded once more, a beautiful man; he could have been a young Johnny Cash. He stood out in the crowd, yet at the same time he appeared rather ghostly. By the time he reached the bar, which was heaving with people who had beaten him to it, his wife was waiting for him holding out a beer.

'Walter,' she said, smiling. 'So talented, big Walter: Siobhan's big man.' This was said with neither celebration nor sarcasm. She hauled him close to her possessively. Siobhan spoke loud enough for most of the gathering girls to hear as she kissed her man on both cheeks. She was a little drunk perhaps.

She smiled with adoration, but her smile was constrained with care. Walter knew exactly what his role was in the context of that kind of event. He could do his job easily, and part of that job was acknowledging the principal currency in which rock stars were rewarded.

Siobhan was quite stunning. Her red hair and her blue-green eyes generated a sense of presence that was almost too powerful to ignore. Some of the men near her at the bar were attempting to do just that – ignore her – and their flickering eyes had jealously flit from her pale skin and slightly lecherous smile to Walter as he had gently pushed his way from the stage through the mass of bodies towards her.

As the two of them met, and kissed, it was immediately obvious that Siobhan was older than her husband. She was just one year his senior, but she appeared to be more mature, and looked older than her thirty years, and despite Walter's road-worn look she seemed more lived-in than he did. In her, the ageing signified a successful decline to greater beauty, if decline is truly how it could be described. In him that night, the beginning of ageing seemed rather sad, because his weary face seemed to signify an even wearier spirit.

In another life – more rock 'n' roll than rhythm and blues – his partner would have been younger, prettier, sillier, and at such a time would have been throwing herself at him, laughing, giggling, kissing him and flirting as though she were meeting him for the first time. Siobhan had never behaved like a trophy wife. She had never worked at it.

I sensed that as she watched her husband drink thirstily she found herself struggling to concentrate, to stay with him in the rather seedy rock 'n' roll surroundings in which they found themselves. Was she thinking, not yet aware that she was now married to a very rich young man, that he had sold his bloody soul to the ridiculous Dingwalls' circus?

And was her greatest sudden fear that he might take her soul with his?

Perhaps, after her father, she was wondering how she would survive yet another self-obsessed man?

I saw the moment when Walter noticed her eyes harden and her mouth narrow. He had told me he knew that she disapproved of what he loved doing so much in the band.

He moved towards her and spoke loud enough for me to hear. 'Darling girl, you don't have to be here. Give me one more kiss, then go on home if you like. I'll see you later.'

Siobhan smiled even more widely, and suddenly seemed sincere. 'It's the Bushmills,' she complained. 'I order it because I'm from Waterford. I knock it back. I don't have the stomach for it. But it makes me feel very good. I'm fine. Really, my lover, I'm fine.'

There was something evasive about Walter's expression. I learned later that he hadn't yet told Siobhan about Frank

Lovelace's deal and what it would mean for them, and that he'd been putting off telling her as he feared it would drive a wedge between them.

I also later learned that Walter had been told, just a few minutes before he walked on stage that night, that as well as the licensing deal to Ford, Frank had sold his entire catalogue of songs outright plus everything he might write in the next five years for on the way to five million pounds. After Frank's commission, legal fees and tax, that would leave a clear two million quid for Walter.

While Siobhan and Walter whispered to each other, Frank Lovelace and I moved away along the bar, to where Crow and the Hansons were waiting. They clearly sensed something was up. And Frank now explained to them all about Walter's windfall. 'You guys will make money too from the use of the band's recording in the TV commercials,' bragged Frank. 'This really is win-win, guys.'

Crow's usually frozen expression cracked, and he looked shaken.

'Holy shit!' As Crow voiced his shock, his wife Agneta looked confused. He turned to her. 'This is bullshit. This is not in the fucking manifesto. We aren't the fucking Who. We don't fucking well sell out. Tell Ford they can't have the fucking music we recorded!'

Frank stood calmly at the bar. Crow didn't scare him. Frank drew himself up to his full height and tilted his head back so it seemed he was looking down at Crow.

'It will be voted on by all of us,' he pointed out to Crow quietly. 'In any case, if you guys don't want your version to be used Walter can record a new one. Why not enjoy this windfall?'

The Hansons meanwhile were looking at each other with quizzical smiles. Leery and curious, they had just been told they were in line for a bonanza, but with no idea what it might entail. From where I stood, what I saw in their faces was a realisation this might be the moment that would set them free and allow them to move on to greater things.

Crow looked at the couple and seemed to read their thoughts. 'The fucking Everly Brothers will be turning in their graves.'

Steve Hanson cut in. He too drew himself up to his full height, and at over six feet tall he suddenly seemed imposing and even a little dangerous: 'I don't think they are actually dead, Crow. That might be your problem, thinking you control the copyright to every great song you've stumbled on from the halcyon days of R&B and American pop.'

'Oh, you creep, Hanson,' sneered Crow, refusing to back down. Agneta took his arm to try to calm him. 'You'll be talking about the benefits of heavier cable for our PA speakers next, or suggesting some guitar-player mate of yours who is good at shredding, whatever the holy fuck that is. You fucking nerd.' It seemed to me that despite all this bluster, Crow was intimidated by Hanson, and was beginning to see that he was going to be overruled by Steve and his wife. It would be a first for the band, and one Crow would find difficult. To say he slunk away to a different part of the bar would not be correct. He swaggered, but he seemed hangdog and a little pitiful.

At that moment Selena walked up.

The resemblance between Selena and Siobhan was obvious; it was also obvious that Selena was much younger. If Siobhan looked older than her thirty years, Selena seemed to try hard to look younger than her twenty. Her hair was auburn, worn long in soft ringlets with two short plaits either side to frame her face, and she had the air of a sixties hippy about her; around her neck she wore a garland of beads and small flowers, and on her ears large loops of pink plastic. She'd told me that she believed she was an angel, divinely inspired in human form, who worked with real angels, guiding not only the spirits of the people around her, but also working in concert with the secret masters of the universe. This made her no less attractive to me or any of the men around her, and many of the women too. She was captivating, with shining blue-green eyes and a wide and luscious mouth.

Her mother had died as she gave birth to Selena, ascending to the heavens on her wings. Why wouldn't Selena have had a screw a little loose? In any case, I knew better than anyone that a loose screw here and there could mask a different shade of genius, and if Selena was in any way a genius, she was even more a beauty.

She was a flirt too. According to her I myself had been subject to a few of her flirtations when she was eighteen, and running from man to man excitedly at Siobhan and Walter's wedding. But Selena had a powerful presence, and now I watched her at the bar in Dingwalls, laughing like a film star.

In truth, we were all a little fearful of getting on her bad side. When she had been just eight years old she had killed her father Michael Collins with a kitchen knife. Many of the people around her knew the story. She had been forgiven: entirely reprieved legally speaking, even if sanctioned morally behind her back by some of the local nuns back in Duncannon. Siobhan had been bruised, battered and sexually abused by the drunken, foolish man. The police brought no charges, and the social workers soon stepped back. And so in my eyes, and in those of most men who stood near us at the bar that night, when she arrived we forgot Siobhan and saw only the shining, naive, sexual and angelic light Selena emanated, and had flashing visions too of her blooded blade. The strange mélange of light and good and evil and her lack of shame made her a kind of Cleopatra in our stupid, hazy eyes.

She started talking to Frank. As I walked over to join them, I overheard what she was saying.

'Frank, you are number three.' She was laughing, squirming around him as though she were a pole-dancer and Frank was the pole. 'I have already started on Walter. If I can't have him, I'll steal Crow from Agneta. If I can't have Crow, well, I'll just have to make do with you, Frank. You'll have me, won't you?'

Frank was clearly enjoying being wooed by such a pretty young woman, even if he was cast as her third contender.

'And what if you can't have me?' Frank looked at her, only half-joking; he was starting to feel he needed to man up. 'Who's next down the list?'

Selena was laughing, her head in the air, her hooped earrings dangling, her plaits swinging. Had I walked up at precisely the wrong moment?

'Louis!' Selena shouted my name, smiled at me with her Hollywood teeth, and hugged me. 'If Frank won't have me, Louis will take me, won't you? You gorgeous old bunny.'

She tweaked my cheek. 'Isn't he handsome, Frank? Rich too!'

I flushed as I feared she was taking the piss.

Now Walter and Siobahn arrived at the bar, smiling and good-looking, laid-back and cool, unaware that he was top of Selena's list of prospects. Frank and I were relegated, as she turned her light on Walter.

I'm sure Walter felt safe with Selena, safe enough – married to her older sister – to allow her to flirt sometimes, and he responded naturally and openly to her beauty, her light and her natural sexual energy. It seemed to me Siobhan usually looked on indulgently, but always registered the obvious chemistry between her husband and sister. If the attraction had been properly weighed and assessed it would have been clear that Selena worshipped her brother-in-law, and that although Walter liked her, it was, I could see, a rather more fundamental and primal reaction he felt in her presence. She was most overtly sexual and flirtatious

74

around him when he was working a gig, almost unconsciously playing out the role that Siobhan refused to play.

Walter put his arms around the two of them, the sisters. He gathered them magnanimously, and they were crushed together for a moment.

Then, as if he realised he had been clumsy, Walter released them both. Siobhan looked away as though considering her exit.

Selena was excited, playing the part of an adoring fan.

'Walt, you're so great, man,' she effused. 'That last song attracted a hundred angels into the room. Imagine a hundred angels in this dump!' She laughed and her eyes flashed and crinkled.

'Thank you, little sister,' Walter teased.

'I fucking hate it when you call me that, Walter,' spat Selena. 'But you should be celebrating. Frank told me about the big deal with Ford, and the rest. Selling all your old music. You could retire, darling.' She looked at Siobhan with a dark grin and added, 'He could write poetry.'

Siobhan looked grim as she fixed her husband with an intense stare. Everyone at the bar heard what she said.

'Is this true?' She suddenly seemed less intoxicated. 'Have you really let Frank sell your catalogue?'

Walter nodded. 'It's a fucking lot of money too, Siobhan.'

'How did Selena know about all this before me? I am your fucking wife. I'm fucking fuming to be honest.'

Walter began to explain aspects of the deal that he himself had only just found out, that Selena seemed to know about the deal before he did. But Siobhan was looking down at the floor of the bar. A few too many drinks had softened her before, but now she was sober, in the heat of a building rage, her violent father's genes pushing to the surface.

'So you will leave the band?' This was more of a statement than a question.

Walter didn't answer, but turned away and waved at the barman for a top-up.

Siobhan pulled him round to face her squarely and demanded an answer.

'Will you quit the band? Will you give up this fucking shithole? Can we start a new life, work together on a poetry book or something? What about the help you promised me to write a book about Selena and me being brought up by our dad? We thought it might make a play. Bloody hell, Walter, it would be so great to get out of this . . .' She didn't finish.

Walter quickly looked away. Could she see on his face that he wasn't ready to give her what she wanted, with or without a fight? I could tell she was ready to fight him, and her expression must have told him that too.

I think I've said enough to indicate that in my view Walter had indeed decided he might change his life, but not only as a result of his windfall. My feeling was that he was afraid he had no choice but to change. He was either losing his mind or was under a strain he couldn't detect. I doubt his first thought would have been the same as Siobhan's, that he would leave the band. As often happens when important chapters – like strands of delicate silk in a man's life – start to plait together to make an unbreakable rope, by seeming coincidence, four closely linked events threw Walter back on to his own defensive resources.

The first was what Old Nik had told him when they met and walked together in Richmond Park. I believe Walter had told the old man that he was starting to hear strange things whenever he sat down to write songs; conceivably he even read something to him from the first few soundscape descriptions, words that promised music well beyond the scope of his usual skillset. I think that maybe I was the only other person whom Walter had spoken to about this. As I have said, whatever Old Nik advised him changed Walter in some indefinable way.

The second was that Siobhan was obviously beginning to frighten him; her desire to help make him great, and perhaps to live through him creatively was not unwelcome or unusual in a marriage between two people involved in the worlds of entertainment and media, but Walter wasn't ready for it.

The third was surely the idea that with the money that had just fallen out of the sky he could do more or less as he wished, at least for a few years.

Last, when Siobhan smiled, kissed him and said goodbye, clearly unsatisfied that he had not answered her question, both he and Selena felt something final in her manner. And yet I think Siobhan sincerely believed that if she went back to Waterford, he would follow. There were few women like her, she was certain of that. Walter had always been intoxicated by her, her mind, her beauty and her poetry. She couldn't imagine she would lose him. But she was also proud. If he didn't follow, she might never come back. Selena knew that about her older sister.

Frank and I saw it too in the bar that night; Selena – without a moment's hesitation, as though Walter were a baton that had been dropped and must be quickly grabbed and run with, in a race to some finishing line only she could envision – did indeed try to replace Siobhan in that instant without waiting a beat. It was as though for a second time in her life she held a murderous blade, and this time it was Siobhan who would go down for no other reason than that she had married the man Selena – as I learned later – had loved since she was eighteen.

She moved closer to him.

I thought of my poor Rain, who loved Walter too, rather plain-looking compared to the Collins girls, carrying rather more of my genes than were useful when caught up in a contest for a man. She was not cut out to battle against Siobhan let alone Selena and her angels. I must be careful not to place her in the middle of this trio. In the days that followed I would sometimes find myself beginning to hate Walter, just for a moment; it didn't last, and perhaps I was merely envious. He was still only twenty-nine years old, and had been slow to fall in love, if indeed he had ever fallen in love with Siobhan; I began to doubt it. I also doubted that Siobhan loved Walter properly, unconditionally; there was too much at stake for her, I think. Walter was not just a husband, he was a man, a man among and above the other men Siobhan had known, especially her father. Siobhan wanted a gentle man, a poet, a clever man, who never raised his arm or even his voice.

When she had gone – some of us had the sense that Siobhan had thrown down her cards, despairing of the hand she had been dealt – her sister saw her chance.

Selena didn't face Walter, she didn't meet his troubled gaze; she didn't try to engage him. She stood beside him at the bar and her hip brushed against him.

He looked down at her, and wiped the sweat from his lips. She whispered in his ear, grabbed his arm and pulled him behind her towards the doors that led to the toilets.

As we sit watching the sun go down over the mountains beyond Cannes, Bingo barks at a cyclist passing on the road above the terrace. Selena has drunk one too many glasses of rosé. Suddenly she laughs.

'Poor Walter, I really did make a lunge for him.' She went on to tell me what had happened that night.

'I told him I had some great cocaine.'

He followed.

So what she had whispered was not that she loved him, or that she wanted to possess him, or delight him, raise him up through the sky filled with angels, or fuck him; she knew that anything she said that might reveal her exultant feelings and triumph at that moment would not make him follow her. This was Dingwalls after all. She offered cocaine.

I must try to paint a picture of a scene I did not witness, but I can piece it together from what Selena has told me, and from the gossip that later reverberated around the club. The toilets in Dingwalls were scruffy, but old-fashioned, blue and green fired tiles and cracked and streaked mirrors. Walter leaned against a sink, pulled out a mouth-organ and started to play a suggestive rhythm. Selena chopped out some coke, snorted a line and began to dance seductively. A few other girls came in and didn't seem surprised to find Walter watching his sister-in-law gyrating.

The girls related the story later. They felt that if they hadn't been there Walter might have responded sexually. But he did not move, and that made Selena angry.

As he played to her, the girls said, and they agreed he had played wonderfully, she had danced. She had even offered him a blow-job. She had fallen to the floor, exhausted, humiliated and frustrated. The girls and Walter all went to her and tried to help her up.

She pushed them all away, her cocaine high turning bad.

At that point the toilet door opened and one of the bar staff had gestured, tapping their watch. Walter was due back on stage. As he went out to play the second set, the girls, still attending to Selena like courtiers to a princess, heard her curse him under her breath.

'Fuck you, Walter!' she said, her lipstick smearing as she wiped her mouth. 'You've missed the best sister again, you fecking English twat!'

She struggled to her feet, wobbling a little on her high heels. She lit a cigarette and looked in the mirror, and for a moment anyone watching might have sensed what she could see.

Indeed, the room around her was full of what looked like winged creatures. This is what she told me she saw in the cigarette smoke, in the clouds, in the dust thrown up from the sawdust-covered dance floor. She held her belly as though expecting a child.

She cradled herself. No one understood. She turned, shook out her hair and walked proudly from the toilet out into the club.

Walter was at the bar drinking down a long glass of water, the club manager now nervously looking at his watch.

Selena walked straight up to him, and kissed him on the side of his face, forgiving him, and reclaiming him for the benefit of anyone who might be watching.

There was hardly a single woman in the room who hadn't watched her take Walter into the Ladies and was gripped by whatever might happen next. They had seen him hurry out looking sheepish and heard about their little performance from the girls who had caught them together. Siobhan had left only fifteen minutes before.

What slags Selena and Walter were!

That's what they were thinking.

For Selena, looking around at the envious women in the club, it was a brief moment of careless triumph that echoed – whenever she looked back on it – over and over again so annoyingly that it seemed more like a bad dream than a conquest.

For seconds after that moment, Selena's prospects with Walter were dashed.

Indeed her sister Siobhan's marriage was dashed in any case even if she wasn't about to blow it up. Even my daughter Rain's future as her possible replacement was dashed.

Into the club walked a girl I hadn't seen since Walter and Siobhan's wedding some two years before. I mentioned that at the wedding Selena had fluttered around me for a while, and I had been diverted.

This was the girl who had diverted me.

We called her Floss.

Chapter 7

Florence Agatha Spritzler was twenty when we all saw her walk into Dingwalls just as Walter was starting the second set of what would turn out to be his last performance with Big Walter and His Stand. He would probably remember her – if he remembered her at all – as the gawky eighteen-year-old friend of Selena's who hung out with her at his wedding to Siobhan a little over two years earlier.

She looked around and spotted Selena at the bar and hurried over to her side, no doubt so she could feel established safely somewhere in the heaving crowd.

They embraced, laughing, friends from school in Acton from the age of twelve, a few years after the Collins had landed in London. They seemed completely at ease together. It was Selena who had christened her Floss.

The nickname had begun of course as Flossie – after Florence – but taken on its rather dental spin when Floss blackened one of her front teeth falling from a pony when she was fourteen. The damaged tooth was perhaps equal to the deliberate flaw the Persian carpet-maker weaves into his rugs so they do not attempt to challenge God's perfection. With a bright white set of teeth she would have smiled more readily, and if she had done so she would have set the room ablaze. Her natural blond hair used to be quite long but I learned later that she had had it cut very short just the day before.

I remembered her arriving at the wedding; that was before whatever drugs I had decided would improve the day narrowed my vision like a black curtain slowly closing on a brightly lit stage, then blacked me out completely. She was swinging her hair as she walked, which had been an eye-catching feature about her; maybe she felt it helped to detract attention from her mouth. Her nose had a slight upward tilt, and her bright blue eyes set off her classic good looks. She was youthful, and most certainly English, a rose. I say this because her surname was Spritzler, making some people wonder if she might be German. In fact she had been adopted at birth from a convent in Switzerland by Albert, a very capable Austrian surgeon, and his English wife Katharine.

When they were young teenagers, while Selena ran around like a hippy claiming to heal her friends' chakras with angelic powers, Floss learned to ride, and her affluent adoptive parents – relieved at first that she had stumbled on a normal well-brought-up girl's pursuit – bought her a young thoroughbred colt, and a transport box so she could compete in dressage events and gymkhanas. Selena and Floss were best friends who felt centred in the hub of the same wheel. As young teenagers they had been wild, and sometimes had much older boyfriends, but together they were extremely strong, resilient, taking nothing too seriously, laughing at men who found them attractive, intoxicated simply by each other's sense of humour and what appeared to be shared silliness. Beneath the surface they were not silly at all; they both had deeply held ambitions. They each felt they knew what was in the future.

Selena was certain she would depose Siobhan and marry Walter; her angels would guide him to her. I learned later that Floss, not wanting to compete, knew for certain she would never marry a man who wanted to spend his life playing in a band in pubs. She would marry a man who would at least be willing to live close to the green belt of London, near Richmond or Hampstead where she could have horses, and ride every day, perhaps run a stud. So her future husband would need money. In her mind she envisioned a banker, a Stock Exchange trader, or a very capable Queen's Counsel. She knew she might not be posh enough to hook such a man, but she also knew her parents had a wide circle of friends in the medical world, so maybe she would meet a rich young plastic surgeon.

There were other possibilities. For instance, Floss seemed interested in Frank Lovelace. She was whispering to Selena and gesturing in our direction along the bar where I stood with Frank.

I felt sure she must remember and recognise me, and I waved, but she seemed focused on Frank.

'That girl was at Walter's wedding,' I almost had to shout in Frank's ear; the music was suddenly rather loud in the bar. 'Looks like you might have pulled.'

'Florence Spritzler,' said Frank. 'I know her. Friend of Selena. Horsey girl. Doesn't come here much.'

He sauntered over and started to chat to her. His manner was cocksure, over-confident, really quite irritating.

I was fifty-one, and Frank was probably only just past forty, but damn – he was just as much too old for her as I was.

I was deeply jealous. I felt absurd, ridiculous, and reminded myself that my days of drinking, drugging and chasing women half my age were now behind me. Even so, I wanted to be in Frank's place, close to her, to make her smile despite her blackened tooth.

In the months to come I got to know her. There was something careless about Floss, something impetuous and daring that promised adventure. But if she wished she could eat you alive. There was a determination and tenacity about her. Charming, but intensely focused on whatever was in her mind, and to whomever she was addressing or listening to.

Yes, the fact is I found her diverting.

I hardly noticed at first when Crow pulled at my arm. Walter and the rest of the band were already on stage and ready to restart.

I turned to face Crow.

'What have you done to Walter?' Crow's deadpan face was only a few inches from my own. 'He's been hearing strange sounds.'

'I've tried to help him,' I spluttered. I admit to being slightly frightened of Crow.

'Why have you always tried to fill his head with all that New Age shit?' Crow was almost spitting.

'That is not what *I've* done,' I protested.

Crow wasn't listening. He started to poke my chest with his index finger, and it hurt. He had powerful, bony, guitar-player's fingers. 'This band is all I've got, Louis. Don't fuck it up.'

Walter called him from the stage.

'I'll speak to you again later,' said Crow, as he turned to go on stage. 'And I'll kill fucking Frank as well. This band is not about money, or art, it's about truth.'

Crow left me, still muttering, and stalked in his Doc Marten boots like an angry catwalk model to the stage and picked up his guitar.

Chapter 8

The last show at Dingwalls by Big Walter and His Stand would quickly pass into legend. I'd never heard the band play with such ferocity. They played their closing number, their Ford song, as though trying to smash it into the ground, to destroy it, to make it unusable.

> *Freedom on the road, never ready to arrive,*
> *Won't deliver this load, I'll just keep on with the drive.*

A few thirty-plus women at the front pretended to be teenagers, aroused by the metaphors. They were perhaps imagining a man who might give them enough time to orgasm at least once, and half screamed.

Crow looked more and more livid and Frank started to look ill at ease; I'd told him Crow had said he would kill him, and as soon as the song ended Frank left discreetly.

I had found a table to one side of the stage and sat there with Selena. I couldn't see Floss; she had been speaking to Frank most of the evening, and I suspected she had left with him, maybe meeting him outside.

I started to bang my glass on the table with such irritation that I cracked it. I was jealous!

Selena noticed and laughed. It was the right response to my absurdity, but how could she know what I was thinking?

As the band's two crew members were putting away the

guitars, Walter came to say goodbye. He stood uneasily, as Selena tapped the empty chair beside her.

'Amazing show, Walter,' I said.

Walter nodded, not modestly, but agreeing, and accepting the compliment.

Crow walked up. 'Walter.' I could tell he was about to give an order. 'Sit. I need to talk to you. We all need to talk.'

Walter sat, not meekly, but with respect, I think. Crow demanded it, and attention; I had personally never seen him in a rage, but his temper was legendary and it was clear he had something to say.

I made to stand to leave them to it.

'Please stay, Louis.' This was another order. He turned his fierce gaze to Selena. 'Selena, you stay too.'

Before Crow could say anything more, Walter spoke. 'You're wrong about all this, Crow,' he said calmly. 'This is not Louis's fault. It's true that ever since I was a kid he's drummed into me how madness and art can be combined – but I never took any notice. I just thought he was a bit mad, and so were most of his clients.'

Crow opened his mouth to speak but Walter put up his hand. 'Let me finish, Crow,' he said gently. 'Whatever Louis has taught me, or tried to teach me, has never stopped me loving this band, or what we do. It's as important to me as it is to you.'

Crow looked from me to Selena.

'Selena hasn't affected my decision either,' he said, putting his hand on her arm. She shook her hair, got up and walked away.

Crow and I both waited.

I broke the silence. 'What decision?'

Walter shook his head. Then he nodded. 'I need to tell you more about Frank's deal. He's sold one of my songs to Ford to use in a commercial for one of their huge SUV trucks in the States. On the back of that he's sold my entire catalogue. So it's a lot of money and Siobhan, well, she thinks if we have money I should leave the band – because we can afford it. But it's not just about Frank's deal and the money. I've been worrying for a long time now, and my mental health is not good.'

Crow looked grim. This was the end, he knew it was, he could read Walter well; after all, they were old friends. 'Can you at least try to explain what's happened,' he pleaded, some of his anger revolving briefly into petulance. 'What do you plan to do? Are you really leaving the band? What's the matter with your mental health? Just because you've got some cash you're going to leave the fucking band? You just said it was important to you. Do you know what this all means to me?'

Crow gestured at the club, which was beginning to empty – at filthy black cables strewn over the floor, ashtrays and empty bottles everywhere. The most precious place on earth.

'You know I met Paul Jackson,' Walter began.

'Andréevich!' Crow spluttered.

'Let me explain, Crow,' said Walter firmly. 'You want to know. I want to explain.'

Crow sat back in his chair like a scowling teenager. The back of the chair cracked, for a brief second threatening to topple, but Crow didn't flinch.

'Old Nik,' agreed Walter. 'I met him, yes. Louis did arrange it, because he is his agent now, but I wanted to meet him. I've been a fan of Hero Ground Zero since I was a kid. And I was curious. Nik, as he calls himself now, had a breakdown. I feel I'm on the verge of something myself. The pressures I feel are out of all proportion with what is going on around me.'

Crow couldn't help himself. 'Pressure!' He was almost barking, leaning forward, the veins in his neck pulsating. 'This isn't a high-pressure job. It's fun. It's easy. We play pub rock while people get rat-arsed, and we get paid for it. We live well. Where's the fucking pressure?'

'I don't know, Crow,' Walter said, not rising to the bait. 'It might not be coming from what we do here, it might be coming from inside me.'

'So what did fucking Andréevich have to say?' demanded Crow.

'He said something that helped,' replied Walter, but placed his hand on the table, face down, a firm boundary. 'But I don't think telling you would help you to understand.'

'Fuck!' Crow was barking now. 'You are going to stop playing music, aren't you?'

Walter nodded. 'I have to, for a while. My head is swimming at the moment. I feel I'm being taken over, sound, strange stuff.'

Crow stood up, finally really angry, and turned on me again. 'You arranged the meeting,' he shouted. 'What the fuck were you thinking? What could a washed-up old prog rock star who's off his fucking head possibly say that would be useful to Walter? He needs a shrink, not another nutter. Jesus!'

Crow knocked his chair over as he stormed out.

Walter and I sat, watching the crew pack the last few mike stands into a flight case.

'I arranged the meeting with Old Nik because I thought it might help,' I said. 'It doesn't matter which path you take, Walter, but you do have to choose. Siobhan wants you to leave music behind you, to work with her on some grand intellectual project. Crow wants you here, playing what he tells you to play. I want to help you with this stuff you hear – because I believe it could lead you to a new level of creativity. I know what I'm talking about. I have seen it happen before with some of my clients.'

I was very shaken by the tense atmosphere Crow had stirred up. I tried to keep my voice low, and spoke into Walter's ear. I was too rattled, though, to care much who heard what I said. A few stragglers left in the club were looking over at our table.

Walter turned to me. 'Nik was up on Skiddaw for fifteen years, did you know that?'

'Yes, I did know that. He produced nearly a hundred charcoal drawings in that time, which are the basis for my business as his agent.'

'I have always wanted to create a maze,' he said. 'Do you know how long it takes, on average, for even a very fast-growing hedge to be dense enough and high enough to be more than a parterre? More than just a design? A complex you can lose yourself in?'

I shook my head.

'Fifteen years.'

'You're stopping work with music for fifteen years? I didn't even think you would leave the band, although I thought Siobhan was trying to get you to leave. This could be my fault, Crow might be right about that. But the maze sounds great, of course it does, but fifteen years! Walter, you could have a life as a serious artist; what you are experiencing is not madness, not a breakdown, you are connecting with the people around you, with what they are feeling. It's a good thing.'

Of course, I cared very much about Walter as an artist, and appreciated what he did in the band. Siobhan too wanted Walter to be happy, I think, and although I didn't really reckon Walter had much of a chance as a poet based on what we had heard in 'Freedom on the Road', the soundscapes showed that he had a poetic and descriptive flair. At that moment Selena came back to the table with Floss. Walter didn't notice, he was dejected, gazing at his empty beer glass. He was probably wondering why he was feeling so compromised on what should have been a joyful evening. I reached over to him and nudged him, so that he would at least acknowledge Floss who stood nervously waiting. He looked up at Floss and his eyes flashed from Selena to her friend, back and forth, stopping long enough to gaze at Floss, without speaking.

'You're Floss,' he said, holding out his hand, then getting to his feet. 'You were at the wedding.'

'That's me,' she replied. 'It was a good day.'

'You're the rider girl, yes?'

'Right again.' Floss tossed the missing blond hair she had sported the day before, now cut short. It was a strange but delightful action.

'Do you ride?' she asked. 'Ever had a pony?' She looked at Selena to share the joke, to make it clear that she, being a girl among girls, was teasing him a little. But Selena was starting to look furious.

'Not me,' Walter said. 'My parents used to ride, but I am a bit frightened of horses, always have been.'

'We shall have to fix that.'

Flashes of golden light make the sound of cymbals and gongs, brief and splashing. A tower made of thin metal girders wavers in a powerful breeze. A young woman gasps. The entire world around her is vibrating. Another building falls. This time it is a building made of metal, girders, bells, tubes (like those from xylophones), tautened wire, tightened strings of cable, booming sheets of hanging aluminium sheeting, walls made of cable-stretched skins of exceedingly thin metal membrane wavering and vibrating with the gently moving air. As it collapses the mixture of metallic sounds is cacophonous and shocking – a far more disturbing noise than the collapse of the glass cathedral. At one point one of the long, ringing, shining stainless-steel tubes, tipping slowly from upright, falls against one of the thin membrane walls and begins to tear through it; the noise is excruciating, teeth-rattling, spine-curdling. All this is punctuated by the enormous low-frequency thuds of huge steel girders collapsing, and the rising whine of cables being stretched to their limit, twanging, flipping, spinning, whirring and whipping, and then finally breaking. When a really large sheet of plate metal begins to lean, breaks free of its popping restraining bolts, falls and hits the ground, the noise it makes is quite unusual. A clean sound, without the anticipated deep thunder. A kind of open-mouthed barking sound, slowed down by some digital device: arrrwraaannggargh. Drawn out too, as it has landed on top of a girder and is almost perfectly balanced, the girder the fulcrum of a wobbling seesaw of a massive, rollingly unstable metal plate as big as a ship.

Siobhan went back to her family home in Waterford that night. She had missed the moment when Floss had usurped her, and without even really trying had ousted her and stolen her husband. Siobhan also missed the moment when Walter fell in love for the first time with a girl who was perhaps his equal in some ways. It would always look to all of us that this moment had happened to Siobhan as though in a scene 'off-stage', a side event that would turn out to be life-changing and humiliating for the great Irish beauty Siobhan was taken to be, and felt herself to be.

The cottage was in Duncannon, a village with a few fishing boats and a rather romantic old fort. The area was quiet, and felt real. Technically in County Wexford not Waterford, but Waterford was the nearest big town. Although she had been shocked by the money thing with Frank, she felt perhaps that this might mean she and Walter could spend some time together at last, and she could get her husband away from the bar at Dingwalls, the creepy women hanging around, Crow's miserable and negative controlling whining, the Hansons' obvious ambition. She also wanted to get her man away from me for a while.

And then there was this floozie Floss. Selena had called her about Walter meeting her again at Dingwalls, and described how obviously taken with her he had been. Weeks later. But had Siobhan experienced even a moment of doubt? I think she believed she would draw Walter back to her. She sat in Duncannon writing a letter as a couple of logs she'd found crackled on the fire. The window was open to the garden, a vixen cried from the copse across the road and an owl hooted. There was no phone, and no email. She didn't even have a radio or TV in the house. She planned to spend her time trying to write poems. In one sonnet she had started she would allow herself to complain to Walter – who was quickly becoming a mere phantom in her immediate daily life – about the way he had wasted his talent helping to sell cars and trucks rather than describing his love for her.

I hoped for Shelley, Byron in your pen
   I longed for you to rise to meet your star
   The songs you wrote moved drinks across the bar
Why would you waste fine words on drunken men?
And wasting once, go on to waste again?
   No sonnet to Siobhan, how could you mar
   Our love with elegies to some fast car?
For money? What can those in love dare spend?
You've sold your talent; then your soul is sold.
   You've championed commerce – why? So you'll be 'free'?
   I love you, and I'll always tightly hold
The hope that one day you might dream with me
   To Waterford! I'm gone! I'll take my heart.
I can't stand by and watch you lose your art.

Pretty good, she thought. She'd used the old romantic Italian rhyming scheme for the sonnet, sometimes used by the sixteenth-century English courtier Sir Philip Sidney, although the modern Irish poets Heaney and Muldoon would always be her real passion. A friend who was a junior editor at Faber & Faber had suggested she write more sonnets; they were becoming popular again. As yet she had not been published, but she felt sure it would happen soon. She thought about completing the sonnet now and including it in her letter. She'd challenge Walter to put it to music and he would try, and probably fail. She smiled, it was pleasant mischief, but she demurred; Walter was probably lost to her for the time being. There would be no point. She had to be patient. He would come to her, eventually. If he did not come, she would divorce him. But he would come, she was sure of it. There was no woman as potent as she was, and if there had been such a woman, she herself would have wanted to possess her.

Chapter 9

It would become clear to us all that Siobhan had overplayed her hand with Walter when she went home to Waterford. She had intended to challenge him. He had decided to quit the band, but he had also decided to quit art in any form. Had she allowed him simply to fade away for a while, and find out what would work for him, their marriage might have been saved. Siobhan had never really bothered to investigate whether Walter's meeting with Old Nik had driven some kind of wedge between them or what the deeper causes of their break-up might be. She seemed completely insouciant as far as I could tell.

I wrote to her with sympathy, expecting her to reply angrily for my encouraging Walter to honour his creative dark side; instead she responded philosophically. She wrote that she intended to leave her job at the BBC; she was fed up with world affairs, politics and research. Walter had given her some money, and they had sold their little flat in South Ealing so she felt secure, at least for a while. She was going to write poetry herself, the now famous *Sonnets*.

She also asked about Rain, how she was, and how she might feel about the possibility she might soon divorce Walter? As I read these questions my intuition kicked in. I had a hunch Siobhan might be asking on behalf of Pamela rather than herself. Pamela must surely want to know how Rain was coping, whether she was happy.

In the letter Siobhan said she knew the nunnery Pamela had entered. She said it was very strict, and visitors were not allowed.

Something about this expression felt disturbing. She used the word 'nunnery' in a way that made it sound as though my ex-wife had started work in a bordello or something. There was an irony there I couldn't quite place. Did Siobhan know where Pamela was living? Neither Rain nor I had heard from her for years.

Walter's wedding to Floss that autumn was a light and carefree occasion. Walter seemed younger. He'd lost his rangy look, his tan had lightened, and he appeared happy and excited. There was something else too: he seemed as though a weight had been lifted from his shoulders. I thought I knew what that weight had been, and I wasn't sure I approved of what he had done, nor did I think it was necessary. He had decided not to make music again, nor would he write songs or poetry nor do anything that might be regarded as 'art' for fifteen years. He later explained that it was fifteen years after Old Nik had had his vision that he returned to normal life. Walter intended to do the same. In any case, I felt what had happened was a significant aspect of what made him an artist in the first place; he had always been special, someone to whom the audience had responded positively. He unlocked their feelings. I'd told him he tapped into their collective psyche. He had money; he could start a new life.

There were cheerful wedding bells of course, the chatter of the guests, cake, and all their friends and families were present. There was no music and no dancing. Walter had wanted a less bawdy occasion for his second marriage.

This occasion was the first for many years on which I had an opportunity to speak with Walter's parents, Harry and Sally Watts. We had been in contact, but my business was doing well and I was busy. Harry was still in high demand too.

By the time we stumbled into each other I was slightly drunk. I should not have taken alcohol. I had sworn off it for years since

Pamela had walked out on me, but I was a little dizzy. What I can remember is vague.

Harry had put on weight. I imagined his arse must look rather ridiculous when he sat on the wide organ stool, shifting from side to side. He had lost a little hair, his skin was rather red, and he looked as though he might have become a bit of a boozer. He looked his age. What were we both now? Fifty-one?

Sally, though, still looked pretty good. She was wearing one of those bosom-enhancing uplift dresses women only get out at weddings to try to outshine the bride, made of stiff material that cupped her breasts like offerings. She smiled like a film star, her cleavage and her perfume distracting me.

'How lovely Florence is,' said Sally proudly. 'Do I remember her from the other wedding?' She laughed. 'I shouldn't mention that, should I, Louis? You were flirting with both the younger girls, weren't you? Selena of course and Florence! Did you ever tell Walter? Shall I? Ha ha!'

My face must have revealed my anxiety; we were at my godson's wedding for heaven's sake!

She laughed again. 'Don't worry, Louis, I won't say anything. I remember once it was you and me who were flirting. Before Harry of course.'

I couldn't remember flirting with the girls. I'd seen them since at Dingwalls several times and they'd said nothing about it. So now I decided I just had to suffer Sally's teasing, although I took some comfort from the fact that she and I shared some secrets too. It was true that she and I had flirted and come close to being lovers when we were younger – and not only before Harry. Occasionally afterwards too. It had always felt normal, human and natural to feel that attraction – old friends who survived the sixties should always consider wife-swapping surely? Even if like me they were usually too smashed to rise to the possibility.

Then she changed tack, hardening slightly.

'How is Siobhan? We liked her very much you know.'

'Siobhan is getting along,' I said, aware that I sounded rather drunk. I hadn't really had very much to drink, but – Christ! – I was actually swaying. 'We exchange letters occasionally.'

'You are as rat-arsed as Florence was,' said Sally, impishly switching back to a topic she had no doubt sensed made me highly uncomfortable. 'You remember that, Louis? At Walter's wedding to Siobhan?'

What *was* she getting at? Harry laughed, perhaps hoping to lighten the mood, but I knew Sally pretty well, and there was undoubtedly a real barb in her words. What a fucking cow she was being!

'What could possibly be wrong with an eighteen-year-old girl, playing bridesmaid, getting a little drunk at a friend's wedding?' My voice was slurred, but part of me felt the need to defend Floss.

Harry changed the subject. How strange it was, he said, that Walter should marry such a horsey girl.

'Sally and I have always been enthusiastic riders,' he said. 'Especially when Walter was a little kid, but at an early age he developed an aversion to horses that bordered on the pathological. You must remember that, Louis. Rain loved horses of course.'

Later, with Sally safely engaged at a distant table with Rain, catching up on the gossip, Harry sat with me.

'I've never understood Walter's commitment to this pub rock stuff. I thought it was a teenage phase. At least it's turned to gold for him. But what is he going to do next? I wonder if he'll go back to horticulture and tree surgery? No bloody money in gardening, that's for sure.'

'He's been doing some very interesting writing, I know that.'

Harry looked away for a moment, musing almost as if he were talking to himself. I could barely hear what he said. 'Might he become a serious composer at last?'

'He might surprise us all,' I replied. 'Especially you, Harry. He could come up with something that advanced the entire way words and music are presented, something really futuristic and audacious.'

Harry's eyes gleamed. 'You mean something scientific?'

'No,' I said. 'A presage. Some kind of sign or signal. It might take as long as fifteen years to gestate, but I believe it will come.'

Harry's look of pride collapsed and he regarded me with disdain. 'Some bloody godfather you've turned out to be,' he said. 'Let's go and get another drink before you fall over.'

Old Nik and Maud had been invited through me, and they were the only ones who failed to show; Maud sent a message that Nik had been very ill. As I read the fax Selena came up behind me and pinched my bottom. It was such an impudently familiar and unexpected thing for her to do, I didn't know how to react. She stood beside me and read the note.

'So Old Nik gets ill and you lose your chance to flirt with his gorgeous wife.' She turned to Harry who appeared quite shocked. 'Floss has stolen my man, Harry. Do you know what that feels like?'

Harry looked bemused. We all glanced over at Floss who was talking to Walter.

Floss had a new front tooth, and was smiling proudly, delighted with her nickname at last. The tooth was set with a diamond.

Selena said it was her engagement gem; she had refused to wear a conventional ring.

Floss came over to where the three of us stood holding our champagne glasses, all yearning for something different to drink no doubt, something stronger.

Floss hugged her old friend and commiserated with her.

'I know you loved him, my darling,' she breathed as she released Selena and held her at arm's length, gazing at her intensely. 'But I love you, so much. Tell me you still love me. We are still friends.'

Selena held her belly for a moment and looked pained.

'Are you pregnant?' Floss laughed.

Selena dismissed the question with a wave. She said her work as a healer and her contact with angels often made her feel bloated. There was a price to pay for helping others: if a healer eased another's pain it sometimes manifested in the healer.

Floss kissed Selena.

'Thank you for being here, my darling,' she said. 'I know it's hard. I couldn't have faced it without you.'

They went to sit together on a bench in the hotel garden.

Selena was suddenly serious. Their voices were loud enough for me to hear.

'I'll never have a family,' I heard her say. 'Fuck knows what it is I always feel I'm carrying. But it isn't a child.'

'I know what you're feeling,' said Floss. 'You're feeling I've stolen the man you lusted after for years.' She laughed, throwing her head back as she did so. 'Cheer up; it's my wedding day. Let's talk about all this again later.'

'Yes,' agreed Selena readily. 'So you're going to be a married woman and do the school run, and shop in M&S and wash Walter's undies?'

'I want to breed horses, not children,' retorted Floss. 'I want to start a stable, and a stud. Our friend Ronnie Hobson – the gay guy from school – he is going to be my business partner.'

'I have always adored Ronnie,' said Selena. 'He'll be a wonderful help. He's funny and camp, but he's incredibly smart. And he's big too. You know he's won most fights he's ever been involved in? He won't abide being teased or insulted about being gay. He'll keep you safe from all those horny old men at gymkhanas.'

Then, his ears no doubt burning, Ronnie appeared, looking as lean, fit and bronzed as an Argentinian polo player.

'The girls!' he shouted, and slapped his thigh a little theatrically. 'Here we all are again. Together. The three mousquetaires.' They all laughed.

'Floss has been telling me about the new business you're getting into,' said Selena, seeming to be genuinely happier for a moment.

'It's going to be *perfect*,' said Ronnie, as the girls made space between them on the bench, and looking back and forth as he spoke. 'I am very good with horses, always have been. Floss is a good rider, but we want to build up a stud. Maybe even bring on some thoroughbreds.'

I stood a few feet away. The champagne didn't seem to be agreeing with me. I was listening to their conversation when Ronnie saw me.

'Come over here, Lou darling!' He was gesturing to me.

I joined them. 'Sorry, Floss.' I feigned regret. 'I overheard you. So no kids, but foals and colts?'

'That's it,' confirmed Floss. 'Ronnie is my man for breeding.'

Was there a hint of *double entendre* there? It was strange to hear Ronnie described as a masculine and capable figure. I hadn't really known the three of them when they were younger, not until Walter's first wedding. And Ronnie had grown since then, and not just in stature. He seemed stronger and lighter at heart.

'Were you and Floss ever an item?' I was amazed to hear the question come out of my mouth.

The three of them laughed, but it was Floss who came to my rescue.

'Ronnie would have been my first love if he hadn't been gay, and I love him still, platonically. With Selena, he's my best friend.' She put her arm around Ronnie's shoulder. 'I hope that Walter and I can be friends the way Ronnie and I have always been.'

Then, turning to me and looking up into my eyes, she said something that touched me deeply.

'And Louis, I've always really liked you too.' She obviously didn't want me to feel left out of their little trio. 'I'm off soon on my honeymoon. Look after these two for me.'

'Well.' I could feel my face was flushed. 'Thanks for that. I'll try. And good luck with the stud. I'm sure it'll be a lot of work to get going, but you two seem the right couple for the job.'

'Will it be expensive?' Selena asked the pertinent question.

'Walter has money now,' Floss explained. 'He has agreed to help set us up.' Floss saw that Selena was looking distracted.

'Don't be jealous,' she pleaded, reaching out and holding Selena's hands in her own.

'Don't be daft!' Selena dismissed the idea. 'Just don't hurt Walter. My sister was a complete bitch to him. She was an intellectual snob. It was as though Walter was never good enough for her. You must know – I realise this is not the right moment, but Walter was terribly shaken when Siobhan left him. He was deeply hurt. He looks tough, but he isn't. You know I tried to help him. I saw it all coming but I was the wrong person. The little sister, dammit. Floss, make him happy. He deserves it.'

Not long after our conversation ended, and Floss had gone off to find Walter, when suddenly, cameras whirred all around. Confetti filled the air. Floss looked stunning. The diamond in her front tooth glinted, but as her hair shone, and her eyes sparkled, such synthetic adornments were of little consequence. As I've said, Walter seemed lighter, and settled; he had a new dignity. They got into a massive limousine, waved through the lowered windows, and were gone in a cloud of dust thrown up from the gravel drive.

Chapter 10

I was probably the only person close to Walter who had some inkling of the reason for his absolute withdrawal from show business once he was married to Floss. Many of his friends looked to her for an answer, citing the rather elite life she led riding and breeding horses. But I knew that Old Nik had said something that had triggered a reaction in Walter, even frightened him.

At his home with Siobhan, Walter had always had a small studio with a piano and recording equipment. Now in his new house with Floss he kept only the piano, and he played it rarely. Music, once such an enormous part of his life, fell into the sidelines of his days. Walter didn't even listen to music any more. What was so strange about their home, and I was invited there only occasionally, was that they had no television, no music system, not even a radio. Instead they had a small cinema in the cellar, where they watched movies on DVD. If you tried to get Walter to discuss a movie, he would pretend to remember nothing much. The only interest he spoke about with enthusiasm was his garden.

After their marriage Walter and Floss had rented a five-bedroom thirties house in the leafy part of Sheen within walking distance of Richmond Park, and just a pleasant stroll away from my apartment. I visited as often as I was allowed. There were riding stables by several of the gates into the park, which suited Floss well, and Walter had chosen a property with a garden, laid mainly to utility lawn surrounded by a few mature trees needing surgery, that the owners were delighted for him to bring to life. The house was set back on a road that was fairly quiet even at rush hour. When legions of local mothers collected their kids from the various schools in the neighbourhood, there were occasional snags, but Walter had no reason to venture out. In any case, he rode a scooter. Floss used their big Volvo 4x4 to get to and from the various stables she used, or walked through the park to the one nearest their new home. Walter had few distractions. Planes flew low overhead on their way to Heathrow, but he quickly got used to their noise.

He had found his home with Siobhan in South Ealing more amenable in some ways, he told me. He had liked the variety of ethnic types who lived there, whereas in Sheen Walter felt entirely surrounded by the British middle classes.

This was my manor. Up in my flat that doubled as a gallery on Richmond Hill, I became a familiar figure in the area to young trendy people interested in the Outsider Art that celebrities were starting to collect. I held my exhibitions in various local buildings, such as the White Lodge in Richmond Park and Orleans House on the River Thames. In fact there was a large Swedish community in the area, and a fair representation of Japanese and Asian business families. However Walter, with no children at school, would have little occasion to meet them, and wasn't really aware of his neighbours in the usual ways. So he lived among them but, unlike me, at a distance. Walter was rather isolated, and deeply involved in creating his complex garden maze using faux hedges of woven willow rods and various creeping plants rather than the slower-growing yew.

The overall mood of the area was one of gentility under assault. Bordered by a few housing estates and hemmed in between Richmond Park and the railway line to Waterloo, its position on the South Circular Road meant that the traffic in

Sheen could sometimes be an annoyance. But without needing to take part in the school run Walter and Floss could pick and choose when they travelled. It seemed to most of their friends that they lived a peculiarly quiet life.

Crow Williams retained the band name and continued to work the pub circuit, playing many of the old songs written by Walter. He rechristened the band the Stand, but it became known, and billed, as Crow Williams and His Stand. As he was not about to adopt any kind of gimmicky Walter-inspired posing on stage there were some disappointed customers. But he surprised everyone by taking over the microphone and proving himself a good singer. He also wrote decent songs. Given the chance, he would complain a little about Walter's defection, partly because he felt Walter was missing out on the pub rock ethic that was like bread and water laced with nectar to Crow.

On one subject Crow could be prone to outbursts that shattered his otherwise super-cool demeanour: the Hansons had insinuated themselves into Andréevich's affections and obtained permission to use the defunct band name Hero Ground Zero once used by Paul Jackson. They were on the verge of filling stadiums with their extremely ambitious progressive rock that veered into baroque classical music and artful jazz. Three of the original band were included, despite their age; they gave the revived band dignity. Crow, the only one left in the Stand's original line-up, was appalled, and said so.

'Why would anyone even bother digging up that old Hero Ground Zero bollocks?' He remained friends with the Hansons, especially with Steve with whom he'd grown up, but he was always scathing, even to his face. 'It isn't new. It isn't even fuckin' old. It's rambling, self-indulgent, self-glorifying and egoistic.'

Selena meanwhile became a professional healer and worked in specialist clinics set up in the NHS with the sanction of Prince Charles. Despite this dignified role, she still appeared to be crazy to most of her friends. No man had ever taken her on, despite her prettiness, except for a wild night, or at best a wild week. I think she often felt lonely, and was one of the few of their old friends who saw Walter regularly and that was because she remained so close to Floss. But whenever she could, when she had access to Walter alone, discreetly behind Floss's back, she would remind him that she would always love him, and would always be willing to take him. Of course it was years later that I learned all this from Selena, but I had always wondered what Selena's motive for visiting Walter had been. It wasn't obvious, it didn't seem to be about trying to seduce him, not then. I believe that maybe she simply wanted to be near him occasionally. And no doubt she missed Floss, her childhood friend. She put on a little weight as the quiet years passed, and her angelic references became increasingly bizarre.

'Yesterday I realigned the universe,' she once said to me in passing, looking as though it had been as tiresome as doing the laundry. 'I was one of a thousand angels conscripted for the job. It isn't easy being me.'

But on the other hand she really did seem to help people when she set her mind to it, whether it was with hospice care, emotional or creative blockages, or even mundane medical problems like back pain.

She decided that Walter was creatively blocked, and was always trying to persuade him to allow her to spend time with him as a healer. I came to accept that she simply wanted to help, just as I did.

Of course I knew Walter was not really blocked; he simply blocked anyone who wanted to draw him back into his old musical world, or into art in any form. I had helped so many visual artists to break through their mental problems and become successful artists that I felt I was failing Walter in some way. But Walter was a musician and that was not my area. Yet there were famous musicians in rock and pop who had done such amazing work, either because they were mentally wobbling or because of stress, or drugs or whatever pressed them into new and extraordinary worlds.

Syd Barrett had simply taken too many drugs – and, sensitive artist that he was, he eventually broke down. Nevertheless, we were all the beneficiaries of his talent and his wild mind. His early work with Pink Floyd had been sublime and anarchically adventurous.

Peter Green had been a founder of Fleetwood Mac before they became so huge and one of the greatest blues players of the sixties. He simply found success was not what he wanted, nor could he cope with it. We used to see him wandering the streets near my gallery in Richmond, his fingernails allowed to grow so long that he could not play guitar.

Syd and Peter had dropped out of the music business and never made it back in.

Walter worried me, and I found him frustrating too. I felt that he was on the brink of some kind of useful madness, some kind of visionary capability, something close to the Asperger's syndrome so common among my Outsider artists, but, as I say, I was concerned I was failing him by being unable to help him take the next step.

I also felt that part of Walter's journey, in an odd way I didn't fully understand, was that his memory had sharpened. When I went to their house he would lead me around the extraordinary garden he had created in suburban Sheen, and list flowers, plants, shrubs, insects, birds, butterflies, worms, beetles – extinct and extant: the list was never-ending. Quite apart from the maze the garden itself was a complex and evolving design, with spirals and alleyways and cul-de-sacs and vistas that were infinitely and finely detailed.

In a way he had cheated by making dense trellises on which he grew climbing plants, which defined and provided density in the maze several years before the slower-growing hedges caught up. The climbing plants also filled the air with perfume and the garden with spring colour. Finding oneself lost in the labyrinth was never claustrophobic or unnerving; when it happened to me I wanted to remain lost for hours, and finding the way out always felt a bit deflating. If I could have transformed Walter's garden into a painting it would have been magnificent.

So although I worried about him, I also believed that he was trying to manage his creative explosions through the work he did as a gardener.

And I knew that he was still hearing something, something remarkable, or disturbing.

Somewhere between the wind and the waves lies the collateral for the second movement. We have heard the fall of a glass cathedral and the collapse of a building like an airport terminal. To lead from the first movement to the second, a voice, almost human, wails a continuous note. The voice, if in fact it is a voice, is racked with pain, is gargling blood and chewing regurgitated flesh. The sweep of the wind, for that is what it is, caresses with broom-like fronds of air stroking over an endless landscape, gently at first, stirring the trees, the leaves, the dust from the woodland paths. Then gusts break up the soothing, hissing breaths, each one harder than the one before. Building to thunderous, house-shaking punches. Punches that, at the very moment they deliver a thrust of pressurised fresh air, knock every last gasp out of the lungs. Then that ancient whistling howl, from eternity: whooooowwwow, whoooooooowwwooooow, whooooooooooo. Like an air-raid siren over London in the Blitz, and equally portentous. This tempest can blow us directly into the jaws of hell, fan its flames, and feed its fire. Then the crash of a wave so huge, a tsunami-like wall of water falling on to the wind like a huge hand waving away an insignificant skein of smoke. The earthquake in the first movement has created this terrible wall of water? Perhaps. There is more than one wave, there are more, each more complex, more developed than the last. Crashing, folding, weeping, seeding, sanding, flowing, pebbling, rolling, whooshing and fading. Receding. The voice that remains now, after the tumult of the second movement, is human, no doubt about it now. It is the voice of a child, a little girl, of about seven or eight years old, and she is singing happily. She is using a language for her song that is completely made up. It sounds like a mixture of French, Italian, Spanish and some Mandarin Chinese. As she sings we can hear that she is playing with water, and possibly sand, on a beach or in a back-garden play-sandpit. She pours water into the sand, sand into the little container of water, back and forth.

Book Two

Chapter 11

A moment of silence...
      While we imagine the fifteen subsequent years during which Walter avoided making music, and Floss bred horses in order to avoid making babies.

Can I can bring myself and my family back into the frame again? Rain recovered from losing Walter. She remained friends with him, but it took a long time to forgive Floss; Rain had been interested in horses but – like many teenage girls – had given them up suddenly when boys came along. She continued to work for the BBC as a radio correspondent, but later when she had time off, she often worked at Floss's stud and sometimes she stayed with me in my apartment in Richmond for fairly long periods.

One evening, the sun going down like a red orb over Heathrow Airport in the distance, we sat at the open window and she sipped a glass of wine. Rain was in silhouette, and something of an aura framed her face, the effect of the sunset behind her. She looked older than usual; my daughter had become a strong-looking and powerfully attractive woman, perhaps not in the Irish sisters' league, but she had her own special mystique.

'Dad,' she said suddenly, her eyes moist. 'You know I don't hate Siobhan.'

I didn't really know what to reply. Before I could think of something she continued.

'I don't hate Floss. I don't hate Selena and I don't hate you or Mum.'

'I never thought for a moment that you did.'

'I think you probably did, Dad.' And she was right of course. She continued: 'I did dream I would marry Walter, and when he married Siobhan I did hate her for a while. But she has been a great friend to me, and to Mum.'

'That's good to hear,' I said, sorry that was all I could come up with.

'When Siobhan went back to Ireland and Selena jumped in I fucking hated her too, for a while. God, Walter seemed such a twat, sitting in Dingwalls waiting for women to throw themselves at him. When Floss beat Selena to the punch what really hurt was that, once again, Walter had not sensed that I was there waiting, and always would be.'

'You are like a sister to him.'

'We once kissed, Dad,' she protested. 'I remember telling you about it. We were still young, but we kissed for two hours, tongues down each other's throats. I was in ecstasy. I would have made love to him. He just stopped. It was as though we were playing a game of Monopoly together, and he got bored and folded up the board. A few minutes later he was playing his mouth-organ with his head in that huge plastic bucket that he used to make himself sound louder.'

'Rain, you lived with me, and with Harry and Sally, we were a family, you were like brother and sister. He was blind to that part of you. You will find a man, Rain; you just have to let Walter go.'

'I have let him go.' She nodded her head with certainty. 'That's what I'm saying. I've let all the men go. And I don't hate any of them any more. Men or women. I especially don't hate Siobhan. She's been great to me, and great for me. Do you understand what I'm saying, Dad?'

To be perfectly honest I had no idea what she was talking about. Was she trying to tell me she had fallen in love with Siobhan?

Rain occasionally went to visit her old boss in Waterford for what I took to be consultancy sessions and I had begun to wonder if they were lovers.

I felt quite worldly about all this. I had arrived at a place where I was unruffled, serene, and even rather proud of whatever Rain may have done with her sex life.

So my pride was pricked, and I was caught unaware, and felt a little foolish too, when a few days after our talk in my apartment, I heard from Selena that Rain's trips to Waterford were not only to spend time with Siobhan, but also to visit her mother, Pamela, who I had been told lived in a convent somewhere in County Wexford.

You will remember that my own affliction, my aberration, my visions, had been seeing what I believed might be the faces of frightening screaming heads in the grain of the walnut headboard of the old French bed, the one Pamela and I had bought a short time before she despaired of me and left me. It was Rain, trained researcher and qualified historian, who had gone out of her way to find out something strange about the journey of the bed itself. What she unearthed helped me to feel that I had not been entirely mad about the visions that I felt emanated from the old bed.

Its provenance was the castle city of Béziers in the south of France; the bedhead had been carved from a massive wooden gate to the city. Béziers had been the home of the gentle Cathars of the Languedoc region, who had refused to convert to Catholicism and brought down the ire of Pope Innocent III in the thirteenth century.

'Dad.' Rain caught my wandering attention. 'That bed from Béziers. You know I tried to convince Mum, despite my journalistic scepticism, that your nightmarish response to it had not been caused by drug abuse alone, but also by some intuitive facility you have. You remember, Dad, that the Pope's military commander, Simon de Montfort, slaughtered twenty thousand occupants of Béziers. Mum is a Catholic. It wasn't what she wanted to hear. At first she thought I was trying to trawl up the bloody history of the Catholic Church to try to break her faith and her vows. When she realised that I was just trying to generate a truce between my mum and dad, she understood.'

It was good to spend time with Rain, and feel closer to her again. She'd been away a long time, on and off.

A few months later Rain arranged for me to go to Ireland. I was to visit Siobhan and hoped to reconnect with Pamela.

The trip to Waterford is an easy one when you fly from Heathrow to Dublin, and then take a car down the motorway. You don't see much of the sea on the way south, so the arrival in Duncannon is especially uplifting. The sea, the sky, Waterford across the estuary. Rain had arranged for Pamela and me to meet at a little café that overlooked the small fishing port at Duncannon.

I looked at the redhead, wanting to see her as the amazing ginger Wonderwoman I had once known. What I saw was a mother, a concerned and slightly shamefaced one at that. But it was me who went first. I played my hand, which was not a good one. No kings, no queens, no jacks or aces. Just numbers.

'Did I fuck things up for Rain?'

Pamela shook her head, but I could see she didn't feel entirely happy.

'You know I did nearly enter the convent, I was almost a nun.' She looked at me as though waiting for me to laugh. 'Oh, I know it sounds mad. But it was partly my lust that drove me to it. I'm a Catholic. It was OK making love to you, but you weren't enough. I'm sorry, Louis. You were my mistake. Rain was our mutual triumph, but I couldn't stay with you. Not after . . .' She didn't complete the sentence.

'What did I do wrong, Pam?' I sounded pathetic.

'If you don't know now you never will, Louis. Let's just move on, can we? It's been torture for Rain having to lie to you, to keep my life here secret.'

Pamela wouldn't tell me where she was living. Clearly she didn't want to see me regularly. But despite the discomfort we both felt, we were at least friends again. Rain was delighted of course. She only knew she had gone a long way towards repairing things between her parents; she knew nothing about what had really separated us. Neither did I. Not then.

Rain then took me to visit Siobhan in her cottage. Rain had stayed with Siobhan maybe once or twice by that time. Whatever enmity had built up when Siobhan had married Rain's childhood crush seemed to have evaporated.

It was a charming house. The two ground-floor rooms had been knocked together to make one large space that included the small kitchen at the back on one side of the fireplace. Siobhan had transformed the room into a generous space with two large and comfortable sofas strewn with cushions, and a thick rug on the stone-slab floor that somehow always felt warm. A huge inglenook fireplace had been tagged on to the back of the house when a new staircase to the upper floor had been constructed along the back wall. The house had originally been a farmworker's cottage, one of three. The other two were closer together and had been combined and converted into a home by Siobhan and Selena's parents, when times had been better, before Selena was born. Siobhan's house still looked quite plain from the outside. The windows were modern-looking, of metal and double-glazed to provide some resistance to the winter wind from the Irish Sea less than a mile off and which was visible from her bedroom. The roof was of unpleasant and rather cheap tiles. But Siobhan had coaxed flowers to bloom around the front of the house, partly by planting a high protective hedge of laurel. Some of the plants she had kept in pots, moving them in winter into a basic glass greenhouse at the back of the house. Now most of what she had planted had grown strong and vigorous and had been transplanted into the beds.

The way the upper floor was arranged confirmed my suspicion that Rain and Siobhan were lovers. There was evidence of two women living together: two sets of clothing strewn around carelessly, and in the bathroom two toothbrushes, one electric, Rain's preference. Siobhan's behaviour with Rain was affectionate and intimate, like a doting and patronising aunt perhaps, but also slightly lascivious. At least that's how it all seemed to me.

At the top of the staircase the entire floor opened up. A massive double bed, again strewn with cushions, took up one end of the room and had been raised on a plinth so its occupants could see the view of the distant estuary while lying back. The bathroom was a part of the bedroom, the tub in the middle at one end, with an open shower tray to one side, and a small toilet in a semi-enclosed area to the other with a sink where I'd spotted the toothbrushes.

Of course, I would have felt very uncomfortable interrogating my own daughter about her sexuality. Rain was no great beauty, I suppose, but she had a very good figure, and a strong presence, lovely eyes and a wide mouth. I knew from her mother Pamela that some men's sexual insatiability is unequal to that of certain women. We blokes literally run out of blood, we fail to swell after a time; such troubles are never a problem for a healthy woman. Rain was not Pamela, but may well have wanted more than she got from her first few male lovers.

As I looked around the bedroom, the inevitable question to my daughter was on my lips: have you found someone, at last, that doesn't stop?

Siobhan joined us, as if to deflect my rather tacky curiosity, and as I looked up after bending to look out at the sea, she was standing with her arm linked with Rain's.

The message I received, right or wrong, had at the time been very clear.

Your daughter is mine now. This is where we sleep, and roll, and spoon, and sometimes things go much further.

Fifteen years had passed. Fifteen years earlier, Floss had walked into Dingwalls very soon after Siobhan had walked out. Walter had met Floss and married her. In the interim I had sold painting after painting, making the most money from Old Nik's extraordinary, visionary work. Walter worked in his garden, the maze becoming ever more dense as the years passed. Floss grew her equestrian business with Ronnie into a hugely lucrative concern. Ronnie and Floss spent a lot of time together, which was still the subject of some gossip, born back in the days when they ran the riding stable in Sheen. But with their later venture, one lucky thoroughbred colt they entered into a race at Newbury won by a mile and was sold for stud for several million pounds to an Arab from Dubai. The colt's progeny went on to become winners themselves. As Walter's money ran out, Floss's filled the void.

Walter still contacted me occasionally and we got together to catch up a few times over that period. He said that from time to time he tried to make music based on his writings from the days when he started hearing the anxious thoughts of the front-row audience at Dingwalls. But he rarely heard the kind of disturbing sounds he'd heard back then. He was beginning to get out and about too, getting to know some of his neighbours. Sometimes he had a chat with the Iraqi fellow who ran the local convenience store. His name happened to be Hussein, which he told Walter was incredibly common among Muslims.

In the autumn of 2011 Walter came to visit me to ask what I thought he should do to celebrate his fifteenth wedding anniversary. I recommended flowers and he ordered them by phone.

'Fifteen years! That's lovely,' cooed the woman in the florist's. 'So what have you been up to in your retirement? Don't you miss the band?'

'Yes, I do miss it, but I've moved back to my first career. I'm a garden designer. It's inspiring. Creative.'

'I hope you still do music,' she insisted.

'I still hear it!'

Politely fielding the woman's questions, Walter laughed, ordering the pale pink peonies that he knew Floss adored. But as he put the phone down, he seemed to feel a wave of anxiety sweep over him. He asked if I would spend an hour with him.

We went for a walk together in Richmond Park, and I tried to comfort him. At the same time what he told me filled me with an excitement that I found hard to contain; after the fallow period of fifteen years, in which he had concentrated on gardening while Floss got on with her equestrian business, Walter was now hearing music again.

The soundscapes were back. Was Walter now going to return to the music business?

What I heard him tell the woman from the flower shop was that he was doing some creative work at home. Up until that moment he had convinced himself that was precisely what he was not doing. By gardening he had felt he was avoiding creativity and art, dealing only with the soil and the elements.

As Walter began to describe what felt to him like a crash, I began to fly a little. After all, I live by the madness of others, and my own madness had yet to be redeemed.

'I hear what people are thinking,' Walter said quietly as we slowly walked along the sandy bridle path near Richmond Gate, where Floss occasionally rode Dragon, her favourite Highland pony. Not a good horse for dressage, but sporting an extravagantly long 'blond' mane, just like she had once worn her own. And he could jump pretty well.

'Walter,' I reminded him, 'you spoke to Nik about all this, not to me. You explained what you were hearing to him.'

'Every morning I walk to the main road to buy milk and a chocolate bar from my friend Hussein,' he said. He smiled his handsome grin and looked at me, pausing for a moment. 'Got to keep my energy up.'

He produced a sheet of paper. At first sight it looked like a kind of manifesto with short paragraphs. He handed it to me.

'Is this for me to keep?' I was pleased to be trusted again. It had been a while.

Walter nodded. 'My face is familiar enough locally, to people who saw me perform, or know my face from the papers fifteen years back, or documentaries on the telly – whatever – and they chat to me. They seem to feel I am a friend. It's wonderful in a way. It makes me feel as if I live in a small village. Or I overhear them talking to Hussein. Later, I write down what they say. Sometimes, before they speak, I can already hear and feel what they are concerned about, I can hear it as sound. Everyone is worried, Louis. Frightened.'

'Fear is the normal human condition, Walter,' I said, turning the page over. 'So this writing is not a description of what you've been hearing?'

'What I hear is much harder to describe. I don't think I'll ever be able to compose music that comes close to it; some of these paragraphs connect with what I hear and some don't.' He tapped the page I held in my hand as he spoke.

We crossed the busy road and walked towards Petersham, and then in Richmond Park sat on a bench that allowed a view of St Paul's Cathedral eight miles away in the City, just visible through the haze. I began to read. The title of the page was written in longhand, using an old-fashioned pen: 'The people behind the soundscapes'; the rest was printed from a computer.

I worry about the planet, this strange weather.

When I wake up I feel my dreams must have been disturbing, but I can remember so little.

I find it so hard to reconcile the gentle Christian beliefs I know you've all been taught with the violent demands of the hard-line Muslim clerics at our local mosque. Why should my kids have to face all that intimidation, those threats and censure? They haven't done any wrong, at least not yet.

How can music and dancing be wrong? Surely they are expressions of the heart?

Where have all the sparrows gone? When I was a child there were thousands of them, everywhere.

Robots will take over the world; I know they will.

Hurricanes. When will this wind cease?

Why can't things just remain as they were? Why is there always someone who wants to change things?

'It's incredibly sad, isn't it?' I looked over to Walter who was gazing into the distance, his strong, handsome profile belying the fragility of his mind. 'Who are they, all these frightened people you have as acquaintances?'
Walter did not reply.

'Do any of these inspire music?' I said, trying to imagine what Nik would have made of all this.

'Read the first one,' Walter said. 'Read it aloud, and then close your eyes and see what happens.'

It was a strange instruction, and I felt a little embarrassed as I began. '*I worry about the planet,*' I read haltingly. I gave a small cough to clear my throat. '*This strange weather.*'

At this I looked into the sky. It was a bright Autumn, a bit of blue, a few clouds, the sun hiding somewhere. I continued reading aloud.

'*When I wake up I feel my dreams must have been disturbing, but I can remember so little. I find it so hard to reconcile the gentle Christian beliefs I know you've all been taught with the violent demands of the hardline Muslim clerics at our local mosque. Why should my kids have to face all that intimidation, those threats and censure? They haven't done any wrong, at least not yet. How can music and dancing be wrong? Surely they are expressions of the heart?*'

Walter looked at me; I looked back. I understood why a devout and extreme follower of Islam would turn his back on music, even proscribe it, but both of us would find it hard to believe music was an expression of evil.

'Who said this?' I asked.

'Funnily enough it was Hussein himself, who runs the shop.'

'Not a radical then.' I smiled.

'No, but he is sincere, devoted to God.'

'Worried as much about climate change as he fears the hardline mullahs?'

Walter shook his head, but he was affirming what I'd said.

'What – or how – could hearing such a statement possibly cause you to hear it as sound?'

I was not as incredulous as I may have seemed, but I pressed my godson. 'What could it chime with in your own heart? Are you afraid of climate change, or of radical mullahs? Do you have a soundscape – as you call them – that evokes what Hussein said to you?'

The singing child is crushed by the fall of a hundred massive rocks that come down from the sky like grossly overgrown hailstones. They are in fact part rock, part ice, and as they smash into the ground – covered as it is by the broken glass, the tangled metal and the sand and rock-pools of the two previous movements – stone and liquid concur to create a new noise. It is the sound of avalanche, and in the midst of it all is the farting noise of a thousand rubber bags being squashed, their putrid contents expelling in globs and gobs. Ice and shit. Or is the burbling, bubbling sound that of lava burping in the heart of a volcano? Introduced now, in this revolting and heart-rending scene, is the first violin. Ralph Vaughan Williams in his Lark Ascending used a solo violin in the most perfect impressionistic way possible. Here, the solo violin represents a vile whiff of methane escaping from the cesspit of foul lava. At first a growl, a scrape, then a swoop, a cascade, and then a rhythm that allows the construction of a simple fugue. The soul of a lost daughter, a child never born, will rise, almost like a lark, from the stinking recesses of the abyss.

Chapter 12

Walter had predicted that fifteen years in the garden would be enough. Floss still came and went, always shining, always alive, riding close, riding away, riding here, riding there. She would come home from a day at the stables covered in mud, her blond hair in wisps around her face; sometimes she chewed a plait or scratched her nose, and she'd walk into the garden which after all his work was in some ways as impenetrable as a jungle. She wouldn't call him, she would search until she found him, draw him to his feet, put her arms around him, bring his face to her own, and kiss him so tenderly and affectionately that he never had a moment's doubt how much she loved him, how she trusted him, and how much she appreciated the freedom he allowed her.

He had tried to tell her that he needed to escape, he too needed to fly, to jump from a window and see what he heard as he crashed to earth. He couldn't find the words. Now she kissed him again and again, repeating that they had been together for fifteen years. In the patterns, the whorls of the lawns, the spirals of the flowerbeds, the planting of the trees, Walter had echoed and celebrated and exalted that number: fifteen. So that day, the occasion of their fifteenth anniversary, with his beautiful wife in his arms, he knew that he had to leave his garden.

In the house they made love and Walter wept. He cried the way a woman might if taken to a new height and stamina of orgasm, and cannot contain her emotion or her gratitude; not grateful to her lover but rather to the miracle unleashed in her own body. Then Floss wept too, though her sexual arrival had been more sudden and brief. Sexually then for a moment they had changed chemistry, taken on different elemental names, and swapped roles, his arrow down, hers up.

'I might play the piano again,' Walter said. He lay back on their bed, his chest bare, still moist from shared sweat.

Floss smiled, and tossed hair that had grown long again.

'You could take your mouth-organ out into the garden tomorrow,' she said with a laugh. 'See what happens.'

Walter pulled the pillow from under his head to swipe her, but she was too quick. As she walked naked to the window he gasped at how beautiful she was at the age of thirty-five, how slender and fit, and yet on the edge of being voluptuous. She turned to look back at him and even in the mist of sexual afterglow his breath quickened at the curve of her breast.

'You must do whatever makes you happy,' she said. 'I know what you've been hearing is not about happiness necessarily, but you need to live. That's all.'

She ran back and threw herself on top of him and they kissed again.

'Do all men need to make things?' She was laughing. 'Walls, holes in the ground, songs about trucks?'

'We like songs about sex best,' said Walter, thinking about Crow and finding his thought quite wrong. 'In the band I wrote pretty much everything. I think I was too embarrassed to write anything about sex. A garden is all about sex.'

'What!' Floss laughed. 'What do you get up to?'

'I meant birds and bees.'

'You watch insects while I encourage Dragon to cover a visiting Highland mare,' she said as she gathered her hair into a muddled bun.

After fifteen years they were more deeply in love than ever. But Floss told Walter that she suddenly wanted to create something as well. And so both these beautiful young friends of mine, my godson and his wife, had survived a period of suspension, a time they had lived in stasis, riding, digging, staying close to straw and sweat, the earth and fertiliser. Now they were ready to start again.

As Walter and I walked in Richmond Park he confided to me his renewed love for Floss and I was glad. But there was something more I needed to know.

I turned to him, blocked his path, put my hands on his shoulders, and then lifted my right hand to his cheek.

'What did Andréevich say to you?' I asked him as firmly as I could. 'Since then you've ploughed all your creative energy into your garden.'

Walter took out a slip of paper and showed it to me. He had written down what Old Nik had said.

You must learn to wait. The moment will come. Waiting is the black art of creativity, not inspiration. Be ready. Be alert. Always. And then when the moment comes, you will be waiting, and you will have nothing else to do, nothing better to do than to fall in love all over again. As I once was, you are the mirror of everyone around you. You are their conscience and their voice. Look to the future, whatever you see will come about, good and bad, it is inevitable. Look to the light.

'Fifteen years ago,' said Walter, 'I wasn't really ready to accept such an idea.'

'It's beautiful,' I said. 'And makes good sense. Are you ready now?'

'I'm not sure I'll ever be completely ready,' he said, smiling wryly. 'I've never been brave enough to face the job of making real and tangible what I hear.'

* * *

Fire. Flames. Crashing timbers. Roaring whoosh of air. Crackling, metal expanding and creaking. Small explosions. Then a huge and thunderous eruption. The cries of firemen to each other, the beeping and snatching white-noise gasps of their radios. The sweep of the hoses. The sound of the generator in the fire engine. Glass shatters and falls. Occasionally what sounds like fireworks fizz and whizz, but it's just various bottles of household chemicals exploding and each doing their unique chemical incineration thing. We hear the footsteps of a man, crunching over debris. The kid is alive, he says. A miracle.

Somehow, all that time alone in his garden, building a safe retreat for himself, a kind of spiritual hub around which the suburb of Sheen might have turned, Walter had not understood that he would never be able to shut down his connection with his peers, nor shut out their subconscious thoughts. For fifteen years of creative lock-down he had continued to be steadily filled with their emotions, their rage, fear, shame, resentment and tendency to judge, their need to try to shift the blame for everything that was wrong with the world, and everything they might have done but had failed to do, failed in their drive to try to right significant wrongs.

He had first become aware of this starting to grind away in him in the months before he had decided to quit the band. Because it was at that time that Siobhan, mistaking his genius for the scrupulous industry of a poet in the making, had forced him to review his creative process, and in so doing he had stumbled upon this *second sight* of his, that both frightened and appalled him. And so he had run away and hidden. Sometimes when two people love each other, and adore and respect each other as had Siobhan and Walter, one of the pair is left utterly alone. She had known instinctively that Walter had some great mission before him. She had also hoped to support him, encourage and guide him to some extent. But then she had lost him.

Floss, by contrast, rode horses, brushed them and mucked them out. It appeared she did very little else. She was always awake at sunrise or earlier in winter, and arrived at her stables near Richmond Park at seven in the morning. Sometimes Walter would be awake before she left the house, and would be able to share tea or coffee with her. Usually he slept later, until about nine or ten. The rock 'n' roll time clock was hard to change.

In fact, Floss played a big part in running the house. They had a single helper, a cleaner who doubled as housekeeper and came in every day but weekends, and only for a few hours. She shopped for the couple, and cooked, but did so according to recipes, menus and shopping lists created by Floss. Floss went to snuggle up to her horses at weekends as well.

In the fifteen years they had been married they had never taken a holiday abroad. Floss entered gymkhanas and won prizes. They had a splendid compact horsebox with camping space that was kept parked at the stable. Walter joked that it would have served well as a bandwagon.

Walter was still not comfortable with horses; there had been the incident when his parents rode up to him on a beach when he was a child, and then rode quickly away. This had not exactly traumatised him, but it had made it impossible for him to regard horses as anything other than instruments of escape. His parents had escaped their duty to their tiny son by riding away; was Floss now to do the same? This innate suspicion was always picked up by any Equus he approached; it was not appreciated.

Walter was all the while immersing himself in his stunning garden – to keep at bay the overwhelming sounds he might otherwise hear. Floss lost herself in her work with her horses, and especially the breeding work at her small stud; was this to stifle any instinct to have a child of her own?

I'd met Floss's partner at the stables, her old school friend Ronnie Hobson. I knew Walter liked him, and trusted him around Floss partly because he was gay. He was exactly the same age as Floss, so about nine years younger than Walter, very striking-looking, slightly effeminate in speech but powerfully built. His back was straight and strong, he rode a horse like a Prussian colonel from another era, and I'd heard since that the predominantly female customers of the stable tended to describe his smile as 'melting'.

Ronnie looked after the accounts at the stables, and the business made a profit. As well as being an accomplished horseman, he was something of a horse-whisperer. He had trained Floss's favourite seven-year-old Dragon, and taught the extremely nervous horse and rider to jump. With another horse, Santana, a thoroughbred gelding they had acquired from a stud in Wiltshire, he added some gentle but effective dressage tutelage, bringing Floss's teenage skills to the highest class. He coached Floss in all the important details of preparation that led to gymkhana wins and to the rising reputation of the stud. Floss adored Ronnie.

I knew that Selena claimed that Ronnie was 'accompanied by a ghostly entity'. Floss joked that this was true, and that Ronnie's 'entity' was one Clive, a beautiful young waiter at All Bar One whose hair and skin were so pale, so lovely, that he might indeed have been a ghost.

The mothers and daughters of Sheen who availed themselves of Floss & Hobson Livery were fascinated by the intimacy between the business partners. Gay or not, when Ronnie flirted with Floss, she responded. The watchers believed they could see that something was not right. For years Walter ignored all this and the gossip it inspired, but when he started to try to compose again, he began to notice some electricity, some energising spark between Floss and Ronnie that he had never felt in his own relationship with his wife.

No longer secure in his garden, he was bombarded by the buzzing pheromones and energies that Floss seemed to bring home with her after work. She was alive, completely. He had some way to travel to arrive at his own destination; he felt it might turn out to be precisely the opposite end of the spectrum of *joie de vivre*. Second sight as the Celts had known it was sometimes a precursor of death – not a premonition, but a vision of death as inevitability for the human race and every individual human soul, as in Old Nik's vision on Skiddaw. But what Walter began to hear and feel as he opened his heart to his creative soul was not simply death. Rather, it was a connection with the fear of death felt by those around him. One can come to fear fear itself, and that particular fear seemed to be what Walter emanated when he tried to compose.

The soaring song of a lark sounds across the breathing din of a hundred-acre field. No wind, or else we'd hear nothing at all of the distant bird, but the low and thudding hubbub of a dozen tractors binding bales, or speeding cars and white vans on the motorway five miles across the hill, just beyond the steepled church. Of course, in the even, gentle breeze there is the sound of moving trees; once noted the sound is the familiar swishing that has a multitude of different degrees from a kind of crackling to a simple hiss. All this is the backdrop to the sparkling rising dipping falling call of the swooping bird. A goose from Halifax, Nova Scotia, lost his way home this time, challenges three others for the lake. He cackles, screams and barks, and splashes, trying to seem insane. They hoot back at him, determined not to give way. Intermingled are the laughs and giggles of a girl of about fifteen. She whoops as she runs, shrieks with joy and abandon. We need this water too. A single gosling rushes out, the reason for this fit of pique, like some demented child on speed, or clockwork toy with wonky rudder, steering first this way then that, snapping flies perhaps. The noble mallards do their usual thing, a quack it's best to call it. There are variations on the basic quack of course. Quacks come in threes and fours, all expressing some degree of mallardic irritation and impatience. The honk of a dismayed heron whose concentration simply cannot, must not, be disturbed. This may look like fishing to some who can be so amused, but this chap behaves as though he's meditating for some Buddhist edge, some Sufi path, some perfect moment with a golden carp with bones removed and scales rubbed dry. The pigeons hoot like idiots, always fools, just one sound for every kind of emotional charge. The tits, the robins, jays and rooks all jockey for the sky, the bush, the slug, the worm, the fly. The magpies search in packs like wolves, for eggs to steal. And then without warning the twitcher's world explodes, indeed becomes a proper world, and every flying thing we've ever seen and heard attempts to take some charge. For those of you whose hearing is, like Walter's, a little smashed, the sound of some of these small birds, if slightly slowed to bring it better into the range of human hearing dimmed by years of blues and timpani booms, is a wondrous thing. Even lower then it will need to be for those of you who liked to shoot, to eat the bag, spit out the lead; you're mutton, mate, that's what we say. In all this high-pitched singing, all for love or space or food or flight, there is more music. From my tower I can reach out, no hair to hang, but still can touch the fairy tales of nature's most prodigious collection of collectives. A startling of pianos; a pudding of Steinways; a persuasion of Marshall and Roses; a mesmerisation of Bosendorfers; a consternation of Bluthners. Tweet. How did that single word ever come to mean the sound of bird? Anyway, anyhow, anywhere. Like flutes and pipes and reeded horns in flight, a concatenation of Charlie Parkers. Light. Stars. Magic.

Chapter 13

I am tempted, as I continue to confess, a narrator, to talk about myself. I am aware that in groups of people – friends, families and associates – trends of thinking can spread in an unhealthy way. I am also aware that good and positive energies and theses can be shared as well; faith in nature, and in human potential for good can be nurtured through conversation and enthusiasm for art and literature and the fine works of great men and women from history.

Rain was an exception. Once she let go of any notion that she might one day marry Walter she took off like a lark. Freed from one man she found many enthusiasms. She was in love and beset by infatuation and in love again almost every time I saw her – each time with a new and fabulous conquest that I had to remind myself could be either male or female. If she was Siobhan's lover it was clearly not a monogamous relationship. As Rain was my daughter, my girl, Walter was my son – a godson, but my boy. I continued to do things for Walter, I helped open in him doors of perception and creativity that his father had failed to do, despite the fact that he was a musician himself. I encouraged him to develop that sense of the people around him; his immediate peers, appointing them as the commissioners of his role as a creative writer and composer – working entirely on their behalf, for their pleasure and enthralment. I guided him in the business of listening and waiting, the two most important abilities for a composer.

What I did not do was prepare him for the deleterious side effects of madness.

Gasping, moaning, cries of orgasm, women weeping and panting in the pain of childhood, men reeling from punches, children crying, laughter, gulping air, shouts, screams, hollers. What is this sound? Humanity, making its noises. Babbling conversation in a hundred languages, singing, chanting, a face being slapped, a slash of a blade, the sound of a fall, a slip, a slide, the crash of a human body as it lands after a fall from a high building. Oof! Ungh! Aaah! All those exclamations gathered from a million comic books, a dozen Elmore Leonard crime novels, all sounding in a single minute of time. Calls, one to another, in panic or in friendship, a mother to a child, a child to a lost mother, one child to another, one football player to another in the middle of a game. The sound of a kiss being started, broken. Entreaties, endearments, pet names in endless and absurd lists, meaningless, puerile, sweet, silly. Orgies, battles, streetfights, audiences at rock shows, the circus. Shouting loud enough for God to hear. Silent muttering prayers, litanies, under-the-breath aspirations and requests, hopeful pleas. Shouts. Then a painful birth, remembered as an echo in an explosion of brilliant yellow rays.

Summoned to Walter's music studio in his garden at Sheen I admit I felt a mixture of excited anticipation at what Walter might play me, and anxiety about his mental condition. On the telephone he had sounded scattered, confused and unfocused.

'I'm doing creative stuff again,' he said. 'But I also have an old feeling; I sense I'm losing Floss somehow. It feels as though this marriage could go the same way as it did with Siobhan unless I'm really careful.'

'Don't be daft,' I soothed. 'You love each other. Floss has her work, you have yours.'

'But in the entire fifteen years of this marriage I have never before exposed myself to the kind of trouble that composing seems to bring up for me.'

'You're worried about what you're hearing?'

'It's making what is already difficult even worse.'

'Don't let yourself get lost,' I advised. 'Try not to isolate, don't get self-obsessed.'

Walter laughed. 'You have been nagging me for the last few weeks to throw myself into this, to allow my compulsive drive to emerge. I have some basic music now. Do you want to listen to it?.'

'You are an artist, Walter,' I reminded him. 'Whether you work in the garden, or composing. It's the same.'

'I don't think the price is worth paying if I lose Floss.'

'Every woman wants a song,' I teased. 'Didn't Siobhan just want one sonnet? And you couldn't even do that?'

'I *wouldn't* do it,' replied Walter. 'Should I compose music for Floss, about her, that reflects her, rather than what I am beginning to feel?'

'It can't hurt.' I laughed.

'Floss wants me to do what is right for me. Not knock up silly love songs. I'm feeling a new load placed on me. My peers are all fifteen years older since the days of the band, just like me, but most of them have young children. They carry a sense of duty, responsibility, and both the burden of the past and the weight of the future. They all have money troubles and huge concerns about the environment. They want to see a safe and secure future for their children.'

He laughed loudly. 'Louis, around here we are surrounded by human breeders, yummy mummies and their City boy husbands who want to have lots of children. But these are scary times to bring up kids. You must know that.'

I understood. Walter's peers were a lot younger than me, but we all had access to the same dreadful information. I was moving towards the twilight of my life; I knew that if I were younger with small kids I would not feel so sanguine. Indeed, Walter's contemporaries carried the weight of the planet, not just of their own immediate environment. Nature was now redefined; nothing natural was unaffected by the explosion of the human race and the threat of the actual explosions it might unleash if they all failed to agree on who God was, if indeed such a personage existed in any shape or form.

No, he could not write for Floss, because as an artist he could not contact her. He had become creatively imperious.

When I arrived at the house in Sheen I walked into a dilemma that I prayed I might be able to help Walter to solve. However I couldn't disguise my fizzing excitement at hearing what he had composed in his new and disturbed state.

Walter, in my opinion, had found in himself a streak of genius. His songs with the Dingwalls band had been good. Hearty pub rock was hard to beat, and not easy to make. His new work, his soundscapes, would surely be the kind of art I knew how to engage with, penetrate, analyse, value and market.

Closed eyes. Blindness. Then flashes, an infinite universe, layer after layer of stars, each promising a new beginning. A clarinet plays scales, disciplined and regular, obviously read from a book for practice and fluency of eye and hand. Gentle, the soft, reedy, slightly honking sound of the lower notes rings across a small suburban room, setting glasses rattling on the table. The player sometimes leaves his position at the music stand, and when he feels familiar enough with a section of the music approaching begins to walk around the room, raising his instrument to the ceiling. Over this cascading, regimented and predictable non-musical music comes the sound from the next room: a baritone saxophone, wild, playing with no boundaries, barping, stopping with glottal clicks, the rattle of the complex brass key system adding a percussive rhythm to the scales and extemporisations. Among all this swooping music is what sounds like a swooping light, like a kind of electronic ray, wooshing. Then a piano, in the wrong key, or is it in any key at all? The player is using mainly his right hand, his left framing random chords at the beginning of every four bars or so, and then flies all over the chord, up and down, like a bird soaring, sometimes like a trapped animal trying to escape from a cage, or a fly trying to batter through some glass to the light. Then a door seems to open and the piano breaks free, the baritone sax catches up with the clarinet and for a moment, a brief moment, they concur, and flow. Then they each veer off on their separate flights. Now a double bass sets up a rhythm, so strong, so insistent that it demands not to be ignored, but it is ignored. The fingers plucking are replaced sometimes by a powerful bowing, percussive and mischievous, rising high on the strings, sometimes sounding like a viola or cello both slowed down into a new and sonorous range, but also sped up in an emulation of the inevitably clumsy and staggering patterns only a double bass can express. Then drums clatter along, then more saxophones, thin-sounding trumpets, joined by electric guitars being played far too fast, trying to sound like saxophones being overplayed hysterically. Next electric instruments join in, organs, Wurlitzer pianos with their characteristic knocking, buzzing reeds. Synthesisers swoop in, playing in impossible clusters of harmonically forced intervals, fourths, fifths, sevenths – creating a modality reminiscent of another world, but somehow echoing the strange timbres of those dusty pipe organs in old churches pushed into overtones. This is the history, the mystery, the hysteria of jazz rattling and drifting in incoherent rusty waterfalls across the landscape. Then suddenly, without warning, everything stops and an alto sax is all that can be heard, a player disconnected from his soul but somehow connected to the universe.

I think it is clear by now that I took my role as a godfather seriously. Perhaps too much so. The vows one is asked to take in the baptism service (and Harry was a Catholic) were of a religious rather than spiritual nature. But it was in the matter of Walter's spiritual state that I felt most responsible. I wanted him to be fulfilled, to be happy, and to be able to bear with equanimity the frustration and difficult times when creativity was not free-flowing. I guessed Harry knew I would be better at this stuff than he would. Yet I wanted to offer practical help too. Walter had attempted to musicalise the written soundscape descriptions. As he played a few chords on the piano, and sang some plaintive phrases, it became clear that he hadn't got very far with it. As a composer he couldn't capture what he heard in his head, what he had so eloquently and poetically described on paper.

'Walter,' I said, 'this is very interesting, but you need someone to remind you how to write music again.' I laughed, trying to reduce the impact of my negative review. 'You need a kick up your musical arse! I hope you don't mind me saying this.'

Walter smiled, and shook his head. 'You're right,' he confessed. 'I'm trying my best. I seem to have lost the knack. Or maybe this is just too big a task for me?'

I decided to ask Crow to visit Walter, as there was no one more down-to-earth, more practical. No one was better than Crow at kicking musical arse.

Chapter 14

Despite the fact that Walter was no longer performing at Dingwalls, I continued to go, and quite often. I had many friends there, and Frank Lovelace still managed Crow's new band.

I couldn't really work out whether Frank was a villain or really cared about music. I knew that like me he loved the company of the women at the bar. Selena was sometimes around, still beautiful, mad as ever and very entertaining. Crow's wife Agneta would sometimes be there too, and she always had charming and becoming Swedish girlfriends in tow, but on this occasion she was absent.

Crow's band was terrific, and true to his R&B thesis to the letter. Walter was missed, but Crow was a strong front man and his singing and guitar playing were cohesive and convincing.

I loved talking to Crow. He never seemed to change. That evening he came to sit with me and brought me a Coke.

'So Walter's maze is finished.' He smiled. 'Does he still have his head in a plastic bucket?'

Selena saw us and came to join us, having overheard Crow's last question.

'Playing the mouth-organ,' she said with a laugh. 'He loves the sound inside that bucket. Louis told me he started doing that when he was boy, didn't you, sweetie?' She looked at me. 'He used to say it made him feel as though he had a microphone, and a bit of reverb.'

'How is *your* work going, Selena?' Crow's question surprised me. Was he really interested in her strange world?

'I am starting to bear the ravages of healing a few too many of my friends, including your fabulous wife, Crow. She had arthritis, you know. I fixed it.'

'You did,' accepted Crow.

'And there are those who ask for healing but the problem I can see is that they have entities living within them like parasites.'

Crow laughed. 'Fuck off, Selena! Agneta doesn't have parasites.' He got up and stalked off.

Selena looked at me, her arms spread out. 'Did I say Agneta had parasites?' She pulled an incredulous face. 'I said I helped her arthritis.'

My impression was that Crow had become more narrow-minded than ever in fifteen years. He was so hard to talk to about anything other than music, and even on that subject he was a fanatic and a pedant. Some might say that he was more focused; Crow was brilliant, especially if working with younger musicians where his historian's view of music from the late fifties to the mid-sixties always found a willing ear, and added context and effective constraint to otherwise undisciplined young minds. On his own, driving his own small band, his playing just got tighter and tighter, his repertoire narrower and narrower, until in the end, his longish scraggy hair going suddenly grey within a single month, he was a happy anachronism. He used a regular introduction that his fans had come to anticipate with glee. *Here's one some of you may not have heard.* He would then launch into 'Susie-Q', or 'Cathy's Clown', or some other classic well known even to someone who had recently walked out of a jungle in Borneo.

I called Crow the next day at two in the afternoon and he was obviously still in bed, and hung over.

'Hey, Lou,' he said, hiccupping. 'What d'you want?'

I heard a female grunt in the background. I was pretty sure it was Selena. I wasn't sure how I felt about it.

'I want to speak to you about Walter,' I said. 'Who's that with you?'

'Mind your own fucking business,' he cackled. 'It's Selena of course. Like a rat up a pipe.'

He later confessed that Agneta had left him without warning a week before to marry her boss at the bank where she worked. Selena had offered 'healing'. My guess was that she and Crow would surely become an item, but their sex life might be frustrated by Selena's dream of getting Walter into bed.

In fact, I suppose I'd better admit it, at the time it really annoyed me, Selena sleeping with Crow. I was jealous, or envious, or something. Selena always gave me a bit of a hard time, I felt.

'Anyway, about Walter.'

'Oh yeah?'

'He has started to write again.' I sensed this might not be a smooth negotiation. I wanted Crow to look at what Walter was doing. 'It isn't quite music, not yet. It's descriptions of music, and sound. I think it could be the basis of something pretty amazing. It could be really cool.'

Crow wheezed as he lit a cigarette, and started drawling with no preamble.

'In your day, Louis, back when you were at art school in the sixties – with the benefit of grass – everything probably felt cool in music, everything seemed new and fresh. It was all flooding over from America: R&B, Tamla Motown, New Orleans, Memphis, Bob Dylan. You probably called music "sounds", like the Yanks.'

'True.' I laughed. 'It seemed to carry some kind of message.'

Crow gasped between puffs of smoke.

'Who cares about a message? Sounds. It's a good word. Sounds are all I want. Cool sounds. Simple sounds.'

I could sense him pulling himself up, leaning back against the bedhead to allow him to give more force to what followed.

'How arrogant does a fucking pub rock star need to be to believe they can carry a message to the audience?'

He was probably referring as much to the Hansons and their work in the revived Hero Ground Zero whose latest album had been the bestseller of the year. But perhaps he was also digging at Siobhan's futile attempts, fifteen years back, to refine what Walter had been doing in the heyday of the Stand.

'Sounds,' he barked. 'That's all it is. It's all it ever was.'

I explained that Walter was hearing sounds, real sounds, amazing sounds. He was reflecting the anxiety of the people around him.

'In a way he is composing,' I went on. 'But it's just written descriptions at the moment, and very rough music demos. He's hearing a grand mixture of sounds. He's writing a kind of score, or libretto if you like. He calls them soundscapes.'

'This is even worse.' Crow laughed, breaking into a broken smoker's cough. 'It sounds like he thinks he's fucking Stockhausen.'

I knew that the kind of sounds Crow was talking about were not like Walter's sounds, but I was determined to get him to go and see his old friend.

'Crow,' I urged, 'you need to see Walter. He needs to see you.'

It might not work out well; I knew that. Crow would listen to Booker T and the MGs playing *'Slim Jenkins' Place'* and he would classify the track as 'sounds'. He would look at what Walter was doing and might classify what he saw, and what it might produce as music, as 'a nightmare made real'. Even so, I knew that bringing them together was what I needed to do next. It occurred to me that the ally I needed to persuade Crow to visit Walter was Frank Lovelace. He might see a reunion in it for the Stand, or some kind of opportunity to make money. All I cared about was that Crow reconnected with Walter, and would look at what he was doing.

A large wooden wheel rolls through the dust of an unmade road. The cart creaks. The ox pulling it wheezes. The driver mutters as he snaps his straight whip at the ox's seesawing haunches. A street seller shouts his wares, peanuts and biscuits, in Gugarati. Children giggle and laugh as they pass, neatly dressed, on their way to school. The blare of an overdriven radio pumps out bhangra-style dance music, distorted and colourful, energetic and rhythmic, lilting and swaying but with deafeningly vibrant drums. Sacred cows wander in front of hooting petrol-driven three-wheeled rickshaws, their bells clanging sombrely in the racket. The pit-pat and stuttering across the square of a distant tennis match on a hard court, laughing voices in cultured England-educated Indian accents. A thundering, rocking, overloaded bus drives past, several ghetto-blaster radios playing at once, Qawwali, Bollywood, Indian disco and more bhangra. A mullah calls the Muslim faithful from a distant tower, his voice amplified in the distance. Birds squawking, flapping and fighting over a dead mouse in the road. Darkness. The flicker of a candle.

Steve and Patty Hanson had sold fifty-three million of several albums over fifteen years. Hero Ground Zero, the band started by Paul Jackson aka Nicolai Andréevich in the sixties that the Hansons had revived in the nineties, was a prog rock band of the old school that broke all records in arenas and stadiums around the world. Patty had stopped playing the drums and stood up front in a wispy dress banging a tambourine. It was rumoured salaciously that she performed without underwear. The light show was legendary, her body was legendary, her tambourine playing was Royal College of Music Grade 10, but it was her voice that made the band so huge. She sang like a husky siren, her voice almost without vibrato; it was a cold sound, but still passionate and vulnerable. She and Steve together wrote ambitious and audaciously pretentious songs. They wrote about Kings Arthur and Alfred, the Greek myths, beautiful cars, dreams, nightmares, colour, science and even fashion. One successful album consisted of a series of songs based on early Hollywood movie titles.

They respected no conventions, broke through all boundaries, sneered back at anyone who dared to sneer at them. They took drugs, they drank, they crashed cars, Steve Hanson even crashed a small plane and walked away. Patty spent more on dresses that would reveal her (alleged) lack of underwear than she did on drugs, but on their last recording session she had (allegedly) run up a bill for three hundred thousand dollars with her cocaine dealer. Also managed by Frank Lovelace, the Hansons were high in the Rich List.

But by 2011, when Walter was trying to emulate the sound he was hearing every day in his head, Hero Ground Zero were burned out, creatively depleted. They were still filling large venues and attracting bids for festivals, but I could tell they could not write songs any more.

After I had spoken to Crow I called Steve and got Patty on the phone.

'Louis,' she sang my name. 'How fantastic to hear your voice, my darling.'

She still sounded like a music teacher, slightly posh and had obviously risen at six and spent the morning practising the cello or whatever. She also sounded slightly exhausted; perhaps I was projecting on to her voice what I wanted to believe: that they needed Walter. I asked how she and Steve were doing.

'We're a bit like Abba, my darling.' She laughed. 'We are still married but have other things going on, if you know what I mean. Louis, you don't want to take me out to dinner, do you? That would be wonderful. You could take me to Le Caprice. I haven't been there for years.'

'I'd love that.' I wasn't being entirely truthful, but Patty was still a very beautiful and sexy woman. 'I wanted to let you know I've got some interesting news about Walter.'

'Is he still working on that peculiar labyrinth thing in his garden?'

'He calls it a maze' I corrected.

'Take me out, Louis,' she pleaded. 'We can talk over dinner.'

After speaking to her and arranging to meet her at Le Caprice that night I knew intuitively that where Crow might need a hard sell to go back to work with Walter, the Hansons would hungrily consider what Walter was now creating, and might rediscover hope for their old band.

As she smoked a small post-prandial cigar that enraged even the sophisticated folk in Le Caprice, Patty fluttered her eyelashes at me. Did she think I wanted to fuck her?

I wanted to explain my real reason for needing to see her. I told her all about the soundscapes and ended by saying I was sure that Frank would feel they could trigger a band reunion. That seemed to alert her.

'So Walter is hearing anxiety, and wants to make music out of it. It all sounds interesting, Louis. Most intriguing.'

I coughed, and she laughed at me.

'You're a saint, Louis, really,' she showed her amazing white teeth as though posing for a press photo. 'But you do need to speak to Frank about this. Not me. The business stuff is all so boring. I'd love to hear one of these soundscape thingies though. I've completely run out of new ideas myself and Steve is no better. Walter always was a dark horse.'

* * *

145

A mathematically organised arrangement of notes cascades rapidly from a slightly out-of-tune upright piano. The patterns sound like an attempt to evoke a Bach Partita or prelude. In a major key, the patterns hardly come close to melody but are pleasant, like the sound of a waterfall. Light reflects from the surface of the rippling pool; the sun is reflected. The first piece is short, quickly followed by another in a darker and more sombre mood. Again, there is a Bach-like modality to the composition and a two-handed elegance to the performance. This piece too is short, followed by another, very fast, optimistic and eloquent set of passages that ends suddenly with an ostentatious and flamboyant flourish.

I contacted Frank and he felt, as I had predicted, that we should try to bring Walter's band back together. I would rely on Frank Lovelace to run things once I had planted the seeds, since it seemed to me that in order for Walter to survive the embedded and indoctrinated musical ego of Crow on the one hand and the grandiosity of the Hansons on the other, he would need a more musically adept mentor than myself.

I spoke to Maud from time to time. Old Nik's paintings were selling very well and were still the backbone of my business as an art dealer. He painted the same scene over and over again with small variations: a sweeping field of human souls presided over by vast angels.

Once when I called I said, 'I thought it might be a good idea if Nik could spend some more time with Walter, which could help him harness and unleash his own angels and demons,' I suggested nervously. 'Walter's are sonic ones of course.'

'I'm afraid that won't be possible,' said Maud. 'Nik is dying. He has advanced leukaemia.'

'Bloody hell!' I was stunned.

'He is reliant on intravenous morphine, and is surviving, but it's reset his clock. He's also even madder than usual.'

I couldn't help thinking that the old hero was about to live up to the name of his old band and was approaching ground zero.

This was a shock to me on many levels. I had come to depend on the sales of his artwork, which provided a steady and reliable income. I had come to adore Maud, a woman who carried some sweet quality that continually attracted me to her. I was at ease with her, she was my age, and I found her still beautiful, serene and immensely kind. This jarred with another emotion I often felt whenever I saw her face after a long hiatus: sexual arousal. I never acted on this, but I know she was conscious of my vulnerability around her. She didn't take advantage of me; once she laid a hand on my knee while consoling me about some small personal crisis and my heart started to beat so quickly I thought I might be having a stroke.

I was aware that this attraction might well have been leading me by the nose from the very first day we met. Old Nik's paintings could, for all I knew, have been produced to order from a factory in Lahore, the Pakistani city with at least one excellent art school. Equally, they could have been knocked out in Taiwan. Neither I, nor my clients, would give a hoot. Nik's esteemed Tolstoy-inspired signature was all that was necessary to validate his process.

'I've only met Walter in passing,' Maud reminded me. 'I'd very much like to speak to the young man. If he's been so influenced by Nik, it would be good for me to have an hour or two with him.'

I felt a pang of jealousy and promised myself that such a meeting would not be a show I mounted.

Chapter 15

The show I did manage to mount began with Crow rolling up in Sheen on a Wednesday afternoon in his black 1956 Lincoln Continental Mark II at two in the afternoon. There were no free parking spaces in the street, but Floss was at the stables, so he pulled up on to their small driveway and left the boot of the coupé hanging over the pavement so that the local mums with pushchairs had to divert into the road. It was not a sunny day, but it was warm, and he and Walter hugged each other at the front door, with a degree of uneasiness on both sides.

Soon we were sitting drinking coffee just outside the entry to Walter's maze, and catching up. Walter was clutching a laptop computer nervously. Crow spoke about his divorce from Agneta, while Walter spoke fondly about Floss. Crow talked about his band, and the fact that almost nothing had changed for him in fifteen years, and how rapidly the time had seemed to pass. Walter talked about his garden and then showed Crow around it. Crow was a businesslike fellow; he had no time for niceties. He could be blunt, but he held no grudge against Walter. He quickly cut to the matter at hand: Walter had been composing. Crow wanted to hear what Walter had recorded.

Walter prevaricated. There was a lot of nervous preamble. He was aware that Crow wouldn't know what to make of the demonstration soundscapes based on what he had been hearing. He himself felt they were unfinished, tinkling piano, inadequate as a true reflection of what he hoped to achieve given more time and resources. Walter knew that Crow was far more broadly educated about music than he appeared. It was only with the Stand that he had insisted on the very narrow manifesto that gave them their power.

'Please remember this is all work in progress, Crow,' he said. Crow nodded, looking down. 'Would you read the descriptions? They give a far better idea of what I'm hearing.'

'Give me some credit, Walter,' he barked. 'I know what you can do. I worked with you for years. Just play something. I'll read the descriptions as we go. Soundscapes you call them? The first syllable works for me. You could give the capes to Patty.' He laughed his smoker's gasp that was almost a wheeze, and his joke cleared the air.

'I will,' said Walter. 'I'm sorry. But what you will hear is not conventional. Not songs as such. If I sit to play the piano, as soon as I find some good melody or interesting and enticing set of new chords, my mind flies off into chaos and disorder. If I fight it, it gets worse and I simply have to stop work. If I allow myself to accept what I'm hearing it begins to take shape, and I can write down what I hear, and then later I can try to gather sounds and record a mélange.'

'A what?' Crow knew perfectly well what a mélange was. 'A blancmange?'

Walter opened the laptop.

'You're not recording on a fucking computer now, are you?' Crow was laughing again. He sat back, and let his old personality shine through. He was the Luddite pub rocker. For him 'recording' would always involve reels of tape, a mixing console with controls like a wartime aeroplane and a lot of cigarette smoke.

'When I left the band,' explained Walter. 'I gave away my funky old recording gear.'

'Can you work all that stuff?' Crow looked at the coloured patterns on the laptop screen.

'The learning curve was steep,' admitted Walter. 'Remember, I've been digging in the garden for so long. I usually only turned this thing on when I wanted to order plants.'

He told Crow that he had tried reading inspirational books, and worked programmes intended to help artists who were blocked.

'I needed to find a way to unlock the art.'

Crow was now trying not to laugh. He didn't like musicians using the word 'art'. Music was music. Art was something else. Art was what music critics looked for in all pop music, including pub rock, yet became irritated if any artist aspired to deliver it. Defining what was and what was not art was not for the musician. It was down to the critic.

'You should talk to Siobhan,' he said, not without a little sarcasm. 'She was the one who always thought you could be the new W.C. Yeats. She knows what *art* is.'

'You mean W.B. Yeats, I think,' corrected Walter. 'I don't really contact Siobhan that much. Louis speaks to her sometimes. Selena of course.'

'I'm teasing you, Walter.' Crow laughed again. He exchanged a look with me. I knew he had bedded Selena. He winked at me as if to make sure I kept quiet about it. He lit an American Spirit and blew a cloud of smoke into the air. 'How's it going with Floss? Still in love?'

Walter blustered a little. 'Yeah,' he said quite shyly. 'Still good. All is well. We spend a lot of time apart but it seems to work.'

It was unconvincing. The gossip about the separate lives he and his wife led troubled him. He trusted Floss, but her friends and stable clients didn't. He knew Crow was teasing him and he had forgotten how to handle it. He clearly felt the need to go further, to be more positive.

'I'm really happy with Floss,' he said. 'She's a complete star, so incredibly beautiful too, and always glowing; vibrant. Still riding, working at the stud and teaching too.'

Crow leaned forward; did he sense that Walter had something to say that might require him to stop acting like a jerk?

'I always seem to be waiting for her to come home,' admitted Walter. 'She's a great rider. Does all the biggest meetings and horse trials. Badminton and all that.'

'Oh yes!' Crow made a lascivious face. 'Tight riding pants. You should cheer yourself up while she's away by reading Jilly Cooper novels.'

But Walter was serious; he couldn't properly pick up on Crow's clumsy levity and didn't try. 'I've only just started to feel that life is slipping by, that something is missing.'

However Walter could sense that Crow was glazing over, leaving the room. If he didn't play him something soon, he would put down his coffee and drive away. Walter was not desperate to be judged, but up to this moment no one had heard what he had started to record. Not even me. I'd just pretended I had to get Crow and the Hansons to reconnect; so far I had only read the written soundscape descriptions, which were impressive.

Walter led Crow and me through the maze, where for fifteen years he had been creative in a way that was natural, easy and spontaneous, and into the gazebo-like garden room he was now using as a studio. The sound of their footsteps echoed slightly, and at first sight there was nothing in the room but a Yamaha grand piano and stool. Through the window I saw Walter set down the laptop on a little table in the far corner beside some small digital boxes. Crow looked around for a sound system. I saw him realise that Walter had had speakers buried inside the walls, like someone who wanted music but didn't want large loudspeaker boxes and wires cluttering up what had earlier been a middle-class living room. This was not a musician's sound system, he was probably thinking. It was an interior decorator's notion. He said nothing. There was nowhere to sit but on the piano stool, which he took. Walter stood nervously by the table, and hit a button on his computer.

Walter had called me afterwards; he said he was pleased with the way things had gone. Crow hadn't liked the primitive and arty music demos. They were full of electronic twittering and white noise interspersed with strange discordant piano. But Walter didn't really like what he'd done either; he was still struggling to make music out of what he had written down. But he said Crow had taken it all seriously. With the descriptions of the soundscapes on his lap, reading and listening at once, Crow was the first to read and hear a crude approximation of what was going on inside Walter's head whenever he tried to write a song.

'The best part,' said Walter, 'was that Crow asked to take a copy of the essays home with him. He wanted to share the entire thing with Selena. He said she would love it.'

Blinded. There is only sound. Blinded by light. Burning light. All around there are small whirring creatures, mechanical, sounding like sophisticated mini-robots, but with clockwork motors inside them, slowly, steadily running down. Massive airships, driven through the whistling breeze by buzzing motors that seem far too small for the job. Flying geese, honking and squawking territorially, like the real thing, but obviously powered by some kind of complex multi-geared engine. They swoop, honk and crash, one by one. Small ships, pressing through the ice floes. Grinding to a halt, then being crushed inevitably by the encroaching ice. Tiny insects, also powered artificially, buzz, flap, zing and whistle through the air, bouncing off windows, walls, then spiralling to the ground. Mechanical men, as real as men, walking sedately with a flowing and even gait across the roads, their slick, mechanical hydraulic motors hissing and fizzing almost imperceptibly.

Artificial voices, having conversations about art and life, and emotions and feelings, the phrases slowly becoming incoherent and unravelled, the language more absurd. The sound of an approaching Ice Age, the increasing hiss of freezing wind, and crackling frost. Finally, a small snow-sled, unmanned even by a mannequin robotic controller, out of the control of whomever once guided it, careers down a frozen street, skidding on the black and white ice, and smashing into a tree. A few more feeble revs of its petrol-driven engine, a few more slurs of its caterpillar tracks, and it dies. A trio of singing penguins, or ostriches or emus, or some such upright walking bird, with absurdly feminine voices in uneasy harmonic approximation, trip down the street, slipping and sliding, giggling and laughing, their song a kind of crazy laughter in itself. They are stopped by something unseen, their singing ends with the little surprised and disappointed noises of children interrupted in a favourite game for bedtime: ah, oh dear, oooh, ooo-ah, poo, pah, bah, no, etc. This is the last we hear of the mechanical world of a fridge door, an automated gate and a computer-controlled toy car. It is in fact the end of the toys, of the robots, the non-thinking, non-feeling machines; we are hearing the last of our little helpers. Helpless.

Selena told me that Crow had taken the soundscapes back to his house, where she waited for him, ready to fuck his brains out if he was ready. He threw them to her as he walked in.

'There you go, sweetheart,' he taunted. 'Your beloved Walter's latest brain-farts. Actually, I must admit it isn't half bad.'

I would learn later that Selena had known exactly what to do with the soundscape descriptions. She has confessed as much. On reading them she said she knew someone who might be able to help guide Walter.

'Siobhan will be thrilled to get her hands on this stuff,' she said to Crow. 'She'll know how best to develop them.'

Crow let her make copies of nineteen or so pages, and she – and it seems obvious now – sent them to her literary sister. She would know people. In her days at the BBC she would have built up contacts throughout the world of the arts as well as journalism.

When first reading the soundscapes Siobhan knew straight away that Crow couldn't really help Walter. Frank Lovelace wouldn't help, while Steve and Patty Hanson would try to turn them into a rock opera or something. And Floss was too busy with long weekends of dressage or maybe un-dressage if the gossip were true.

Siobhan was another who still loved Walter and still hoped to see him rise again. No doubt she despaired of me and my clunky attempts to inspire and focus my godson with embellishments of his madness and its potential, and she did indeed know what to do.

'Selena,' she said excitedly on the phone. 'Can't you see?'

'See what?' Selena was baffled.

'Walter's father Harry,' she said. 'He's fucking perfect for this.'

What an act of genius! Harry. When Harry called me a few days later, after he'd received the package from Waterford, he was excited at seeing what extraordinary creative outpourings his son had come up with, and was already beginning to think about how to contribute. Harry realised his son had at last done something that he could be a part of, that he could under-stand and develop, and – beginning with organ partitas remi-niscent of some of the most extreme music he was ever asked to perform – started to compose orchestral scores. Harry Watts, organ supremo, for once in his life could do something for his son that no else could. He could compose serious, dark, audacious and fearlessly accurate and impressionistic music that would bring to life what Walter had described. A gift from father to son.

'This stuff is nuts,' he said, 'but it's beautifully written. It's audacious. Parts of it are rather sophomoric, overdone, but it's been easy to use the descriptions as briefs for music. I have already composed the first three pieces. I'm using organ (of course), and conventional orchestra and choir, and some unusual instruments that others have used before like thunder sheets and so on. I'm having a ball. I am connecting with my son emotionally, intellectually and spiritually for the first time in my life. Move over, Louis! God bless you!'

It was a poignant time for me. Within a little over a month not only had Harry composed the bulk of the most clearly described soundscapes, but also made stunning orchestral recordings of them. As an organist, orchestra leader and choirmaster he had everything at his fingertips. He told me later he had spent around thirty thousand pounds on it all.

'The least I can do,' he said with a laugh. 'I've taken it out of what I am leaving Walt in my will.'

In early 2012 Walter sat to listen for the first time. I was there with him at his studio when he finally listened to all the pieces as one, but it would probably be impossible for me to try to explain his reaction. Suffice to say he was transported. His father knew what he had been feeling, and had captured the immense intensity of his strange connection with the fearful folks of Sheen. The recordings were literal transcriptions of what Walter had written, music made from what he described. Of course it might not have been exactly what Walter had himself heard, but it was damned close. Father and son had connected, perhaps in a kind of hell. But a hell of art, science, social conscience and political empathy for the people of west London with whom they shared their daily life.

And so there was a second listening session in the garden room for Crow, who was quite proud of the solution he had engineered for Walter via Selena. I attended, nervously. Anxious to mediate if needed.

All around there are small whirring creatures, mechanical, sounding like sophisticated mini-robots, but with clockwork motors inside them, slowly, steadily running down. Massive airships, driven through the whistling breeze by buzzing motors that seem far too small for the job.

When the partly realised soundscape was finished, I could see that Crow wanted – desperately – to break the ensuing painful silence with a joke. He wanted to say, right, Walter, very nice, let's get your leather jacket back out of the wardrobe and I'll see you on stage at Dingwalls at nine thirty tonight. Instead he got up, walked over to Walter who was looking at the floor, and put his hand on his shoulder, and did so surprisingly gently and kindly.

'This is your father's work, isn't it, Walter?'

I jumped in quickly. 'What Walter has been experiencing has been extraordinary. He's connected to the people around him. Look at the soundscape descriptions.'

'I have looked at them,' said Crow. 'I see my old buddy in them. But I don't hear him in the music. Selena fixed this. Siobhan passed it to Harry. Brilliant.'

He turned to Walter.

'You always worried too much about the planet, mate.'

He gestured to the computer and the speakers. 'You can't orchestrate for violins and brass, or classical organ. But you and your dad have made Stockhausen sound like Abba by comparison. Same old shit, but really heavy shit. Great sounds.'

There was no greater compliment for Walter from his old bandmate.

'Steve has to hear this stuff, Walter,' Crow continued gently. 'He'll know exactly how to make it work for a band.'

Walter looked up and there were tears welling in his eyes.

Crow broke the spell. 'And of course we need some fucking songs to hold it all together, and to lighten the fucking mood. Leave that to the other grown-ups in your past life. Me and Steve and Patty will make this work.'

Crow left quickly and returned later that same day with Hanson in tow. Walter and I were waiting.

'Walter,' breathed Hanson, holding his old friend in a bear hug. 'How the hell are you?'

Hanson was looking slightly bloated and his thinning hair was long. He seemed a little dizzy as he walked around the room and I got the feeling that at any moment he might just fall over slowly and gracefully, like a condemned chimney. At one point he took out a silver cigarette case that was obviously full of pre-made joints, then had a last-minute rethink and snapped it shut. His eyes were bleary. He wasn't drunk; he just seemed luxuriously and dissonantly worn out, like some grand Russian duke from the time of the Romanovs. His coat was more like a cape, and was lushly embroidered with threads that glinted with gold and silver.

The three men from the old band fell easily into the same kind of catching-up chitchat that Crow and Walter had had earlier in the day. This catch-up was a little easier for Walter because Hanson's band was famous, always on television and radio. He was perhaps also of the opinion that Steve and Patty had been happy to move on, and had found what they wanted.

After these preliminaries, Steve swung around in a circle taking in the almost empty room. He was holding a bottle of Evian, and waved away the offer of a hot drink.

'Patty told me you were doing brave new stuff.' He gestured around him at the clean, open space. 'I love this! Just a piano and a laptop; it must challenge you to get new ideas down.'

He sat at the Yamaha grand piano and performed a flourish evidently meant to show off the piano itself and the reverberant sound of the room, rather than his own skills. But despite his world-weariness he was obviously still an incredibly adept musician.

'Great sound in here, nice piano too.' He nodded as he stood up, tottering very slightly like an old tree in a strong wind. 'Inspiring.'

Crow looked at Walter. His friend was standing quietly, not moving. Crow looked down at Walter's hands and saw that two of his fingers were moving, fluttering in a nervous motion. Still treating Walter with uncharacteristic gentleness, he put his hand on his friend's shoulder.

'Are you OK?'

Walter nodded, and looked up and smiled. He turned back to Hanson.

'And you and Patty,' he said quietly. 'You've done so well. How are you guys?'

Hanson was clearly trying hard not to brag, but as he spoke easily about Hero Ground Zero and the triumphs they had enjoyed in the preceding fifteen years it fell to Crow to bring him down to earth.

'It's all on fucking tape these days,' Crow sneered. 'They don't play live on stage!'

'Computer you mean.' Hanson was unapologetic. 'Not tape. Everyone uses computers now. You have to use them to synchronise the video.'

'Oh, yes, the video.' Crow laughed. 'We're thinking of smashing some television sets at Dingwalls to remember the sixties.'

His jibes were on one level affectionate, but they were also accurate: Hanson had made a lot of money and sold huge numbers of CDs but times were changing. In any case, Hero Ground Zero were fucking awful in Crow's opinion. Hanson laughed, relying on Crow's affection, but everyone who had followed the extreme divergence of the members of the Stand after Walter's departure knew Crow would never hold back. He would say what he felt was true. Hanson would never return the criticism because the Stand had been his band too, and for many years he had been a passionate advocate of what they had done. He wasn't immovable like Crow. He never said much. For those who are as successful as Hanson there was nothing much to be said to detractors. Better just to let them rant. Where Crow had driven to Sheen in an absurd and anachronistic old American car that polluted the air and used ten gallons of fuel to get there from Camden Lock, Hanson had driven in a powerful sports Lexus hybrid costing as much as a Porsche. Walter later told me he thought they were both nuts, but then he never drove anywhere except to the local horticultural nursery, and he went on his scooter, and had his purchases delivered to his house.

'Hanson,' Crow said with a laugh. 'Fifteen years and really nothing has changed at all. You're still avoiding the main thing. We are just musicians. That's all.'

'You're right, Crow,' agreed Hanson, seeming to give in. 'We both feel we've been off in a wide circle, a great arc, and we're back facing the basics. We need great songs. But you know that for Patty and me this was all inevitable. You can call our journey pretentious, and you may be right, but we did what we had to do.'

Walter seemed content to stay out of the discussion. Perhaps he was surprised at how easily he had fallen back into his old role as the front man of their band and felt some of the dignity of that position returning. Then Crow, impatient as ever, turned and looked at him.

'Will you play Hanson that stuff you played me?'

Walter knew what was expected of him, and what he had to do, and was surely aware that Hanson would be a far more receptive listener than Crow.

As Walter touched the space bar on his laptop to start playing the soundscape composed by his father, the mix of music and sound effects mangled together and disturbing, he realised how strange was the day he found himself in: his old bandmates gathered to listen to something he had 'written' after a fifteen-year hiatus. This was friendship, if nothing else. I could tell he trusted his two old compatriots to be kind, but to be honest. He knew he was making himself vulnerable, but he also knew he was being true to who he really was as an artist, and that he had changed, for whatever reason. Steve Hanson's expression as he listened to what Walter had put together was telling. His face first hardened, then his eyes narrowed and took on a gleam. When the sound stopped, he turned to Walter, glanced at Crow, then back to Walter.

'Fuck, man!' Hanson took Walter again in his theatrical bear hug; then he held him at a distance with two strong arms. 'Crow was right. This is really heavy shit.'

He had echoed Crow, but with an entirely different angle: it was clear he thought he had discovered the Holy Grail.

A clap of thunder shakes the horizon, even the clouds seem to shudder. Lightning sizzles as it flashes, earthing down to the steeple of the distant church, barely visible through the teeming rain and blown spray. Huge trees crack, branches falling. Wind buffets the windows, rattling them with deadened thumps as though large wet cushions were being hurled at them. There is nothing to see; there is only a greyness, a kind of darkness illuminated by sound. The wind carries flotsam, leaves, sticks, fir cones that crash against walls and trees, and it all splashes into the lake. Small buildings, sheds and the like, are blown down, and then their fragile parts lifted up into the sky to spin and whirr until they clatter down. Over the lake the rain drives down on to the surface of the water so powerfully that it flattens the spray it generates as soon as it has whipped it up. Hailstones clatter on the tin roofs of the remaining barns; the animals are uneasy, cows, sheep, horses, pigs, moaning and frightened. The Collies from the farm begin to howl, tethered in the open as absurdly it is still summer. They are drenched, huddled down, utterly miserable. Dozens of blinding flashes of lightning illuminate the underside of the trees as they bounce, reflected up from the lake, and lighting up the black and deep grey clouds at the same time. The clouds seem to be moving, folding and unfolding at high speed, like a fast movie. The wind whips water off the grass near the house and hurls it at the windows so hard it sounds like metal chains being lashed at the building. Water overruns the gullies, backs up the drains, washes over the brick pathways and runs in rivulets over the grass. Thunderclaps sound in machine-gun series, impossibly rapid, impossibly deep, impossibly impossible. A freak wave of water so monstrous it seems as large as a huge meteor crashing in from outer space drops from the sky and hits the ground so violently that time itself seems to miss a beat, then recovers and ticks on relentlessly. Space is being bent, curved, by the lightning, the rain and the thunder. Nature, created by some manifestation of God, is challenging that very same God to stop her, to snicker at her: 'This too will pass.' For it seems as though this storm will never, can never pass; since it began it has only grown in intensity and volume, without a second of let-up, not a hint it might desist. Then, the most frightening single clap of thunder ever heard since the beginning of time, louder than any that has gone before, seems to burst our ears, and the storm is over.

Chapter 16

I found myself in the dear old Caprice a few days later having lunch with Selena. Permissible, I think. I was a single man. I felt flattered by her invitation and her company, and I was pleased to see the envious looks of the men around me and the evil glares of their female companions. Selena was quite clearly half my age. She was one of those extraordinary women who seemed to rise above the ageing process. She had never looked young, even when she was young, and now she didn't look any older, despite having made no apparent effort with her hair or make-up. At the age of thirty-six, she simply looked slightly overweight, but still beautiful. I felt smug, I suppose, sitting in a quiet banquette against the mirrored wall in the bustling Caprice.

She had been the one to summon me. She wanted me to know she was not with Crow. She had slept with him just once, and she knew I knew. Was that all? I wondered. There was more. She told me that Walter had an 'entity'. That is, a disembodied soul tagging along, living vicariously through him whenever it got the chance. Like Ronnie's entity? No, not like Ronnie. And she was very serious. Walter, she felt I must have known, was the one *lifelong love of her life*. That was how she put it. She knew I would understand, where others would not. I worked with artists who claimed to be visited by angels, or demons, or heard voices. I took them and their work seriously; surely I could see that Walter was subject to the same kind of possession?

Something had happened to change him; a door of perception had opened in him that he had been unable to handle. That's why he had quit being creative fifteen years before, except in his garden.

Selena could be difficult to read. I could see her obsession with Walter was still strong, but why was she turning to me? It was almost as though she were giving me a warning, to prepare me for something terrible she could see ahead.

I am an art dealer, but I can't pretend that I understand what the people I represent are going through. I had my own experiences, of course, and I knew that it was too easy to put everything down to drugs. Drugs had opened a door for me too, and slowly, as that door had closed, I settled down and managed to live a more normal life. But I could not forget what I had seen, what I had experienced. I could not set aside the fact that the practical Rain, an journalist no less, had followed a trail leading from the walnut bedhead with all its screaming faces right back to the brutal and appalling inquisitions of the Pope in the thirteenth century. Intuition and psychic rawness had operated in me at some level, and the facts gathered by Rain seemed to support that; the facts followed the feelings. It was irrefutable evidence as far as I was concerned.

So was it possible Walter was 'possessed' as Selena claimed? Who was I to argue? I wasn't entirely sure it mattered as long as Walter was alive and reasonably content. Yes, it was true Walter was struggling with his new art, battling with the rigours of his return to composing, albeit in collaboration with his brilliant father. But why would Selena be so solicitous? Selena, who always said she could see angels, who apparently had an angel who accompanied her at every difficult turn of daily life, who was not getting a little overweight, but was instead 'pregnant' with forthcoming angelic expositions, the backed-up logjam, she said, of voices attempting to speak to a wayward society, lost souls. I understood what Selena was saying – after all, I represented Nik and I took seriously the visions he had seen up on Skiddaw – but what the hell did she want me to do?

Selena must have noticed my mind wandering. The waiter had brought my main course a few minutes before and I hadn't touched it.

She leaned closer to me as though to block out the chatter of the other customers in the Caprice, her pretty face inches from my own as her voice dropped to a paranoid and conspiratorial whisper.

'Floss,' she breathed, 'has secrets.'

I was more unsettled by this idea than the image of Walter with an 'entity' following him around.

'What secrets can Floss possibly have?'

As far as I could tell Floss was a simple soul, a jolly girl who bred horses, albeit with a diamond in her front tooth.

Selena settled back in her chair and I thought with a flash of anger that I would probably get no more out of her.

'What about Walter?' I asked. 'What do you want to do? What do you want me to do?'

She shook her head as though to indicate that I needn't worry about Walter. 'Floss might need you, Louis,' she warned. 'She might need you very soon.'

She turned away and took a sip of wine as though the action might offend me. It was dismissive.

'Why? What would make Floss turn to me?'

I was getting irritated by this all-knowing seeing-eye charade.

'Oh, I think you and Floss share a very special bond, don't you?' She leaned towards me again, not quite so close this time, and lowered her voice once more. 'And Floss might need you and your support because ... well, I am – at last – going to steal Walter away from her.'

Oh that! Yes of course. Always. For ever. Yes. I found myself nodding as though in approval when in fact I was relieved to see that Selena had remained in the same familiar track, and that nothing had really changed.

Then she said something that really did ruin my lunch. 'I know you're still troubled by awkward circumstances in *your* past, Louis.'

'What do you mean?'

'Seventeen years ago, at Walter and Siobhan's wedding.'

'I was there,' I said. I'd been so drunk I remembered very little about it. 'Of course I was there. I am Walter's godfather.'

Selena leaned back and, gently caressing the phantom promise of her swollen belly, delivered her best and most unexpected shot. 'I know you are ashamed of what you did.'

'I don't know what you're talking about.' I refused to rise to her dark insinuation, but it planted an uneasy seed. I had a vague memory of Selena and Floss, Ronnie too, running around at the wedding looking precociously pretty, slightly drunk. But I had been on the edge of blackout. In the recesses of my mind, a sliver of memory, there were drugs that I had supplied and plied, ketamine the worst, and there was lust, but probably for Sally, who was more my kind of woman.

'Don't try to kid me, Louis. I saw you together, getting it together, Louis, when you thought no one could see you.'

My head was spinning, but I was alert enough to realise for the first time that Selena was trying to exercise some kind of control over me, even blackmail me over something I may or may not have done at Walter and Siobhan's wedding. I sat there expecting accusations of perversity, for her to call me a disgusting old fart even for agreeing to take her to lunch. Then suddenly she surprised me.

'Louis,' she said, with a sweet smile. 'Do you like me? Do you care about me? Do you love me at all, as a friend?'

'Of course I do, of course,' I said, relieved she had modified her tone. 'We are friends, of course we are.'

'Then help me to win Walter. Please.'

'I have no intention of actually helping you to win my godson!' I tried to laugh her proposition away, but she faced me with a very determined expression.

'Of course you want Walter and Floss to remain together,' she almost sneered. 'You and Floss have a very special bond, don't you?'

I tried to calm her down. 'But I would never stand in your way if they split up and you and Walter were to find love.'

I wasn't sure I had placated her, but we managed to complete our lunch in a slightly more settled mood.

The thud of a baseball bat hitting a melon. An axe whizzes through the air and strikes a tree trunk. A machete chops at thick, leafy undergrowth. A spade buries its tip into the soil. A blade slashes at the throat of a pig, blood gushes noisily as the animal squeals. A rain begins, of billy clubs, falling on to shoulders, cushions, heads, smashing windows, on to bone, skull, cheekbone, forearm, back of hand. Footsteps fleeing, footsteps following. A chase. A clearing. A cleaning. A cleansing of woodland, jungle, wild animals, human body and soul. And then the clunk, click, clank of huge switches being thrown, the buzz of brilliance and electrons. Blinded again, by brilliance, the future, by fear, by anxiety and shame.

Walter told me later that the very next day Selena had summoned him to the same table in the same restaurant. Floss and Ronnie were away at the time on an organised hack, strangely enough in the same area of the Lake District over which Old Nik had wandered like a tramp for many years. What Selena shared with Walter was as disturbing to him as everything she'd told me.

'Ronnie has an entity.'

Walter had laughed, and turned to fiddle with his shoulder bag, trying to find his credit card to pay for lunch.

'He's possessed by a dark spirit that I can only see when he's walking away from me. It lives around him like a shadow, literally. Ronnie is a good-hearted man in many ways, but he is a fraud.'

Walter said he could hardly believe what Selena was trying to tell him.

Selena crashed on: 'Ronnie pretends to be gay, but in fact he's a full-blooded heterosexual man with a long string of female conquests among the customers at the stables.'

Walter looked incredulous. Ronnie had recently started to wear items of women's clothing; he especially liked high heels, and had even started to joke about transitioning.

But Selena had not yet delivered her final blow.

'Ronnie and Floss are lovers. Everyone knows.'

Walter's deepest insecurities had been triggered at that moment.

'They are probably making love right now.'

Walter felt sick. Selena was reinforcing all his most paranoid fears.

'How do you know?' he snapped. 'What have you seen? Or is this just gossip?'

'I don't need evidence,' Selena said quickly, defending herself haughtily. 'I won't listen to tittle-tattle. I simply know.'

Walter had always been determined to keep Selena at arm's length. He regarded her like a wayward little sister – and perhaps as a bit mad. He and Floss had enjoyed sex only rarely for quite a long time now – and he was only human. He was vulnerable, envious that Ronnie spent more time with Floss than he did.

Selena could see her chances slipping away, so she went further.

'You too,' she had told him confidently. 'You also have an entity. I can see it now. This parasitical disembodied soul is expressing itself through you. It's what is making you feel crazy. It's colouring and distorting your creativity.'

Walter had not been convinced, but on one level had been longing for some explanation of what had been happening to him.

Selena saw her chance. As she leaned forward, her loose dress opened slightly and Walter said that he could hardly take his eyes from the new voluptuousness of her cleavage, and the lust-ful light in her blue-green eyes.

'Believe me, Walter,' she said. And somehow, the combination of her persuasive psychic magic and the swelling of her pretty breasts gelled; Walter told me later he was seriously afraid he might weep.

Twenty minutes later, the bill settled, Selena took Walter by the hand and led him to her car, and drove him to Sheen. Later, separately on different occasions, they both told me what happened next. When they arrived outside the house, she parked carefully in the driveway sheltered by shrubbery, turned off the engine of her battered old VW, pulled up her dress as though gathering herself to get out of the car, and kissed him deeply, hungrily, passionately. At last she knew for sure she had begun to close the circle that had started its lustful arc back in the bar at Dingwalls fifteen years before. She was about to seduce her number one candidate. Walter flushed, his heart beating; he could probably taste Siobhan on Selena's lips. I'm sure he was aroused by memories of lips and taste and familiar flesh. They got out of the car and walked into the house.

Later, Walter decided that maybe after all Selena had been correct about him being taken over by some kind of jinn. For as he reached his orgasm, swimming in the genuine loving adora-tion that rained down on him from Selena's entire body and being, he suddenly felt nothing.

'Oh God,' he gasped. 'I'm sorry.'

It was as though his orgasm had been hijacked, stolen, completely erased.

'My darling,' cooed Selena, holding Walter's sweat-covered face in her hands. 'What happened?'

In what should have been the afterglow of their illicit passion, the morphine-like swoon that Selena had felt, Walter clumsily blurted out the truth.

'Not what I expected,' he said. 'I'm so sorry, but for a moment there I felt as if I'd left my body.'

'That sounds amazing!' Selena didn't really grasp what Walter meant, but was beginning to understand something wasn't right from the frightened expression on her lover's face.

And then Walter said something so unexpected, so badly timed, so brutal, that it quite took away her breath.

'How can you cheat on Floss like this?'

Walter's question was not so much an accusation as an outburst of real curiosity; or was it that entity inside him? Much depends on whose version of events I might believe. Selena, Walter knew, adored Floss. But his question shocked him as much as it did Selena at such an intimate post-coital moment, and he realised he still felt rather disembodied.

Selena could easily have turned the absurd question back on Walter. He was cheating on his wife after all. Instead she brought her face close to his, held him, and looked deeply into his eyes.

'We are all cheating now. Floss isn't just cheating on you with Ronnie.' She was angry and turned to gulp some wine and light a cigarette. Her breasts swung as she flopped back on the pillow blowing smoke into the air. How breathtakingly beautiful she must have been at that moment.

'What do you mean?' Walter's heart had started beating again, overtime. 'There's someone else? Another lover? It isn't just Ronnie?'

Selena shook her head. 'Not another lover. Floss has kept something from you. It's so important, and she's kept it from you for the entirety of your bloody marriage.'

'What do you mean?' Walter was on his feet now. His body was lean and muscular, and at the age of forty-five his face still handsome and rugged. But his expression was that of a young boy who had seen a ghost. He didn't smoke, and had never been much of a drinker but at that moment he whirled from side to side, as though looking for some prop that would see him through the moment. There was none.

'She's my friend,' said Selena. 'It's not for me to say. I shouldn't have said anything.'

She suddenly lunged at him, starting to cry, the impact of what she'd done beginning to sink in.

'I love you, Walter,' she spluttered. 'I always have. You know that. I am the one you should be with. Floss is whoever she is, I can see why you married her, but you two are not the same. She's never here. You need someone different—'

Walter interrupted. 'An Irish girl?' He was laughing, but there was a manic element in his eyes. 'I think I tried that one!'

Walter pulled on his blue jeans, furious. His mind was filling with flashes of realisation that popped up like newspaper headlines. Hypocrisy, manipulation, gossip and intrigue. She had already betrayed her friend. How could he know whether any of this was true?

'Please' – he was almost screaming now – 'please don't tell me you got all this secret information from your damned angels.'

When that was precisely what she began to do, he abandoned all hope that he might get any sense out of her. He pulled on his T-shirt, buttoned up his jeans, slipped on some soft shoes and ran from the house, leaving her lying in the bed that he had only ever shared with Floss.

This was not what Selena had hoped for, but now she accepted that what had happened was inevitable. She had waited for what felt like her entire life to make love to Walter. Sometimes her own power frightened her.

Months later, Selena gave me her version of what had happened that day. She had asked herself how the extraordinary love that she'd felt for Walter for so many years could have become transmogrified into such vengeance?

Her confession, and her question to herself, made me look back at my own life. Had I ever loved Pamela, truly? Or had it all just been about how sexy she had been when she was young? I was young then too, all testosterone and libido. I could forgive myself if I had never loved her, but when I asked myself the question, what was so sad was that I didn't know the answer.

Selena had seen Walter, wanted him, and remained fixated on him for the rest of her life. But I wondered if she could be certain she really loved him?

I had never experienced such certainty about Pamela, about any woman.

I think Selena really did offer herself to Walter unconditionally, but his indifference to her drove her to extreme measures. In any case, he was not entirely indifferent to her. I believe he was as attracted to Selena as she was to him; he simply had some way of controlling what he felt. He was not obsessed by her as she was with him – and yet she could exert power over him. That suggested some vulnerability in him that was not entirely sexual.

Behind all of Walter's artistic complexity was a man, just a man. And that man would have been close to a saint if he had been able to resist what few men since the dawn of creation have ever managed to successfully and completely repress – the lure of the sister. To his credit he had resisted Selena until now. The problem was that Selena saw his resistance as evidence of how much he valued and respected her; indeed she regarded his resistance to her as evidence of his love for her. She may well have been right. So in my view, whatever he had done, he could not have resisted Selena for ever. And the people around him, the chatterers, would have condemned him as a predator, a cheat, a liar, an adulterer of the worst kind. I can't get completely inside Walter's mind. I can't tell you quite what he was feeling as he ran from his house leaving Selena – both triumphant and uneasy – swooning in her best friend's marital bed. But when we met, when he eventually came back to London, he did describe the events of that afternoon with Selena.

I have a fairly good hunch that by sleeping with Selena he had realised that he did in fact love her almost as much as she had always loved him. And yet, if he was a man like me, I can hazard a guess that the love he discovered – and then had to acknowledge – did nothing to reduce his old love for Siobhan, or his love for Floss.

Men, although not all, can love many women; you don't have to travel too far back in history to find that this is true. Neither are all women innately monogamous or instinctively sexually loyal. It is all down to convenience. Men want to have certain women entirely to themselves. Certain women are willing to sign up to that deal if they are sufficiently exalted and protected. At the basest level, men want to exert power; women want evidence of that power and their ability to channel it. Selena was not so much a new woman as one who had taken up the blunt weapons usually employed by men. She was not a feminist in any sense, but she understood real power. Is any of this love?

Selena would have shared Walter with Siobhan; she would certainly have shared him with Floss. Walter, just like any man, would have been unable to share any of them with anyone else.

Had I consistently given my godson bad advice at every vital crossroad of his life? Had I made a similar mistake when I had suggested back in 1996 that Walter, suffering from distracting and disturbing sounds in his head, should meet Old Nik? Did I make a similar mistake sending Crow and Hanson to hear his new compositions in early 2012? It seemed that perhaps his father, whom I had cast as a man who had been unable and unwilling to help his son, had in fact contributed so much more than I had.

If I had guided him my godson clumsily, I had done so sincerely and specifically in the matter of his art, and only that.

Of course that is not entirely true: I had hoped that when Walter first met Old Nik he might see that his marriage to Siobhan had been a mistake. I hoped he would see that not only was he destined for greater things than Dingwalls, but also greater things than writing a few nifty poems that only two or three hundred people on the planet would ever read. I had often asked where Walter's father was while I played God, but Harry had been there all along.

Bingo looks up at me now as I write; at least for my beloved Collie I am a reliable god of sorts. Bingo certainly taught me the value of waiting. He waits constantly for an opportunity to work. Catching a ball of discarded paper that I toss towards the basket qualifies as a matter of vital importance, and he always catches it elegantly and efficiently without fuss in mid-air and quickly returns it to my feet. He stares at the ball, with shifty glances sideways in my direction, without moving his head. His art is fifty per cent in the catch, fifty per cent in the alert but patient waiting for the next throw. Sometimes the Collie's waiting weighs on me, a distraction. Is it possible to wait, when someone or some animal is waiting as you wait? So it was with Walter. Having advised him to learn to wait, and now at last – after years of labyrinthine gardening – to act, I had thrown a ball, tossed out a challenge that was rapidly becoming too complex for him to negotiate, and too intimidating a problem for me to act as guide. I would be no help.

* * *

Exploding stars. War. Distant explosions, cries of pain and horror. German soldiers. French. British. Afghan. Iraqi. American voices. Holocaust, apocalypse, war, terror. Planes diving, shooting. Tanks manoeuvring. Rockets screaming. Engines. Marching boots. Running, scuffling, skidding. Falling walls. Children's voices. A correspondent reports on a mobile phone. Data sounds from the past-present-future, so ticker tape, Morse, mobile phone sounds. Closer explosions. More cries of pain. Cries of triumph. Victory parades. Cheering crowds. Then an even bigger explosion, a massive one. The fall of radioactive rain. More cheering. More crying. Distant speeches across a crowded city square. Dictators, peacemakers, pacifists, warmongers. The sound of families pleading with their loved ones, do not go, you will never come back, my duty, my duty, my duty, my religion, no God but God, the only saviour. More explosions. Bells ringing. Rising to an incredible cacophony. Then a single bell, mournful.

From the shameful bed he had shared with Selena it seemed to Walter that there was only one place he could go. Floss and Ronnie had driven the horsebox to the hack in the Lake District, so the Volvo he so rarely used was at the back of the house. He had grabbed the laptop containing his father's recordings of the soundscapes he had been hearing, picked up the car keys, a credit card, and started driving towards Wales. Over the next ten hours he passed through Holyhead, over the Irish Sea to Dublin, and on by road through Wicklow to Wexford. Then from Waterford to Duncannon.

When he later described to me his arrival at Siobhan's father's cottage he invoked a scene that could have been the setting for one of Constable's paintings of gloomy and portentous cottages. He stood outside the building, a sepulchre to Siobhan's father, the drunken bully, as the sun sank behind gusts of wood smoke from the chimney. As he moved towards the front door it opened, and in the shadows a man wearing a beret, grey jacket and high-necked dark blue jumper emerged. Before Walter could see his face he turned to kiss Siobhan on the cheek then mounted an old pushbike and rode through an arch of roses to the footpath and the road back to town. He didn't acknowledge Walter. He may have heard the Volvo.

Siobhan smiled at him as she walked out into the dimming light, her red hair still luxurious, her blue-green eyes glinting, her teeth the spectacular white he remembered. The first thing he noticed was that her bosom, always generous, was larger; like her sister she had blossomed. Still fresh from the lascivious entanglements of his time with Selena, and connecting again with his body for the first time since he left Sheen, he felt a lustful continuum. Siobhan swayed towards him, her arms outstretched.

'Hello, Walter,' she said. Her voice was as beautiful as ever, as sonorous and lilting. He felt a jealous pang as he realised her voice sounded smoky and tinged with the huskiness of sexual afterglow. Who was that man he had seen?

How could she look so young? Walter was forgetting that once a man knows a woman she remains for him almost frozen in time, unless she is tragically struck down by illness or too much smoking, food or booze. Siobhan looked the same to him. He had imagined she would be wrinkled, with a belly, her hair full of grey. Of course she was subject to all those changes, but Walter could see little evidence of them in the evening light.

'Hiya, Siobhan,' he said. 'Sorry to drop in like this. Not feeling so hot.'

He had not seen his first wife for over fifteen years. She looked the same. She looked better in fact. This was not what he expected.

'So you came to me.' Siobhan laughed. 'Am I your mother now?'

Damn these Collins girls, he thought; he had indeed hoped for a maternal shoulder – advice, scepticism and pragmatism. Instead he was plunged straight back into the romantic mist Siobhan had always emanated around her, and he knew his visit might be a mistake.

By the fire, over wine, they shared the essential details of their respective experiences of the past fifteen years. They had communicated a few times by letter in that time, but there had been no explanations, no recriminations, no melodrama and none of the old intimacy. Now, face to face, Siobhan seemed genuinely interested in what Walter had been doing, whether he was happy, whether Floss was happy and if she was still close to Selena.

'It's a fucking mess, Siobhan.' Walter was not a self-pitying type, but for a second his eyes threatened to fill with tears.

'You had sex with Selena.' Siobhan had obviously received a call from Selena who had guessed where Walter might head after their argument.

Walter did not reply.

'She's always wanted that,' Siobhan said with a smile. 'Maybe now she'll grow up and leave you alone. She always wants whatever I have. You should have fucked her years ago, instead of building yourself up in her eyes.'

Walter still said nothing. He was grappling with Siobhan's bald female logic and trying to put out of his mind that even if she were right she was talking about her sister, not some unknown groupie.

'Selena called. She told me what she told you. Do you believe her?'

'I'm afraid I do. There have been rumours for years about Floss and Ronnie. I used to discount them.'

'Because Ronnie is gay?'

'I discounted them because Floss loves me, loves our life and her work, and on top of everything else because she adores Ronnie.' Walter suddenly began to make some sense of the situation. 'She wouldn't hurt Ronnie, or threaten their career together, by having sex with him.'

'I agree with you. So you don't believe Selena?'

'I'm not sure.'

'Did she tell you how she knows what happened between Floss and Ronnie?'

'No, she wouldn't give me any details. It was absurd. After ruining my life she then said she couldn't betray her best friend.'

Siobhan laughed. 'Selena played you, Walter, she doesn't really know any more than you do. Not for sure.'

'She said there was more going on. She said Floss had a secret. Some awful secret.'

'Walter,' soothed Siobhan. 'Selena is so jealous of Floss it has eaten her up for years. But Floss is maybe her best friend too. She's so torn. You know that when you and I split up she thought she could move in on you.'

Walter interrupted, 'You left me.'

'All right,' said Siobhan gently. 'Let's not make this worse. Can I get you another drink?'

They shared another half a bottle of red wine. Walter did not ask who the man was he had seen as he arrived, and Siobhan did not volunteer anything. Eventually they both quietened.

Walter found himself gazing at her, hoping she didn't sense how beautiful he found her.

Instead, she was the first to stroke.

'You look good, Walter. You look handsome. All that dirty work has had a good effect.'

Her barbed humour almost made Walter smile. Did she mean dirty work in his garden, or fucking her sister?

She went on: 'You've lost your stringy cheekbones and developed some real muscles. You've put on some weight. It all suits you.'

This opened the way for him. 'You look wonderful too, Siobhan. I'm not here to seduce you, but you do look extremely sexy,' he said quite shyly. 'Is an ex-husband allowed to say such things?'

'No, he bloody isn't.' Siobhan laughed. 'And you won't seduce me, Walter.'

Siobhan made it clear that in fact there would be no romance, no bed-sharing, and the solace of her curves was not going to be available to him. Much of this she said with a smile, but Walter needed to hear it.

Walter told me when we met back in London that he had decided then and there that the drug that really did it for him was not sex but music. It was something of a revelation for him. It explained why he had managed – for most of his life – to be true to his two wives, and in a very important way to himself and his own ideals. His father and mother had spent long periods of time apart while Harry was on tour, but they had stayed faithful to each other.

I had to fight back an impulse then to jump in and tell him that back in those days, his mother Sally and I had spent many evenings alone by the blazing log fire, her drinking red wine, me in a heroin haze. I had often thought the only reason we had never drifted into having sex was because my drug of choice made me completely disinterested in physical embellishments to my 'Little Mother' heroin jag.

Back when they were young teenagers, Walter, as Rain had told me, had experimented a little with my daughter, but after thirty minutes of kissing, where she would be breathless, ready to move to some new level, Walter simply felt a light swoon, rested, serene, and deeply happy and at ease.

So if had he learned that the drug that worked best for him was music, it didn't seem to me to be providing him with many kicks. He just looked good at what he did, and it appeared to come easily.

Old Nik had conveyed that when he was ready he would fly higher as his creative work began in earnest. Siobhan had always understood this, and knew that the way she could penetrate Walter most deeply would be through his creative work. She had waited a long time to play this role, the only one that really interested her.

'You are writing,' she said. 'Selena sent me the pages. You know it was me who sent them to your dad?'

'Yes. Thank you so much. It was an inspired idea. I brought the music he has written.' He pulled his laptop out of his old grab-bag. 'You still have our old sound system? I can plug it in.'

Siobhan nodded. Then she laughed. 'Yes, play your music, but you know I will always be more interested in the words you write. That will never change.'

But she listened, and as the room filled with the dark and profoundly disturbing music, the thunder sheets, the bull-horns, the dissonant choirs and the thrilling and experimental violin solos set against the backdrop of Harry's church organ imitating both birdsong and nightmares, she was mightily pleased to hear how well her idea had worked.

As she listened Siobhan pored over the pages of the nineteen soundscapes that formed the main body of his work since he had emerged from the labyrinth.

Afterwards Siobhan looked up at Walter, and the flash of delight in her eyes told him all he needed to know.

'You know this is amazing stuff. But as wonderful as it's turned out as music, all this terror of the future is a kind of arrogance.'

'What do you mean?'

'No one knows for sure what the future holds.'

'I am just writing what it is I can hear in the air around me.'

'So you're like Selena now!' Siobhan smiled, but there was some anger in her voice. 'You're a psychic. You can hear what people around you – the audience – are feeling?'

Walter brought his eyes up to hers defiantly enough to make it clear he would not back down.

'You're not psychic, Walter,' barked Siobhan. 'It's absurd.'

Siobhan disappeared for a few minutes into the kitchen where she clattered plates, cups and glasses so loudly that Walter remembered when they were married that this was her way of letting him know she was angry with him. After a while she came back in, holding two cups of black coffee.

'You don't know what is happening, Walter. No one does. You may feel you can connect with the anxiety of people around you, but you can't. Each of us has our own little world. It's our duty to maintain each other, raise each other up not bring each other down.'

'So says the foreign correspondent,' said Walter with a laugh.

'Ah, now that's different, Walter. That's truth, not whimsy.' Siobhan believed she knew the difference. She had never faltered like so many of her journalist colleagues and ended up writing fiction, just some excellent poetry. 'And you have to accept that the truth about Floss may never be reconciled with Selena's so-called facts.'

'What?' Walter was confused.

'Trust her,' said Siobhan. 'Until you know for certain. Then when you do know something, you may find it is unimportant to you. That you can survive it.'

'The rumours . . .'

'Who cares if Ronnie is really gay or not? If he's bisexual then . . .' She stopped short of adding that he could join the club of which she was a contented member. 'If Floss is going to betray you, nothing you can do will stop that happening.'

Walter knew that his ex-wife was right. He felt like a boy in her presence, as he always had. How strange that this woman might be the one who would reassure him, and help him find acceptance of his situation.

'The stuff I've been hearing does make me feel anxious,' he said quietly. 'Louis has been bullying me to try to turn it into art.'

When Walter was telling me about this conversation with Siobhan I was surprised to hear him suggest I had bullied him. Is that what he really felt? Siobhan had defended me.

'Louis a bully? I doubt it, Walter. And I have no doubt that fucker Frank is trying to get you to reform the band!' Siobhan laughed again. 'Stop worrying, Walter, what you hear is what you hear. You grew up with your head in a bucket playing a mouth-organ. You've always been a strange fellow.'

'What I'm hearing is not my doing, Siobhan. It comes into my head uninvited. It feels like some manic *schizo* shit.'

'Let it come,' soothed Siobhan. 'That's my advice. Accept it.'

'That's what Nikolai Andréevich advised,' Walter cut in. 'Fifteen years ago, when I first started hearing this stuff.'

'He's right then. Allow some affection for the people around you whose troubles inspire you – they are good people; all people are good people. Fear and art are entangled, sort of intertwined. It's always been that way. It's easier for me, Walter. I'm Irish. We know how to *kiss the dark*. But at last you've found some artistic ambition; you have a function over and above those evenings teasing Selena and making all the boys at Dingwalls jealous.' She laughed, and Walter laughed with her, easily, for the first time that evening.

'Walter.' Siobhan held his hand. 'Do you like your father's music? Do you like what he's done with your words? Did I do the right thing with this – just once?'

Walter looked at his ex-wife, and smiled. 'Oh yes,' he said. 'Yes, yes, yes!'

The sound of galloping hooves on hard ground. Thudding rhythmically, two horses, breathing hard. Jumps. The whip. Faster. Faster. Then splashing through muddy, shallow water. Climbing a hill, until reaching the top the two exhausted horses and their riders stop to survey the sight we cannot see, but that through this soundscape we can hear. A valley, a distant country, made of the sounds we have been hearing in the play so far. This is the sound of the portents of the end of the world, the death and fading of everything, everything good and bad and in between, everything natural and everything man-made, nature and the environment – all of it. Again there is a strange kind of blindness, blindingly, fiercely brilliant and warm. Clumsy, grop-ing, lost – but making it easier to hear, and to be able to focus on what can be heard. Then finally all the most disturbing sounds resolve into the most musical, into the jazz, the fugues, the song of birds. Ultimately the piano, and Walter's one song for Floss.

One thing was becoming clear as Walter sat listening to Siobhan discount all his anxieties: she knew him better than anyone, better than any of his friends, no doubt better than I did, and almost certainly better than his parents.

She was the one who asked the most important question, one he probably would never have framed himself.

'How well do you think Floss knows you, Walter?'

'How well do I know Floss?' He was countering, hypotheti-cally now.

Siobhan leaned forward earnestly. 'That's not the right question.'

She knew he hadn't come to see her to consult her about art or religion. He'd brought the laptop containing his soundscapes as an offering to her, in return for some emotional solace and advice.

'I don't want to lose Floss the way I lost you,' he said sadly.

'You never had me,' she scoffed, but with a kind smile. 'Not in the sense you have Floss today.'

'I must ask you a question.' He was feeling embattled. 'Who was the man at the door when I arrived?'

Siobhan smiled conspiratorially. 'Why assume the person you saw was a man?'

Walter surrendered. Siobhan might know him, but he hardly knew his first wife, and at last realised how wonderful that was. He was her friend, she was wise and knew him well, and could advise him without conditions. She had never taken anything from him, never chided him, and never tried to constrain him. She had only ever pressed him with her passionate conviction that he had potential as an artist.

They drank two more bottles of red wine, and when she nudged at the fading embers of the fire with a poker, and then kissed him and climbed the stairs to her bed, Walter realised that all he had learned by coming to see his ex-wife was that this time he could not turn back.

He lay back on the luxurious sofa, his head surrounded by cushions and the scent of the woman he still loved and respected, and perhaps the additional contrasting scent of a man or woman he might never know, and drifted into a deep sleep. It had been a long, long day.

Chapter 17

The long days turned into the better part of a week. Walter lost track of time. No landline phone. No radio. No television. No internet. For two days he let his mobile battery go flat. He didn't leave the cottage.

He was awakened one morning by Siobhan, holding a cup of tea, and gently shaking his shoulder.

'Walter,' she whispered. 'Wake up. Something has happened.'

Walter pulled the blanket over his legs and sat up, rubbing his eyes like a child.

'Floss has had an accident.' Siobhan held out the cup and Walter took it, slow to wake up completely. 'You must go to London immediately. Call Selena. She called your mobile. I charged it up for you last night.'

Walter descended into a panic unlike any he had experienced in his life. His heart pounded, but still did not seem to pump enough blood to his brain to stop him feeling dizzy. He held his breath for thirty or forty seconds at a time. The feeling of dread in the pit of his stomach almost prevented him thinking rationally; it was as though his body had taken over his brain.

Siobhan passed him his mobile phone and ordered him to call Selena. He realised that having to make the call was partly to blame for the intensity of his panic.

'What's happened?' he demanded, spilling the tea on the blanket as he dropped his cup. 'What kind of accident?'

'I don't know the details, Walter,' said Siobhan firmly. 'Selena just called, crying and upset. Phone her.'

Walter's mind began to race as he threw the mobile phone aside and pulled on his jeans. Selena was, as usual, at the centre of things. This thought made him angry. He spoke aloud. 'She always seems to know so much more than anyone else about what Floss is or isn't doing.'

He heard his own voice and was embarrassed for a moment. He asked himself questions silently instead, preparing them for Selena. Had Floss fallen? Or had she and Ronnie had a road accident in that bloody awful horsebox?

However frightened he was of finding out what had happened, he was dreading having to speak to Selena. Why did he have to confer this power on her? He had hoped simply to put her out of mind, and to refuse to face the gossip she shared about Floss and Ronnie. And what was the lifelong secret Floss had kept from him?

Siobhan – now holding his phone out to him as he pulled on a T-shirt – had successfully re-focused him on the importance of his work, the absurdity of imagining that relationships, love, sex, marriage, divorce and even death mattered when art was on the table. Now, all she had done to steady him and settle him was blown away. He saw that it had always been so; Siobhan could be, and would always only be, his creative mentor or amanuensis. She could never go any further in her ministrations. She loved him, that was clear enough, and had immense respect for him, but it was the younger sister who probably better understood his connection with the darkness in his mind, in his aural world, in his soul.

He took breath after breath, and handed the phone back to Siobhan.

'I can't do it.' He was finding it difficult to breathe.

She dialled Selena for him and gave him the receiver.

Selena wasted no words. 'Floss is in the Critical Care Ward in Ealing Hospital.' She was weeping.

'Tell me what happened, Selena,' said Walter. 'Please stop crying. You didn't do anything to Floss, did you?'

This seemed to galvanise Selena. 'Don't be so fucking stupid, Walter. She fell off a fucking horse, a week ago. I only just found out. Ronnie tried to call you.'

'Sorry,' Walter said meekly. 'He left a message but I missed it. How is she??'

'I understand she suffered some kind of stroke while in the ambulance.'

Walter was amazed at his detachment. As his heart slowed to normal he knew that hearing this news from Selena was probably a good thing. She had after all been the one who told him that Floss had been unfaithful to him, possibly for years. He had generated such an emotional distance now through Selena that he almost felt as though he were listening to a report of a tragedy in some far-off place, unconnected to him. It wasn't that he felt no sympathy, nor was it that he didn't care; he had been tempered, hardened, by what Selena had told him about his wife's affair, and even more hardened by his own lapse with Selena.

Selena broke the silence. 'Are you OK?'

'I'm trying to work out why I'm shaking so much, but I don't feel anything.'

'What are you doing with Siobhan?'

'For Christ's sake, Selena,' he shouted. 'What does it matter?'

'There's something else, Walter,' Selena said quietly.

'There always is with you, isn't there?' Walter was afraid of what she might be about to say. 'More secrets?'

'She lost a baby.' That was a total bombshell. 'You have to hurry, Walter.'

A baby? Walter's first thought was to wonder whether he or Ronnie was the father; who had been the father?

'What baby?' He immediately knew the question was the wrong one. 'I mean whose baby is it? Or rather was it?'

'I don't know, Walter,' said Selena, even angrier now with him in return. 'But I know this baby would have been so important to her. It would have been more important than you could ever imagine. Please, get moving.'

Walter put down the phone, and got to his feet.

Siobhan had gathered his keys and wallet, and handed them to him. She did so with two hands, reaching out and pushing him away as though to urge him to go. At the last minute she grabbed the folder of soundscape descriptions.

He shook his head. 'Keep them,' he said. 'Please. I have copies.'

He looked into Siobhan's blue-green eyes then walked out to the car; the thought came to him that his mother had never trained him to understand women; they still seemed such strange creatures. And if he was any kind of example of men in general, then they were equally peculiar.

On the ferry from Dublin back to Holyhead, Walter leaned against the rail on the deck outside the bar. The sea was rough, the sky grey, and the ferry groaned slightly as its stabiliser fins struggled to keep the massive bulk of the ship steady. Keep it steady they did; despite the waves and the wind the ship ploughed on at eighteen knots as though the Irish Sea were a millpond. Nothing to fear out here.

And yet Walter felt the return of the intense anxiety he had suffered when he first woke up to Siobhan's news about Floss's accident. He could not go to the hospital. He must go home first.

Oh God! He couldn't make himself go to see his own wife who could be dying in hospital after an accident, which led to a stroke.

I remember when Walter told me all this that I interrogated him quite harshly. How could such a good man, and he was that, suddenly become so self-obsessed, hard-hearted and callous? How could he have waited even for a second before driving to the hospital? He defended himself as best he could. He had been in a mist, unsure he should even be driving. He had asked himself whether the panic he felt rooted in was fear. Or was it anger?

He arrived on the outskirts of London in the rush hour. It took him over ninety minutes to drive on the M4 from Reading past the airport. It was after seven in the evening by the time he was level with Chiswick on the A4. Instead of turning off to Sheen he carried on, turning left through Hammersmith and Shepherd's Bush, through Paddington and up to Camden Lock.

Dingwalls. That had been his decision. He needed to stand at the bar at Dingwalls. He didn't even know if the place would be open, but as he drove past it to park in a back street he could see a line of people queuing to get in.

As he walked to the door the first person he saw was me. The evening at the club had not quite started, and there was a scruffy, young local band on stage doing a sound-check. I had gone to meet Frank Lovelace for a drink and to discuss what Walter might do with his new work, as complemented by the brilliant work of his father. We were both standing talking to the bouncer.

We had heard the news about Floss's accident half an hour or so earlier from Selena who had been sitting on the edge of the stage looking up at the young lead singer as though hoping he might notice her. She looked downcast, her cheeks streaked with mascara. Pathetic. She hadn't clocked me as far as I could tell.

Frank spotted Walter approaching and hurried towards him, throwing his arms around him when he reached him.

'What are you doing here, man?' He blocked his way into the club. 'Have you seen Floss?'

'How do you know about what happened? Do you know what happened?'

Frank nodded. 'Selena,' he said, gesturing indoors. 'She's in the club watching the band.'

Instead of turning around and leaving, this seemed to strangely reassure Walter. He smiled grimly at Frank, perhaps making the face he felt Frank would expect to see, and went in and walked to the bar.

I intercepted him. 'Come and talk to me, Walter,' I offered. 'You must be in shock, we all are.'

He muttered that he needed a drink, and while I was getting it Crow, who was doing a show later that evening and was at the other end of the bar, came to join us, holding a Coke. Crow hugged Walter, an uncharacteristic gesture, then shook his hand, and with a shake of his head and a quietly expressed promise to meet soon, made himself scarce. But in that moment Walter had got a tangible unspoken message from Crow that he should not have come back to the club; it would always be his home, but he should not be here now.

Selena joined us at the bar, looking less confident than usual, and less glowing. She put up her hand to him in greeting, but didn't move towards him, aware of his confusion. He looked around him and seemed to lose concentration. He looked dizzy.

Frank Lovelace was giving orders to a girl of about seventeen, who wore dirty jeans, a scruffy denim jacket, and was carrying what looked like a heavy spool of lighting cable. Her face was smudged with what appeared to be engine oil.

'Molly,' said Frank, introducing us. 'I got her the job here on the lights.'

Molly was the tank-girl type who often ends up doing this kind of work. Not necessarily as gender-bending as she might appear, she would have been conventionally pretty but for her messy hair. She was smiling hugely though, obviously pleased to be a part of the Dingwalls world, and especially enjoying the insider proximity to the band.

She looked at Walter as if she wanted to say something, and he responded with an encouraging nod.

Selena looked ready to throw herself into the girl's path, but was just managing to contain herself. The young woman held out her hand to Walter.

'Welcome back,' she said in a confident voice. 'We've all been waiting. I've never seen you play, much too young. Got work to do now. But respect, man! Respect!'

Frank gestured that she should go back to work, so she walked off towards the stage.

Selena tracked Molly's movements, glaring at her. She wanted to let the younger woman know who was boss, it seemed. So I had Walter to myself and we sat and talked. Walter explained something of what had happened between him and Selena, their sexual encounter, and also how confused he was. He was still wondering why he had felt compelled to go to Siobhan for guidance, and apologised for not reaching out to me.

Walter was not one of those predatory men so common in the music business. He had loved Siobhan and now he loved Floss. And yet Floss was not entirely in his mind; it was almost as though he were driving her spectre away: Floss, in a hospital bed, broken and probably distraught.

He looked to the bar where Selena now stood gazing intently at him. His thoughts slowed down even more. Is serial monogamy the answer to the attractions of the flesh? This was the pointless thought that he said now flashed into his head. Falling into bed with Selena had been out of character for him; he knew it and so did she. He could therefore safely acknowledge and accept it when he was attracted to a woman, whoever she was. As he was telling me this, I caught him watching Molly as she reappeared and went back to work. He saw me watching him and in an instant he was found out! It was a poignant moment; Walter was coming to grips with the fact that he was just a man, a human being.

Molly looked like the kind of girl who would confront any man she wanted, and in the brutal parlance of the times *get her needs met*. She also looked as though she might be a lesbian; this was something that maybe troubled Walter further after our discovery of Siobhan's bisexuality. He might be one of those men who wanted to conquer the unconquerable. Just as some young women felt safe in a lively group of gay men, some young men felt drawn to women who like women.

The barman gave Walter a free beer as if for old times' sake.

Selena came over to where we sat, and stood at our table. She didn't try to kiss Walter. She held his hand for a moment, and looked at him with the blue-green eyes she shared with her sister, and it looked for a moment as though Walter wanted to slap her pretty face.

Selena's eyes hardened; no man would ever frighten her again. Never. She lowered her voice.

'I'm sorry,' she said, without a falter. 'I am really terribly sorry we made love. Then this awful thing has happened.'

Walter softened. He knew the accident was not her fault.

'I spoke to Ronnie,' Selena said, and Walter turned to her again, not knowing what to expect. 'He says Floss fell from her horse in the afternoon, but collapsed later. Maybe she suffered the stroke in the shower. At the same time as the miscarriage.'

'Shower?' Walter was almost barking at Selena. 'You never said anything about a shower on the phone. Who found her? Did Ronnie find her?'

'Ronnie was with her,' Selena explained. Her tone was conspiratorial.

'Ronnie was in the shower with Floss?' Walter shouted. 'Is that what you're trying to say?'

Selena lowered her eyes.

Walter slammed down his beer and walked out. As he did so Molly looked across the hall, concern for Walter in her eyes, and threw a disdainful look at Selena and mouthed the word 'slag'.

I quickly ran over to Frank and explained that I needed to leave to try to make sure Walter got to the hospital. As I left the club, I took one last look back into a place I had the feeling I might never visit again. Everything about it was tainted, sullied and tragic. Floss's extraordinary entrance fifteen years before came into my mind; she had challenged Walter to ride with her, as she drove Siobhan from his mind and heart for ever, at least as a lover.

Selena smiled back at me defiantly, left there standing at the bar. I think she was wondering how she could be such a bloody fool. Then her eyes met Molly's recriminating sneer and she smiled at the young roadie, like a grimace, on and quickly off, sarcastically.

Back in his car Walter waited, crumpled, for only a few moments before straightening his back, and as I got into the passenger seat he started the engine, and we set off to Ealing to see his wife.

'Molly is a cool girl, isn't she?'

At that moment of terrible jealousy, when he believed he had been deceived by Floss, Molly's young and fit body had no doubt come quickly back into his mind. I looked askance at him and saw him push the thought away. He tightened his hands on the steering wheel, and drove as fast as he could get away with.

'It's ridiculous, Uncle Louis,' he spluttered. 'None of this feels like me. Is it like me? Am I this fucking shallow?'

'For fuck's sake,' I replied angrily. 'Let's just get to the hospital.'

As he drove I spoke in his defence. No, this was not who he was, not the real Walter. Selena had psyched him up. When she set her mind to it, she could achieve almost anything. Who knew what the truth really was. Errant or not, unfaithful or not, whether Ronnie was gay or straight, and whether Walter himself had slept with Floss's best friend or her worst enemy – none of this mattered any more. He just had to do something right for once.

Looking at the way Walter conducted himself in the next few hours my godson behaved properly; that much is safe to say. As he drove back from Camden to west London, along the A40, over the elevated road above Paddington and Kensal Rise, past Wormwood Scrubs Prison and West Acton and on to Perivale and then south from Alperton to West Ealing, he found himself deep in thought. I knew him so well. I could imagine the questions running through his head.

What had happened to him?

Why had he done all the things he had done?

Why as a teenager had he turned to what Noël Coward had called 'cheap music'?

Was it to annoy his father who had often told him he would never make a professional musician?

Or was it to irritate his mother who had attempted to make herself the sole glamorous female in young Walter's life?

Having succeeded in music, why did he turn away from that career as well?

Not only had he made a living from music, but beautiful women – and their sisters, and their sisters' best friends – had fallen in love with him.

Had everything he had done been driven by some aimless, childish vengeance?

At some level I expect he wondered if the green-fingered skills required of a great gardener, and the performing abilities required to be a great front man in a band like the Stand, had both somehow evaded him. What he was hearing now, the soundscapes, were a reflection of who he really was.

What did Floss think of all this? Would he ever know?

For a second he lost concentration and the wheel of the car caught in the rut of a gutter.

'Fuck! Walter!' I shouted and my voice sounded high-pitched and girlish, and we both broke out laughing.

He quickly recovered and smacked his forehead, then the questions in his mind seemed to appear before me again – I could almost hear his anguish.

How would she be?

The poor, poor girl!

A stroke!

Would she be able to speak?

How would she look?

Would she be able to walk?

He tried to reconnect himself to Floss, in his heart.

Why was it so difficult?

As he drove he told me had never played Floss any of his new work, nor his father's latest developments. She had been away working on the days when he had first played the completed scores to Crow, Hanson and myself. When she was home, she tended to allow him the same degree of privacy in his little recording studio as he had enjoyed – nay, demanded – in his labyrinthine garden. He hadn't even shared with her his written descriptions of soundscapes. He had wanted his project to be complete before he displayed it to Floss. It might have been his gift to her. Today, as he regained control of the lumbering, over-weight Volvo 4x4, the typical 'Sheen-Mobile', he realised that Floss was probably the only person in his limited circle who had no idea what he had been going through, creatively speaking. And he, it now seemed, had known equally little about what she had been doing.

'Our marriage has failed, Uncle Louis,' he confessed. 'This is all such a mess.'

I could see that the question on the tip of his tongue was whether it was too late to mend?

We arrived in West Ealing, parked in the hospital car park in one of the neat rows of cars facing the Uxbridge Road, and found directions to the Critical Care Ward. It was on the top floor of the building, which was more like a multi-storey office block than a hospital.

We travelled up in the lift and as the doors opened I saw a toilet and ran towards it, shouting to Walter that I would catch him up. He was trying to find the ward from the muddling signage on the wall when a woman holding a clipboard accosted him.

He had met her once years before, but didn't recognise her at first. Instead he saw the name at the top of the form she held out to him: 'Maud Andréevich'.

Walter tried to push past the irritating old woman.

'Please!' She was insistent, and blocked him. 'I have a petition here. Please look at it, and maybe you would agree to sign it.'

'I have come to see my wife,' he pleaded. 'I haven't got time for this.'

But Maud just poured out her resentment in a torrent. She was deeply upset, her hands shaking.

'I won't keep you long. This awful hospital has mixed-sex wards, and is open to the public. Perverts come in off the street and hang around in the toilets.'

At that moment I was emerging from the toilet and saw the pair of them, Maud with her face tortured and drawn, pressed as close to Walter as she could. She was holding a clipboard, waving a pencil at him in mid-rant and clearly hadn't recognised Walter.

'The bathrooms are mixed. There are dirty old men walking around with their dressing gowns hanging open.'

For a second I thought she was referring to me, and checked my flies.

'There are young women in hospital gowns you can see through if they stand by the windows. The doctors are all foreign. They're OK, but they're all from bloody India and half the nurses have trouble speaking English. They certainly don't care about mixed wards. Well I do. It's an outrage. My husband has fallen in love with some young woman in the opposite bed. He's out of his mind on drugs and can't help himself. I'm here for him and he doesn't even notice me any more. The whole system is a disgrace.'

Chapter 18

Andréevich. Old Nik. It must be him, Walter's old friend and adviser. He must be here in the hospital.

I had heard Nik had taken to the bottle recently and had tried his hand at hang-gliding again in one last hurrah. In the crash he had broken both his ankles. I had shared a lot of this with Walter a few months before. We were both saddened to hear about it, but my feelings were mixed. Old Nik's passing would stop the flow of new work, but the old work – much of which I controlled – might go up in value. Nik had intended the hang-gliding escapade to be a glorious end. He had been ill with colon cancer that had spread to his prostate and his stomach. Physicians, who had somehow failed to get a true measure of the old man's tenacious and audacious spirit, had given him several short life-sentences. They provided Nik with a self-regulated morphine intravenous supplier, and he used it enthusiastically, reinvigorating his visions of angelic hosts harvesting the lost souls of the forthcoming apocalypse. The end, with no date, no time, no sun or moon, nor tide nor moment: Nik just saw it all coming.

I stood at a distance. I didn't want Maud to see me. As Walter scribbled his name on the petition, Maud pressed his arm gratefully, and was about to allow him to pass.

Then she took a careful look at him. 'You're Walter Karel Watts, aren't you?' Her voice had lost its bullying edge. 'My husband is Nik Andréevich,' she said. 'Old Nik.'

'I realised,' Walter replied, shifting from foot to foot.

'Your old colleague Steve Hanson always tells me that my husband was your guru!'

She laughed then, and absurdly, by that erotic mechanism I seemed unable to control, I swooned a little at this woman whose face had so often touched my heart and triggered my loins.

She mentioned another link. 'Louis Doxtader,' she added. 'Your godfather, I think, is my husband's agent. What an extraordinary coincidence.'

Walter nodded, and I turned my face away, hoping she wouldn't recognise me and slow down our progress to Floss any further. Coincidences often happen in hospitals, which gather people up like railway stations and airports. We tend to run into old acquaintances in such places.

Maud was not so commonsensical. 'No,' she corrected herself. 'This is not a mere coincidence. It's meant to be. It's like a circle, and it's closing. How wonderful. I'm Maud by the way.'

I could maintain my distance no longer. 'Hello, Maud,' I said, offering my hand. 'I've brought Walter here to see his wife.'

Maud held out both hands and we each took one.

Then, suddenly looking her age, she broke down in tears. Walter moved to comfort her and hardly heard her confession as she fell into his arms and sobbed.

'I had his child,' she wept. 'He never knew.'

Walter seemed not to register what she was saying. Probably all he could think of was Floss in a coma, after a stroke, perhaps disabled for life, having lost a child.

Walter allowed Maud to pull away from his arms slowly.

She looked to the floor.

'My husband,' she said, 'is behaving absurdly. Wickedly, though he can't help himself. He's fallen in love with the young woman in the bed opposite his own. He's refusing to die. It's stubbornness.'

Maud turned her gaze on Walter.

'It's so unfair,' she complained, wiping her eyes. 'I've suffered with Nik for so long. I've put up with his crazy visions and his dangerous adventures. Now I can't even watch him die with any dignity. Floss! What kind of a name is that?'

I watched as Walter gazed through the window of the locked door into the Critical Care Ward, and gasped with amazement. What we both saw was especially pleasing after Maud's rant. Like most people, we thought the National Health Service had been in decline, and that this hospital in particular had suffered from lack of funds. However, the entire ward was modern, shining and bustling with dozens of doctors, nurses, orderlies and cleaners. Typically, there was no one at the reception desk outside the locked door, but people were going in and out using swipe cards, and we walked in with one of them who directed us towards a second reception desk inside the ward. That was unattended too. Everyone seemed to be busy.

Lots of staff were moving around purposefully, none of them giving us a second glance. We had no idea which way to turn, right or left. There was a central corridor with about six small wards branching off it, and a few isolation rooms with glass walls. Neither of us had ever experienced such a sense of positive activity in a hospital before. The last time I'd been in hospital was to visit a friend who had had a knee operation, and wanted to smoke a cigarette. We had had to go to a bleak, seedy area set aside for the purpose. It had been an unpleasant experience. But now Walter and I knew that we were looking at the very hub of this hospital, served by powerfully equipped operating rooms. The ordinary part of the hospital was probably much less impressive, and less intense. But this was all reassuring.

Suddenly, Walter seemed to stagger, losing his balance. I held his arm and steadied him.

He looked at me gratefully. His dizziness was caused not so much by panic as by relief. Floss could not be in a better place, whatever Maud Andréevich believed was so evil about mixed wards.

Just then Walter spied Maud at the end of the corridor, walking out of one of the side wards holding some towels. He went towards where he had seen her emerge. How would Floss be?

We reached the ward. There were six beds, five with occupants.

Floss was not there.

Walter had been certain that this was where he would find her, since Maud had said that Floss was in the bed opposite Old Nik's. And there he was, wearing a pair of large headphones, sitting on the side of his bed, listening to something, rocking back and forth. It was shocking to see how much he had deteriorated. He was covered in dark chocolate-coloured lesions all over his face and hands, and his teeth were black. Walter looked at the bed opposite and checked the chart.

Florence Watts. This is where she should be. Was she dead? Oh God. In surgery?

At that moment Nik Andréevich looked up and saw Walter's face. The old man's eyes were full of tears. He looked at Walter and slipped off the earphones. Walter could hear the music, an old New Orleans funeral anthem.

I went down to the St James infirmary, and I saw my baby there. She was stretched out on a long white table, so cold, and fine, and bare. Let her go, let her go, God bless her, wherever she may be. She can search this world over, never find another man like me. When I die, Oh Lord, please bury me in my high-top Stetson hat. Put gold coins over my eyelids, so the boys will know I died standing pat. Get six crap-shooting pallbearers, six chorus girls to sing me a song. Put a jazz band behind my hearse to raise hell as we roll along. Get sixteen coal-black horses, to pull that rubber-tyred hack. There're thirteen men going to the graveyard, only twelve are coming back. Suddenly, the music leaps up a hundred notches, a full classical orchestra follows the rhythm of a huge orchestral bass drum, booming slowly and funereally. Let her go, let her go, God bless her, wherever she may be. She can search this world over, never find another man like me. With every repeat of the two lines the singers become more celebratory. The lead male voice becomes more and more arrogant and bragging, more grandiose, more self-assured. Soon there are thousands of them. A massive choir, straight out of Mahler. A huge organ. The music shakes the world. An old man laughs. A young girl sings, upwards, away.

Walter looked like he was stifling bile; the old man must have been staying alive by the skin of his teeth. But his sunken eyes were alight with something that was tricky to place at first. I was standing at a distance, but Walter told me later that at that instant he realised what he could see in the old man's eyes.

Lust.

Walter called to a nurse who was passing through the ward.

'My wife, Florence Watts, where is she?' His voice wavered with anxiety and concern.

'She's in that bed there, Mr Watts,' said the nurse. 'She's in the bathroom at the moment.'

'How's she doing?'

'As well as can be expected after such a fall.' The nurse uttered the well-worn hospital cliché as she guided Walter to a chair next to Floss's empty bed.

'I understand my wife had a stroke of some kind?'

'I believe it was quite a minor one.' The nurse made to walk away but then turned back to face Walter. 'The surgeon will explain, but she is having trouble with her balance at the moment, and that may go on for a while. She was a keen rider, I understand?'

'She is a professional horsewoman,' corrected Walter, who never knew quite how to describe Floss's job.

'She may not be able to ride again,' said the nurse rather curtly. 'But she is quite well. You'll see.'

Walter shuddered and I knew he must be wondering whether Floss herself knew that she might never be able to ride her favourite horse Dragon again.

'There was a baby, I believe,' Walter mumbled. 'My wife, will she . . .' He couldn't complete the sentence, but the nurse understood.

'She's a healthy young woman. We shall see. It's looking good.' She smiled.

Then she was gone, walking away so quietly and quickly that Walter hardly seemed to notice her disappear. He slumped into the chair by the empty bed. I know he had never thought much about children before. Floss had never seemed to bother about starting a family, she had always been happy with her horses. Now there was a miscarried child. What would their life have been like had the baby survived? Then I saw him look over at Old Nik who was glaring at him. It was obvious he didn't remember Walter.

'You,' he growled. 'Young fellah!'

The old man was calling him over to his bed. Walter went to his side. Nik was whispering. As Walter lowered his head he must have smelled the combined fetid odours of tumours and morphine. The old man grabbed his arm, then suddenly gasped and fell back on his pillow, asleep again.

Chapter 19

Suddenly, there she stood beside him.

Floss. Leaning on a walking frame, with a drip taped to her left arm, the plastic bag hanging from a stand on castors, so that she had to walk in short stages – carefully and tenderly, in great pain, still feeling dizzy.

Walter looked at her; I could see what my godson must be thinking. She was so beautiful. His wife had always glowed; she was a 'shining girl', literally speaking. A strand of blond hair fell over one side of her face, and the white nightie she wore was crumpled. Over it she had on an open blue linen dressing gown that set off a sparkle in her blue eyes. A dark purple-blue bruise on her right temple extended down to her cheekbone. She had recently put on some bright red lipstick, perhaps to cheer herself up, so Walter was confronted with a strange blaze of mixed hues: yellow, blue, purple and red. Floss smiled, beaming at him.

'Floss!' Walter almost shouted her name.

At this, Old Nik in the opposite bed woke up and was pumping at his morphine line.

'Floss,' he exclaimed triumphantly. 'That was her name. I think. I do think.' Nik was starting to yell.

Oh fuck, I thought. It was clear from his expression that Walter really didn't like the old man using his wife's nickname.

'Her name is Florence,' he corrected.

Maud ran into the room to Nik's bed and tried to calm him, looking at Floss and Walter reproachfully. But Old Nik carried on, in a reverie of memory, or perhaps fantasy.

'Florence!! Flo!!! Flossie!!! Floss!' He was laughing now as he tried out all the variations of her name. 'I used to walk you to school!'

He was trying to rise from his bed, his face pale, drained of blood, taking on a slightly green pallor.

He started to sing wildly. Then fell back.

Walter took Floss in his arms as best he could, and led her to her bed where she sat, gratefully.

Nik was still raising hell, and Maud looked over again.

Suddenly, her mood changed. It was almost as though she relented, accepting Nik's delusions. But also, at last, she was able to make the connection between Floss, Walter and me. The pieces were falling together, and she began to see that meeting Walter in the hospital reception area was in fact a much larger and happier coincidence than she had thought. Floss was not the enemy.

She smiled.

Floss smiled back.

Old Nik slumped briefly, appearing to be unconscious for a moment, but then recovered. He reached out, arms outstretched, to Floss in the opposite bed, while Maud tried to restrain the absurdly lustful old man.

His wild eyes moved from Floss to Maud, back and forth.

'Too old to live, too dead to love,' the old man was almost singing now. 'Both you women . . .'

He paused for a moment as if in revelation.

'Both you women are the same.'

Nik's heart monitor alarm emitted a continuous sound – his heart had stopped. He slumped back, his mouth open, his eyes tightly closed. Maud threw herself on to the old man's body and held him. She did not weep, nor cry out.

Walter looked as though he might shout for help, make some kind of fuss; maybe shout 'cart!' as we had seen on hospital television series. But before he could do anything the nurse was there, and pulled the curtains quickly around the bed.

We could hear Maud speaking to her dead husband, asking him a final question as he ascended from this life to the next.

'You said you loved her,' she said. 'Who is she? Who was she to you? Who does she remind you of? You swore to me there had been no one. You swore!'

Obviously uncomfortable to be hearing this, Walter held Floss tightly.

'Poor, poor you!' He was ashamed at how badly he had behaved, how long he had delayed rushing to her side. 'Do you feel OK? Will you be OK? Was the journey here terrible? I'm so, so sorry it took me so long to get here to be with you. I feel like a complete cunt . . . This is all very strange – with Maud and Nik.'

Floss looked up at him and shook her head.

Walter whispered to her. 'The old man had obviously fallen in love with you,' he said. 'Maud was right – he was hanging on to life, refusing to die, almost as if he saw in you someone he had once loved.'

Floss clutched at Walter. This was not her fault, and not a drama she wanted any part of, but Walter was carried away by the unfolding story.

'Maybe you reminded him of someone he had loved before Maud? Or someone he'd had an affair with?' This was clearly what Maud believed. 'Someone called Florence? Could that be why she's so angry with you?'

When Walter looked back to Floss, still enfolded in his arms, he saw that he had been insensitive again. She was shaking her head and weeping. He smiled, and moved so he could look at her face.

'Maud was angry before I arrived,' corrected Floss, dabbing at her eyes with a tissue. 'The old bugger would simply not give up. He wouldn't let go and die. He was in terrible pain. It was awful for Maud. He set eyes on me and seemed to make me the reason to fight back. It wasn't fair to her. He didn't seem to see Maud any more, only me. A couple of times he came round from a stupor claiming he'd been halfway down a long white tunnel. He knew he'd been dying, on the last stretch. He said he'd fought his way back into his diseased and painful body, merely for one last look at me. What an awful honour for me!'

Walter couldn't help but laugh, but he stifled it quickly. There was nothing funny about what had happened, and it seemed like the most extraordinary tragedy for Maud. But of course he knew exactly what Nik had seen in his beautiful, shining Floss. She had illuminated his final days.

'He kept shouting that he had to see my face again,' said Floss. She was starting to cry again. 'My beautiful face; the diamond in my tooth.' She put her hand up to the awful bruise that temporarily disfigured her.

'Nik loved you,' said Walter. 'It was the way he wanted to go. In love with my beautiful Floss.'

'Maybe he just loved life and didn't want to die!' Floss shook her hair, reviving at last.

Maud sat quietly beside Andréevich's lifeless body. She had stopped asking him questions now; she would never get answers. She could hear Floss and Walter whispering in the opposite bed, and guessed they were talking about her husband and his death-bed obsession with Floss, but she didn't care any more. Soon they would cover his face and wheel him away. What would she do then? Where would she go?

As Walter passed his wife some tea, his eyes dropped for a moment, and she could see he was ashamed of something; she suppressed a laugh.

'I know that Selena will always be in love with you, Walt,' she said. Her hand on his arm seemed enormously significant to him in that instant. 'We've been friends for a long time. I know her like a sister. For years we pretended to be twins. Selena says we really are twins, in a spiritual sense. You know what she's like. I forgive her, whatever she's said or done. I love her, Walt. I want you to love her too.'

Walter turned to face her and wanted to speak but Floss put her hands to his lips.

'I can guess what she has been saying.' Floss was smiling. 'Ronnie really is gay. When we were kids and even teenagers, he couldn't really decide. But nowadays he does not "do" women. Never, not at all. He flirts, but that's all.'

Walter shook his head and pretended not to understand, but Floss went on, explaining what had happened.

'I collapsed in the shower in the box.' She meant the horse-box. 'I'd fallen from Dragon earlier in the day. I began to lose the baby and there was some blood. Ronnie came to help me and he was so frightened. Neither of us knew what to do.'

Walter's face was pale; he didn't know where to look or what to say.

'What did Selena tell you, Walt?' Floss pressed her husband's arm, and squeezed it tightly; she could see suddenly that he was hiding something.

'She told me that you and Ronnie were in the shower together.'

At this Floss almost burst out laughing. 'The shower in the box is too small for one person let alone two! If I drop the soap it's too narrow for me to bend down and pick it up.'

Walter smiled; he'd forgotten that.

'She said you two have been lovers for years,' he whispered. Suddenly he felt ashamed that he could ever have believed it. 'That's why I delayed coming here for so long. I'm so sorry.'

He could not tell her yet that he had been to see Siobhan, nor that he had slept with Selena, but instinctively he felt she knew.

Floss kissed him and smiled.

'Selena really does live in a world full of angels.'

'Like Old Nik,' said Walter.

'But she smokes too much grass, does too much coke and tends to gild the lily,' corrected Floss, giggling.

At that moment Floss's parents hurried into the ward. They had been on vacation in some distant place, and had great difficulty getting home. Walter got up, hugged them both and made way for them to move to Floss's bedside to kiss their daughter.

Albert and Katharine Spritzler were in their middle sixties. Albert was, I knew, Austrian, a relatively wealthy maxillofacial surgeon on the verge of retirement. He had practised at the hospital in the past and brought with him a confidence of purpose that perhaps masked his anxiety about his daughter. He had thick grey hair behind a strong hairline, and handsome features, but life had obviously exhausted him, and he looked tired; he was short but had the innate and natural dignity of a surgeon. Katharine was also fairly small, an English woman who in her youth would have been described as a 'rose'. Her once blond hair was now grey, and she wore a fitted grey coat belted at the waist and brown leather buckled shoes. Her eyes were already brimming with tears, but she was smiling. It didn't seem forced: she was, I realised, one of those people who simply smile all the time.

As they talked, and were reassured, Maud emerged from behind the curtain that hid the body of her husband from view. Her face was tear-streaked, but she was smiling with relief.

Walter went to her, and she fell into his arms.

'I'm really terribly sorry about my behaviour,' she whispered. 'It's actually a relief that he is out of his misery at last.'

Floss noticed that her father was gazing at Maud strangely.

'Dad,' she said, touching him on the arm to try to regain his attention. 'Do you know her?'

He seemed mesmerised, and went over to join Maud and Walter.

Walter let go of Maud and Floss's father took up her hands and looked into her face kindly.

'I think we meet again,' he said. Then he asked her, 'In 1976 you gave birth to a baby, a little girl, at a clinic in Bern in Switzerland?'

Floss's mother Katharine had also moved discreetly to Maud's side.

'Albert tells me we three have met before,' she said. 'In that clinic in Bern? Very briefly, twenty years ago?' She gestured towards Floss, her adopted daughter.

The resemblance between Maud and Floss was uncanny.

'You are our daughter Florence's biological mother, aren't you?' Katharine sensed her question was awkward. 'Forgive me. I mean, of course, you are her real mother.'

Maud turned and looked at Floss, face to face.

'Yes,' she said quietly. 'I was in Bern in 1976. I remember you both now. Your daughter is my child.'

Maud must have known at that moment – as did we all who were party to the conversation – why her husband had fallen so absurdly for Floss, and that he had never loved anyone before Maud, or since. He had simply fallen in love with Maud all over again; he had seen Maud in Floss, in the delirium and ecstasy of his morphine-induced swoon.

Walter noticed that as Maud spoke the colour drained from Floss's face.

'You are my birth-mother?' It was precisely the correct expression in the circumstances. She and Maud both shed tears. 'I should have searched for you. I often dreamed of it. I was afraid I would be disappointed.'

Walter tried to comfort Floss. 'You've had a great life, Floss,' he said. 'Brought up by two wonderful, loving people who will always be your true mother and father.'

Incongruously, Floss shook her head. She was not disagreeing, but was unable to take it all in so quickly.

Walter carried on. 'Now you are reunited with your biological mother.'

'My birth-mother,' Floss said.

'It's a wonderful day; we wouldn't know any of this if you hadn't fallen from your horse!' Walter seemed excited.

He could have added that none of it would have come to light had Nik not been in hospital on his last lap. There was a strange air of sadness and joy combined.

Book Three

Chapter 20

This narrator is joined now by his beautiful host here in the hills above Grasse. We grapple over the pen, grab the laptop back and forth, correct each other's mistakes. She has told me so much of the story I have recounted. She has marvellously described so many of the scenes – and bravely too because in various ways she has not always appeared to be an entirely good soul. Without her I would never have written this book, and I am so glad I have.

And of course, regarding that terrible thing I did, for which I must make amends, and from which I must hope for redemption, Selena is the only one who knows what happened. She is the one who has urged me to write, seeking peace. It apparently all took place at the wedding of Walter and Siobhan.

'I've got to the bit about what I did at the wedding, darling,' I shouted. Selena was sitting out on the terrace. She came quickly back into the room, and stood in front of the French window, the sun behind her, her naked body visible under the transparent white shift she was wearing.

Selena was a luminous woman surrounded by angels and sometimes perhaps demons, all-seeing, potent and scary, a killer when she was a mere girl, an arch-manipulator of all the men around her.

'I was just saying, I've got to the rape,' I said to her merrily, as though I were writing fiction and not a confession. 'I am about to describe how you saw it and what you told me I did . . .'

Selena quickly walked over to where I sat, pulled the laptop away from me, sat on my knee, and kissed me long and hard until I gasped for breath.

'Later,' she breathed sexily, somehow combining in the same pregnant word the promise of moral redemption followed later by an evening of great sex. 'Everything will come together later. Take a break. Take Bingo for a walk in the woods.'

I'm taking over the fucking laptop, Louis. You take Bingo for a walk. Let me tap away for a while. Now we are firmly in my territory: angels and demons, and the Astral Plane. But back in the days you describe at the beginning of this story, this would have meant little to you. You may never have suffered from the close-mindedness of some of your peers – those who were certain there were no ley-lines, no God, no ghosts and no astral forces – but if you weren't thinking about sex back then you might well have been thinking about money. You were so materialistic.

I, on the other hand, have always thought of sex as a function of fate, as an aspect of the force and power of the universe, and the will of its physical and spectral agents, whom I can see and feel, but are invisible to someone like you.

You wrote down what little you understood about the things I believe. You advised me that whatever each one of us believes, when we speak of such things in the modern world it is dangerous to reveal too much metaphysical faith. You didn't quite get that right.

You could be the fool. Louis, darling man, you betray yourself with such statements. If you addled your brain and saw and felt some wonderful things, why not own them? Why deny what happened? It's all brain chemistry in the end, the doubters say. But the real question is what is the chemically altered brain perceiving? Is what it sees not there? Dogs hear things we will never hear. Does that mean they never happened?

One thing you did get right was spotting Nikolai Andréevich's genius and accepting the fact of his second sight. Of course, I could also see what Old Nik saw. Since my childhood in Ireland, as early as four or five years old, I saw angels in the clouds. My sister Siobhan and my father dismissed it when I spoke of it. In the end I realised I had to keep secret what I saw, what I felt, what I knew. Later I understood that I was part-angel myself. I could do things no one else could do. I could persuade people to do what I wanted, just by thinking about it. I could move inanimate objects across a table, but only when I was alone.

But in another way I was hardly ever alone. There were always angels around me. One day they began to whisper to me that I had a spiritual twin, and I should look out for her. As soon as I saw her face, they told me, I would know. The first time I met Floss at school, and we ran to each other and hugged, I knew I had found my twin.

Nik's drawings were beautiful, and true, but however many he produced he would never be able to reproduce exactly what it was that special people like him – and me – could see. But with Nik came Maud. I remember reading what you wrote about your first meeting:

'For the first time since she arrived in my apartment Maud looked happy, with a happiness I felt I knew. Again, my heart fluttered.'

Oh, for God's sake, Louis – I wish you'd bugger off with all this 'heart fluttering'. You had wanted to fuck her. Roll around on Old Nik's drawings of angels in heaven, covering them with sweat, with your tongue down her throat. You were transparent. As if, because she was about your age then, you'd be doing some Great Thing by having an affair with her. Ugh. I have to remind myself that back then, when you first met Maud, I only had eyes and designs for Walter. Louis Doxtader? Dirty old man. That's what I would have said if you ever looked my way. Never would have thought I could fall for you. You were bottom of my list of prospects.

But everything changes. When you first mentioned me in this book I was of course one of the 'Collins girls'. But what you did not write was that I was the younger. The prettier. The cleverer. My hair is not red, or ginger, it is dark and lustrous when I don't bleach it. And I did bleach it, and curl it, and put it into plaits in the hope Walter would notice me and want me. I was the only one who understood Walter at a deeper, spiritual level, the only one who could ever have helped him. I knew what he was going through: I could see the dark angels trying to express themselves through him. I could see the shadows. It wasn't that the people around him in Sheen were using him as a channel for their anxieties; he was using them. Or the entities that possessed him were.

What am I? What do I see? What did Nik see? What was Walter hearing? I knew Walter would take a long time even to see me. Your wife Pamela – with her fiery red hair, and phero-mones pouring from her like the overpowering scent from fading lilies – set up your godson, young Walter, to look for a redhead of his own, and my sister Siobhan turned out to be the one. Pamela was such a hot woman, so exciting to Walter, I think, because she was also lost. How could any woman desert her own child the way she left Rain with you? I know why. Only I know why. I made that happen too. In any case, such contradic-tions in a woman always intrigue men. Of course, now we know that she didn't leave Rain, she saw Rain fairly regularly.

Anyway, if Walter had been a bit more of a real rock star, he could have had me. Much sooner. He's no longer number one. You are, my sweetheart. So the first is last, and vice versa.

As I flip back through the pages of this book, I love to read about your relationship with Walter when he was a boy. Reading about this gentle young man makes it a little easier for me to admit that when my sister Siobhan started seeing Walter, I was probably more jealous than even Rain. She was too young for him. At 27 she was still a child really. I was an old soul, and felt a thousand years old.

I am ten years younger than Siobhan, nine years younger than both Rain and Walter. But I feel guilty when I confess that in my heart I put curses on both Siobhan and Rain because Walter loved them, each in a different way. And my curses work. I wanted neither of them to have Walter. He was supposed to be mine. I was supposed to have any man I wanted. I knew how I could hurt them. I would use you.

My childhood and teenage counsellors told me that a woman who has come to control her father – however she has managed it – will always have a distorted view of her power over men. That was certainly true for me. I had stopped my father raping my sister by plunging a knife into his body. When my blade entered his right side from behind, and the icy sheet, the shining plane before him turned red, and the spectacular pain made him feel as though he were roaring even though he could make no sound, he lost sight of my older sister Siobhan entirely. She gasped as our father fell and – where he once had stood with blind rage in his eyes – there I stood, eight years old, holding the long kitchen knife smeared with our father's blood. I was reminded later that I blamed the angels: they made me do it, that's what I said.

I grew up knowing only that my mother had been an angel born at the moment of my birth and her mortal passing. I knew that angels never die, are ever present, invisible, guiding, loving, observing.

Of course, without a living mother I loved Siobhan more than might be normal. She was the principal star in my firmament, but I still thought she was too dyed-in-the-wool for Walter. Too demanding. Too bossy. Too redheaded. Too fecking Irish and literary. Despite all her feminine strength, she was another girl who wouldn't even be in this story were it not for me.

When you were struggling – trying to withdraw from heroin and get clean, trying to save your marriage by accepting the sexual distance Pamela suddenly demanded, and were seeing faces in your old French bedhead – Louis darling, you were seeing real faces, real people, locked in history, imprisoned in the terror and pain of the past, unable to get free. Their screams were real. They needed someone like me to help them escape. You needed me. Pamela was a bitch. You might wonder if she was waiting for a reason to leave . . .

At Dingwalls, as Siobhan went back to Waterford, convinced that Walter would follow her, and I first made my pitch for him, offering him cocaine, and the chance of a blow-job, Louis, you were so right. No one understood what I saw or what I felt.

No one understands today, not even you, not even now we live together and I look after you, and teach you and tease you and try to make you happy. You still don't entirely believe me. I have to show you where to look for those angels, how to see them, and how to find the angel in your own heart and soul. The angels don't care if we are good or evil. They love us whatever we do.

Do you remember soon after, when Floss walked into Dingwalls to catch up with me, her best friend, do you remember what happened? You *do* remember, I know. You were smitten by her as were all the fucking wet-eared men in the club. I always know what you're thinking, sweetheart. You wanted to speak to Floss, to check out whether she might notice you were alive. You'd thrown yourself at her like an old idiot at Walter and Siobhan's wedding.

Did you think she would remember you? Remember the bloody low-grade horse tranquilliser you shared with us? I didn't care much, not that night at Dingwalls. I was still intent on Walter. Louis, this is a good story I think. The hard men who like rock music and think all women are vague, romantic and unfocused will especially enjoy it. But you are telling a story here about five of the most extraordinary women ever gathered in a book like this. You make Maud into a kind of middle-aged sex object; you obviously long for her and you don't know why. And yet she is loyal, smart and determined. She irritates me, because you adored her, but I respect her. She knew exactly what to do with Andréevich's art. She was playing you.

And my sister! God knows she wasn't merely some hippy from the Emerald Isle who wanted her husband to transform himself into James Joyce or Seamus Heaney. She saved my life and I saved hers. Our father was a broken bully, God rest his soul, and I mean that. Siobhan brought me up; she was my mother. And at the same time she brought herself up through college and university and ended up running a department at the BBC. You know, Louis, Siobhan may not have been on the front line of the world's troubles like your daughter Rain, but we had seen plenty of trouble. And Siobhan felt it all deeply. I do believe Walter was a weakness for her. He represented an escape route, back to Ireland, to poetry.

Pamela, your wife, although she was a bitch, does not deserve to be described as a 'nymphomaniac' just because she liked sex with you for a while. I only met her a few times, but what a fantastic and potent woman she was. She didn't leave Rain behind as a matter of convenience, or to give you something to do. She left Rain because she too had a breakdown; right under your nose. You were so full of your own dark visions you didn't even notice. Pamela had a revelation too, and one day you will come to understand its nature. She came out. It was so simple that you missed it.

That brings me to the teenyboppers. Ringo Starr called early Beatles fans that. Teenyboppers. At Walter's wedding Floss and me and Ronnie, we were the teenyboppers. We were running around playing at being bridesmaids. Yes, even Ronnie! We were fantasising about the day we would be married and have brides-maids of our own. We were young, eighteen years old but really immature, and I know we looked and behaved as though we were much younger.

Louis, you can't imagine how strong our friendship was back then. How much can one hurt someone else? Is there any point in hurting a person one doesn't deeply love? Floss and I have hurt each other, we may never go back to where we were, but we will always be soulmates. If we've hurt each other it is a measure of our love. Yes, Floss loved horses. I see angels. Don't imagine that makes us dizzy birds.

So Floss arrived at Dingwalls. I was a bit sad; I admit that. Do you know what I was thinking when I watched Walter's eyes fix on my best friend Floss?

I was thinking that I was an angel, and I conferred with angels. To you men, all of you there that night, that part of me did not exist. I wanted to shout out to you all: 'Bury me, stone me, for I know that not one of you will ever marry me!'

Oh Louis, reading this makes me rather sad all over again. You write about my love for Walter with the detachment of an academic biographer. You can't imagine how desolate I was feeling around those times. I hardly ever managed to see Walter, or give him any help. I rarely saw Floss. I felt shut out completely. When your best friend gets married they have less time for you. But Floss married the man I loved, who had first married my older sister, and always treated me like a bit of an irritation. I started to become normal, as you rightly say. Not good. Normal is not good, Louis. Normality was not what I was born to.

Do you remember when I told everyone about Ronnie? I never cared whether he was gay or not, or that he liked to wear high heels and borrow our bras sometimes. Ronnie had a blurred black monkey sitting on the back of his fekking upright Prussian neck! I could see it.

After Walter had played the stuff his father wrote to Steve Hanson, do you remember writing in this book about our lunch at the Caprice, saying that I could be difficult to read? You said that you could see my obsession with Walter was strong, and wondered why I was turning to you? It was almost as though I were giving you a warning, to prepare you for something terrible I could see ahead.

Oh God! This is so hard for me to write, my darling. It's all true; everything I said at that lunch. I was still obsessed by Walter, and still in love with him like a teenager. But I asked you to lunch because I needed help. I can 'see' what others can't see. Whether that means I'm psychic or barmy makes no difference. Maybe I can just read people, sense their moods, and then some synaesthetic mechanism kicks in and makes peculiar connections.

Walter was in terrible trouble. He loved Floss. No question. But why did she leave him alone so much? Why did Walter trust Ronnie? No one else did! But I also wanted to see you, my darling Louis, and to be with you. I'd realised how you were trying to help. You were being so kind. And you had always been on my list after all. Gorgeous old muffin.

I'm so sorry, Louis, that this story is going to unfold as I know it will. I decided to use you, to take advantage of you. I do regret that now. But I simply had to try to steal Walter from Floss. I couldn't help myself. They call women like me 'home-wreckers'. But Floss and Walter didn't have a real home. Not like this one, the one you sit in these days to write. I made this home for you. This is the real thing. It's turned out pretty well. Hasn't it, sweetheart? Do you forgive me? Can you?

Yes, I seduced Walter. I don't know why he believed me about Floss and Ronnie. It was almost as though he'd known all along that something had been going on between them. I knew a secret that could create terrible trouble for almost everyone in my circle if I spoke about it. Including you if I wished. I felt so powerful at that moment. It was intoxicating. I'm not proud of it looking back, but for me things were only going to get a lot worse before they got better.

And Walter had been hearing all that weird music. It was just the beginning for him. It was going to get so much more overwhelming as his chakras opened up.

And you might ask if it's hard to understand why Walter believed me when I told him I could see Floss and Ronnie making love, in the haze of my super-sight and psychic intuition.

Chapter 21

My name is Louis Doxtader. It seems I have been duped. I'm not sure I can afford to give a damn. Old Nik's funeral came a week after the revelations at the hospital, where Floss met Maud, and Maud understood that Old Nik had only ever loved her, but that he died also loving and reaching out for the woman who was in fact, unbeknown to him, his only child. I attended the funeral of my most successful artist with few regrets. I was sitting on a number of Nikolai Andréevich's finest pictures and I knew his death was more than doubling their value. If I released them slowly over the ensuing years they would eventually increase in value tenfold. It was Maud for whom I mourned most on this occasion. I had seen what had happened in the Critical Care Ward, and the terrible ordeal she had had to endure in Nik's final hours. Floss had only been in the bed opposite Nik's for a week, and in that time Maud had almost lost her mind.

We stood huddled around the coffin, the grave freshly dug and dressed with red velvet curtain material. A few fans of Nik's years with Hero Ground Zero had come, kept at a distance by a pop industry security man so that Maud and the guests could mourn with some dignity.

I kept my eyes on her. She had never looked so beautiful, I thought. I have never tried to hide my passion for her in this story, after all.

Floss, still using a stick, walked slowly over to stand by Maud's side; it was at that precise second that my world started to unravel. The funeral began to feel rather dream-like, and reminded me of a dream I'd had the night before, and I couldn't help but try to recall it. Eventually it came flooding back to me, but as it did a second dream came to mind with equal strength. I tried to bring myself back into the present. Selena has told me that I raped Floss. I can hardly believe it. I can't imagine doing such a thing, but I know that if that Floss, that exceedingly pretty woman, had ever held her arms out to me, and pursed her lips, I could never have resisted.

Louis, it's Selena. My darling, I am taking over again. Before you go too far. There is still so much you don't know. I remember running to your side then and drawing you away from everyone there, into the shelter of a huge tree in the cemetery so that we were alone.

'I can see them,' I said to you in a whisper.

'Who? What can you see? Who can you see?' You were struggling to stay connected to the present.

'I can see several entities using you,' I explained, waving my hands around your shoulders. I could see they were trying to take over your mind, vying with each other for supremacy.

'I can remember a number of dreams,' you said. I knew that of course. That's why I had come to you. Your voice was shaking.

'They feel very real, and they are invading my reality.'

'These entities are actually using your mind.' That's what I told you. I was so happy to be able to explain what I knew was happening to you. I knew you needed my attention, and that you appreciated it. I was looking particularly good that day: black suits me.

I tried to explain to you: 'They are dreaming their own dreams, remembering their own past lives; this has nothing to do with you.'

You started to feel you might see Nik's hosts of angels next, visions from his paintings, and then I had to bring you down to earth with a bump.

'You deserve this, Louis,' I told you. 'I'm sorry, but this is your mind's way of dealing with what you've done.'

'What have I done?' Your head was clearing quickly.

And this, my darling Louis, was when you rose from number four to number one on my list. This was the moment I knew I could hold you. 'You know I saw you. At my sister's wedding.'

It was true, I had seen you; my voice sounded low and conspiratorial even in my own ears. 'With Floss . . .'

'Yes.'

'She was completely out of it with drink and drugs. You took her.'

You looked over at Maud and Floss together. They both smiled. Floss was beautiful of course, but Maud was beautiful too; like Floss grown older.

My name is Louis Doxtader, I am still trying to come to grips with what she has told me, and finishing this book has become so much more important. Was I guilty of giving three teenagers some overly hard drugs, and trying to take advantage of one of them? I know Selena will say anything in order to get what she wants. I know that she comes to believe what she thinks she can see.

After her accusing me of what she had seen me do, we returned to the grave and moved around it as the priest read the sanctification. I was trying to get away from Selena, and found myself nearer to Maud. I felt as if I had strayed into a life that wasn't mine, and I wanted to get back to where I belonged, a place where I was respected and loved.

Maud smiled at Floss, and took her free hand, and – as Nik's coffin was lowered into the grave – mother and daughter embraced.

The wake was held at my flat where we were surrounded by Nik's best pictures. I felt compelled to be the host, because I was Maud's protector, but also of course I was Andréevich's agent.

Conversation inevitably turned to the circumstances of Floss's birth and Maud explained to us all that Nik had never known she had borne a daughter. She had been too young and afraid; it was before they were married. By then Nik had already started to become difficult, having fits and anxiety attacks. Hero Ground Zero had become huge and he was always travelling. There was plenty of money, but the pressure on Nik was extreme and Maud did not want to have a child with him, at least not then, not so early in their relationship. So before she married him, while he was on tour for the last six months of her pregnancy, she arranged for the baby she was carrying to be born and adopted immediately in the clinic in Bern. She had never even seen the child's face, nor held her to her bosom.

Floss's adoptive parents, Albert and Katharine, had been waiting for her there, and brought her up as though she were their own. They never hid from Floss that she was adopted at birth, and even told her the name of the clinic in Bern where she had been born, but they had known nothing about Floss's biological mother, only that she did not want to keep her child. The three of them had seen each other briefly in the clinic, however, passing in a corridor as Maud walked wretchedly away from her baby and they walked joyfully towards her. Their eyes met.

Chapter 22

Six weeks later we were all gathered backstage at a concert at Hyde Park. Walter had been languishing alone in his dressing room for much of the day. The first rehearsal in the morning had gone badly and while the second was slightly better, the mood in the empty park was strained.

I noticed that the road crew included Molly who was operating a follow-spot downlighter mounted high up on the stage structure; in rehearsal the crew had obviously found the soundscapes to be too dark, too serious. They were less cheerful now, just before the concert, than one would expect. One of them told me that he thought the additional music was OK, but they were all worried that Walter was being overly stubborn to refuse to play even a single one of the old songs they used to play at Dingwalls. Steve Hanson and Crow both took me aside and asked me to make sure Walter was all right. I went to see him in his dressing room.

'How are you feeling?' I didn't want to feed into any anxiety he might have about the show, which was a massive endeavour by anyone's measure. 'Hanson and Crow are worried about you.'

Walter looked up from something he was writing. 'I'm worried about them,' he said with a laugh. 'They have much more to do than me in this show. My father has written some very difficult music. My role is just singing, mostly along with the choral parts.'

'Were they hard to get on board, Hanson and Crow?'

'Crow surprised me, I didn't think he would get involved, but Hanson has always been really positive. And rather bullish.' He laughed again, not entirely without irony.

Hanson had always spoken to Walter as though he were a beloved rich uncle, or senior trustee, rather than an old band-mate. Money and success had joined many of the dots that had been evident in Hanson's character back in Dingwalls days. He'd always been made for a grand position in the music business and the arts and was entirely comfortable with who he had become, even if the pinnacle of his career had passed.

'About eight weeks ago,' Walter explained, 'Steve chose a date for this soundscapes show at Hyde Park and started trying to persuade Crow to do it. He was convinced we had plenty of time to get it right and was certain it would be amazing. He loved what my dad and I have done.'

I knew that eight weeks earlier Walter would have been in a pretty bad place: Selena had seduced him, he believed that Floss had been unfaithful.

'Did he ask if *you* wanted to do it?'

'He called. I was on my way to Ireland to see Siobhan. I told him I was in a strange place, and could I get back to him.'

Hanson had agreed to give Walter some time, but in the back-ground Frank Lovelace had insinuated himself into the scheme, seeing both an adventure and an opportunity. He knew precisely how to stage the event. Hanson and Frank had then pushed ahead. Tickets were to go on sale the second Walter agreed. As Walter related all this he looked pained.

I heard later that Crow and Hanson had of course conspired, despite Crow's apparent reticence. Crow had always wanted his old band back, and if he was honest he was sick of trying to make ends meet with gigs in various pubs and clubs around Europe. He had performed a few times in the USA, mainly around New York, but his fans felt themselves part of an exclusive cult, and weren't too keen to share him. Despite a website that had thousands of hits every day, Crow knew that his fanbase was small.

Also Crow liked the idea of making a 'comeback' that would promise one thing and deliver another. The old fans of the Stand, and certainly all the current fans of Hero Ground Zero, even those going back to the days of Nik Andréevich, would go into shock when they heard Walter's latest compositions – if you could call them that. He felt sure there would be songs at Hyde Park, new ones perhaps; but old ones too.

The entire soundscapes idea might be pretentious, but if it was dark then so be it. No doubt Crow believed that in the end he would be able to persuade Walter to play the mouth-organ solo of his life, the crowd would go nuts, and Walter would be unable to restrain himself. He'd run with the adrenalin and endorphins and would relent and do his 'stand'.

'Crow,' said Walter, and he smiled and shook his head. Almost sixteen years had passed and really nothing had changed in Crow's world. Why would it?

Crow, Steve, Patty and Walter all knew this was going to be one of the biggest reunions in rock history.

Walter turned back to the writing he'd been occupied with when I entered the dressing room. He passed me two sheets to read.

'What d'you think?'

> *In two more hours*
> *The light will fade*
> *I wait*
> *For all of you*
> *Ascend the towers*
> *This serenade*
> *Comes late*
> *Nothing I can do*

'Beautiful, Walter,' I said, meaning it. 'But surely you're not suffering all that badly from anxiety about the concert?'

Yet I could see he was in an anxious, darkening mood. How would the audience respond to their grand project, his soundscapes realised by his father, the additional songs and story provided by Steve and Patty Hanson – and the occasional burst of R&B energy that Crow had managed to squeeze in to the otherwise serious and arty programme?

Just then, with three hours to go before the first of the audience would be allowed on to the green, and two hours before showtime, Floss came in to Walter's dressing room. She looked magnificent. She was wearing some very fancy dress, Gucci or Balenciaga, overly embroidered with sequins, that had obviously cost a fortune, and was looking happy.

'Oh darling,' she said sympathetically. 'Are you feeling down?' She sat next to him and held his hand.

'I need to speak to you, Floss,' Walter said. He suddenly turned pale.

'I'll give you two some privacy,' I said, getting up to leave.

'No,' Walter said firmly. 'Uncle Louis, I need you to stay, and I want Floss to have your support if she needs it too. After I've said what I have to say.'

'Fucking hell, Walt,' said Floss, reddening and suddenly quite angry. 'What can be so important that you need to speak about it now?'

Walter motioned for us both to sit down, but then he got up and paced up and down in the dressing room, looking at himself in the huge floor-to-ceiling mirrors.

'I have to tell you, my darling,' he stuttered. 'I betrayed you. When Selena said you and Ronnie were lovers . . . she and I had sex. I'm so, so sorry. Louis knows all this.'

Floss looked down and her eyes filled with tears.

'You have done nothing wrong,' said Walter, facing her and

appealing to her. 'My actions were wrong; you never had an affair with Ronnie. I feel so ashamed.'

Floss suddenly burst into profound and open tears. Walter was distraught too. She was waving both her hands in the air, as she had always done at such times, as though shooing flies away, or dust; she was dismissing him while he tried to apologise repeatedly. I put my hand gently on her arm but she brushed it away.

I wanted to be anywhere else but there at that moment.

Then.

Walter started to say something, but Floss suddenly took control.

'Shut up, Walter! Both of you, listen.'

She was almost shouting, and Walter and I both realised this was something different, that she was not crying over his sex with Selena.

'What?' Walter was confused, and so was I.

'Walter, darling.' She spoke to Walter, but was looking at me, as though it was vital that as witness I should be on her side as well as Walter's. 'There's something I've never told you.'

Walter turned to look at me. I suspected that he regretted having asked me to be present; he had planned only to unload his own guilt. Having endured the paranoia and uncertainty around the supposed affair between his wife and Ronnie Hobson, what could this new revelation be? Infidelity was what sprang to mind. If not Ronnie, who had Floss cheated on him with? If not an affair, what could it be? Financial collapse? Bankruptcy? Simply that his wife was bored with him? Was she leaving him as Siobhan had done? It occurred to me that if she had something to say about what Walter had told me was their rather sporadic sex life, then I was sure he would prefer I was not present to hear it.

Floss was shaking, very slightly. Neither Walter nor I moved to console her. At any other time we would have done so. I stood up and broke the silence.

'Floss.' I was almost stammering. 'Walter wanted me to be here to hear his confession to you. But I can leave now. Surely I should leave?'

Floss shook her head. 'I want you to be here,' she said. 'I feel safer with you here.'

Walter was angered by this. 'You're completely safe with me, darling, don't be so mad. I've never raised a finger to you.'

Floss looked at him beseechingly. 'I don't mean that you would hurt me. This concerns Louis. He is a part of all this.'

Walter was looking at me with complete astonishment, and I found it hard not to look guilty. Was she going to speak about the drugs I'd shared at his wedding to Siobhan eighteen years earlier? I felt a rising sense of panic. Would she confirm what Selena had accused me of? Of raping her. From what Selena had said I had assumed that Floss didn't remember anything about it. But then of course I did not remember what happened and I couldn't be sure Selena was telling the truth when she said she knew. What had Floss meant when she said I was a part of what she had to say?

'Please, you two,' she said, composing herself. 'Just sit the fuck down and stop looking at each other like that.'

Walter and I sat together, but as far apart as we could, on the long grey sofa in the dressing room. She pulled up a chair to face us and sat down.

'You know, Walter, that I lost our baby when I fell from Dragon.' Walter said nothing, but nodded his head imperceptibly. 'Well, I lost a baby once before.'

Walter immediately got up and knelt in front of her. He took one side of her face in his hand.

'When? How?' He was ready to forgive her anything, it seemed.

'I was nineteen. I gave birth to her in the same clinic in Bern where I was born. Fucking catholic parents: I didn't consider abortion. Now of course I wonder where she is.'

'A daughter?' Walter was shaking his head in incomprehension. 'What happened? Did the child die?' Walter was looking at his wife, wide-eyed.

Floss shook her head. 'No. She lived.'

Walter was getting angry, but his anger seemed aimless, wide-ranging.

'Did your parents take you to Bern? Jesus Christ! How could they take you to the place where you were born?'

'They know nothing about this. I found the address of the clinic in one of my mother's books. I told no one. No one knows, except Selena.'

'Who was the father?'

'I don't know, Walt.' I could hear her misery. 'I should never have given her away.'

Walter looked stunned. Clearly he was thinking that Floss must have enjoyed a wild sex life before they married which he knew nothing about.

'Oh, Walt,' Floss protested. 'Don't look at me like that. I mean I don't know who had sex with me at your wedding. I wasn't a virgin when we married, but neither was I a wild child. Selena and I always looked much wilder than we really were.'

Oh my God! My panic was ramping up. Has Selena told her I was the father? If she tells Walter, he'll kill me.

'Who was it?' he was demanding again, more firmly. 'Do you know? Surely you must be able to guess?'

She shook her head. Because unlike me, she had no suspicion at all as to who the father of her daughter might have been. Walter's mood broke, and he drew Floss to the sofa to sit between us, and put his arm around her, pulling her head to his chest and caressing her hair.

I breathed a great sigh of relief, and put my arms around the two of them as they held each other, both with tears in their eyes. But my relief would be short-lived.

Floss knew nothing about what had happened to her baby. She had been running away from it all for her entire life. She looked at Walter then, shamefaced.

'It was at your wedding, Walt,' she said once more, breaking into body-shaking sobs. 'I got completely smashed.'

'As one does at weddings,' interjected Walter, trying to soothe his unhappy wife a little.

'Selena gave me some drug or other. I think it was horse tranquilliser.'

'You're saying you had sex at my wedding to Siobhan?' Walter was starting to see that this was not a story that would necessarily end so badly if only he could contain himself. 'You got pregnant, had a baby whom you gave away. Who adopted the child?'

Floss shook her head again. 'I don't know. My parents met my mother Maud Andréevich very briefly in the clinics when they adopted me, but they knew nothing about her. They had no way of knowing who she was or where she lived. That's what I wanted for myself. It had worked for me, and for Mum and Dad.

'I don't know who the father of my daughter was, and I have no idea where my daughter might be today. I'm still not entirely sure I ever want to know. Selena got the drugs from someone else. I always thought it might have been Ronnie, he'd had some ketamine, but he always denied giving it to me. He never wanted to speak about the wedding. He always said it had been a bad and unhappy day for him. He'd never elaborate.'

Oh my God! I wanted to shout at her that I never gave her the fucking ketamine. It was Selena. It was Ronnie. Anyone but me. Not me. Not now. Oh fuck!

Then I heard Floss laugh through her tears.

'On top of the alcohol, it mixed really badly, and I passed out. All I can remember is that I woke up with someone carrying me to a sofa. Then I passed out again. I can remember nothing. But I think that person made love to me while I was drunk.'

Walter was quick to correct his wife. 'No one "made love" to you, Floss.' His voice was firm, and very angry. 'You were raped.'

Walter now knew Floss had been raped by an unknown man at his wedding to his first wife. He did the maths: he thought, God! Floss had been just eighteen years old. I had to stand there and nod my head.

'Yes, yes,' I heard myself say, aware that I was the culprit. 'Awful, terrible.'

If Floss had really been completely unconscious, I thought, I must have been pretty much unconscious as well.

But a vague memory did come back to me at that moment, of Ronnie being around and Selena too, and I knew we'd all taken a hit of the ketamine I had brought. I'd taken cocaine too, and drunk a fair bit of champagne. At such times I always felt I was merely dabbling. If it wasn't heroin then it couldn't be all that bad. More memories came to mind. I had a shadowy, swirling image of the four of us dancing in a circle with our arms linked. We were singing and laughing. I remembered Selena kissing me, and then her kissing Ronnie. I remembered that I was surprised at Ronnie; didn't gay men find that a turn-off? Did Floss kiss Selena? Did she kiss Ronnie? Did she kiss me?

Then, nothing. No more memories. No images.

Walter's anger switched to Selena.

'What the hell was Selena doing divvying up hard drugs? Wherever they came from. Jeez!'

I was tempted again to shout out in my own defence, but I couldn't break my cover. In truth, I had no defence.

Floss tried to quieten him, pleading with him not to be angry. 'You know the story, Walt,' she cried. 'Selena killed her own father to stop him beating and abusing Siobhan. She was eight years old. That damaged her for ever. She's never had a long-term relationship.'

Walter held Floss's face in his hands. If ever he might have composed a sonnet it would have been then.

With a sudden flash of comprehension, Walter exclaimed, 'Floss!' He was almost laughing. 'The baby you gave birth to in 1995 in Bern, she will still be alive!'

A voice screaming over a huge PA system at some massive public event. 'Welcome to the gates of hell.' Hell. The inferno. Torture. Flames. The rack. Evil laughter. Bodies being beaten, burned, thudding, falling. A ghastly choir. An electric guitar, strangled, itself tortured. A ridiculous organ. The stupid shouting of a football crowd, an Islamic horde, a Pentecostal congregation. A preacher 'casting out devils'. Aspirants speaking in tongues. Crowds of people chanting angrily in many and different demon-strations. Hippy drummers, native drummers, drumming, thun-dering, a building anger driven by the rhythm, transmogrifying into a driving rock 'n' roll band of the old school, playing at full tilt. The sound is huge. This is pub rock, meets pomp rock, meets garage punk, meets prog rock, meets God rock, meets road rock, meets hell-on-earth rock, meets acid, garage, rap. This massive, frightening, disturbing soundscape eventually becomes the rap-rock-pop backing track to the worst excesses of stadium rock, festival rock, heavy metal, death-metal, MTV, guitar smashing and all of that puerile shit . . .

We were all gathered at the side of the stage. The concert was the first time for nearly sixteen years we had seen Walter perform.

An orchestra and a choir were on stage with the band, and behind them a huge pipe organ. Harry Watts was variously play-ing it, or conducting the musicians who were interpreting his orchestrations of Walter's soundscapes. The lyrics, what Walter called 'the libretto', had beautiful moments. Some of the poetry was excellent, I thought. I still had no idea who Harry had commissioned to write it, and in the programme the credit was short: *soundscapes conceived by W.K. Watts, music composed by H. Watts, libretto by S. Watts*. Was it Walter's mother Sally who had contributed the words? Was it possible she was as clever a poet as she was a painter?

As the orchestral music rang out, filling the park with ambitious and audacious modern orchestral music and organ cascades, Frank Lovelace looked extremely worried; the audience was not responding as he had hoped, and as Steve Hanson had promised.

Patty Hanson waved her tambourine and floated around in her flowing silk dress.

Crow looked tough and detached, but I thought I detected a hopeful gleam in his eye. Of course he knew that if somehow he could get Walter to do his famous 'stand' and play his mouth-organ, like in the old days, all would be well.

Walter stood centre stage, singing, howling and – when his father was at the organ – conducting. The musicians Harry had brought played along with Crow, Steve and Patty Hanson, and it was really only Walter who seemed to have little to do on stage. But he looked proud, and moved, and occasionally when his voice was required he used it in an entirely new way. Instead of singing in his old style he used his voice like a musical instrument, and when there were lyrics, they were more like poetry than the songs he had written for the Stand back in Dingwalls.

In the past Selena had sometimes described to me the almost invisible ghosts of the hundreds of entities that she saw in visions and that day, as the soundscapes seemed to open up dimension after dimension, I wondered if I too was seeing them, small shadowy puffs, flitting across the sky like smoke, 'searching for souls they might occupy' as Selena might say. The clouds morphed and evolved and I thought I saw a dozen faces that could have been God up there. And what could that be? I asked myself, stretching across the sunset in shades of gold and grey. Could it be Nik's assembled angels waiting for the Harvest? Was I going back to the days of my old madness, or was I at last experiencing what I had always hoped for in Walter's soundscapes?

After ninety-five minutes the dark and forbidding music ended. As the last soundscape rang out over the park, Selena was clinging to me tightly, almost violently.

As the sun finally dipped below the fairground in the distance, it felt like an uneven and awkward end, partly because there was a sense hanging in the air that the sound might return at any second.

Nothing had been normal about the performance. There had been music, but also a lot of what many in the crowd no doubt took to be simply noise: disorganised, irritating noise. So when the last song finished, there was an expectant silence.

The silence at the side of the stage, mirroring that of the thirty thousand on the green, was broken when Maud asked, 'Is anyone going to clap?' Floss turned to her and smiled, but she shook her head. At that, a few sporadic handclaps did break out, and a few isolated cheers.

There was a gentle rustling. Breathing. I could hear an occasional cough, the clearing of throats, a sneeze. A distant aeroplane rumbled in the sky. No words.

I asked myself if it was possible that the soundscapes had released, confronted and redeemed some of the anxieties they reflected, as Walter and I had talked about? Looking at the crowd, at some of the smiling and hopeful faces looking up at the stage, I felt that perhaps something wonderful and significant *had* happened. Had any of them seen anything like the visions I had seen?

Many in the audience would no doubt have come to hear rock music. But maybe they had been reminded in some way that the music they loved most would always spring ultimately from them, and from what they deeply felt and needed, not just from their musical heroes. Just as Selena described herself as the almost helpless 'Principal Engineer' of all her schemes and machinations, so perhaps the audience were the real engineers of the music they had heard that evening? Although they may have been unconscious that they had elected Walter to the stage that night, they had done so, and he had spoken to them as a true artist – heart to heart.

Could any of this be true? I asked myself again. Or were these thoughts just more symptoms of my madness? Naturally, I told myself, some of the audience would not have been touched at all. That was always the way. That is not to sneer at them or imply they were unresponsive or deaf and blind in some way. They may simply have been confused, or intimidated, left feeling let down by being cheated of an evening of old-time R&B, but also maybe sad they felt unable to rise to what had been offered.

I looked out into the crowd again. A sense of expectancy remained, but also perhaps acceptance that there would be no more. No more music. Walter was not going to blow a note on his mouth-organ and break the silence. He was not going to do his famous 'stand'. There would be no maudlin closing song. There would be no chorus in the sky.

There would be no 'Amen'.

Applause would not break out.

Selena spoke. 'The soundscapes were mind-fucking.'

I nodded. She was right. There was no question that Harry's compositions broke new ground, and had certainly created a deep atmosphere.

There had been such beautiful moments in the orchestral sections, but also very disturbing parts. This was music that reflected an entire range of human emotion and fragility.

Selena held me ever more tightly. Her touch terrified me. She had me in the palm of her hand. She could break me. She could tell Floss – indeed everyone – what she knew, that I had raped her best friend. My control over my life for the past eighteen years, the dignity I felt in my recovery, my sobriety and freedom from drugs all began to crumble. If she talked, I would be finished. My life would be over.

At that moment I felt her left hand move from my arse to my thigh, and then slip around to my cock. She looked up at me, grinning lasciviously, a sly part of me responding, thinking things could be worse.

She waved at her sister who was standing on the opposite side of the stage. I saw that Siobhan was smiling, tears of joy streaming down her face. Selena put her index finger on the programme and whispered to me.

'Siobhan Watts,' she said. '"S. Watts".' It was she who had written the poetic lyrics.

Walter was still standing in the centre of the stage and only a few of the crowd were turning away to leave. There was a kind of buzz in the air, and the lighting monkeys (the operators of the big spotlights up in the gantry) were sweeping the sky.

Selena was in shadow when she looked up at me and said, 'You saw the angels, didn't you?'

I just nodded. I was thinking, Are we united in madness? And with hope flooding in: Does this mean she won't betray me?

The crowd was now finally beginning to turn away from the stage and leave. But as they did Walter came to his senses.

'Don't go!' He was shouting. 'Not yet!'

People turned back to the stage.

'Don't go,' Walter shouted again. 'I have something I need to say. Something I want to ask you all.'

There was a slight pause and the audience refocused on the stage.

'Is there, in the audience, by any chance, a girl born in Bern in Switzerland in the spring of 1995 who was adopted and doesn't know her biological parents?'

At first there was no response.

Walter tried the magic words. 'Is that girl looking for her birth-mother?'

Everyone in the audience looked around at everyone else. What a question!

But incredibly, one by one three arms went up, then four, then finally seven.

Walter laughed. He could hardly believe it. None of us could. What he had intended to be a demonstration to Floss that if her daughter was alive, she would one day be found, had suddenly become infused with genuine possibility. The child might be found. Tonight.

He looked at Floss, who was laughing back at him.

Up in the lighting gantry to the right of the stage, as I learned later, Molly was concentrating on her job. The controlling bar of the huge spotlight she had trained down on him was set at a high angle, and she was stretching awkwardly to keep it steady.

Over the earphone communication system she heard the lighting director give her a command.

'Molly, cut your lamp.'

Cut the lamp? She didn't understand. There were only three stage spots trained on Walter. The rest were spread around the field, another seven 'Super Troupers' as they were known. The entire lighting crew was winging it, being inventive, taking initiative. Everything was turning out beautifully.

This time Frank could be heard on the intercom, more firmly. 'Cut your lamp, Molly. Do as you're told.'

She did as instructed and was removing one of the headphones when the director spoke again.

'Molly,' he said. 'Weren't you born the spring of 1995 in a clinic in Bern?'

Every light operator sharing the earphone system in the thirty-man team heard what he asked. A few of them laughed. Molly had not heard anything Walter had asked of the audience; her headphones were still tight to her head. She had only heard the director.

All her colleagues searched the stage to find her.

One by one all the spotlights in the park found her up on her lighting tower. Nine spots lit her up like a superstar in space.

A girl in a star.

The cherubim hidden in the robes of Nik's darkest angel.

The crowd began to applaud. It was merely a ripple. They couldn't know what was going on, but some of them clearly sensed it was something special.

Walter and Floss looked up, and Molly gazed down at them.

Walter beckoned to all the girls who had raised their hands to come forward. But all of us on stage behind him had seen Molly's face up in the lighting tower. We saw Floss's stunned smile as she looked up at the girl.

Maud's face too caught my eye as she compared Molly to Floss back and forth – mother to daughter – and I knew then that Molly was Floss's daughter. My daughter?

Two long lost children, found within months of each other. I remembered Walter's visions of a child in a star, was it in one of his soundscapes? By some incredible mischance, or perhaps a miracle, Walter's visions were taking on new power, especially as embodied in the music that night. Floss's amazing and tragic life adventures, her own adoption and finding Molly, suddenly took on operatic significance. Could it be a mere coincidence? Maybe . . . but in the context of the concert, it was full of poign-ancy and momentousness.

Then I saw that Walter knew what he had to do. He positioned himself like a statue, his mouth-organ in his right hand ready to play, held in what appeared to be an attempt to keep light from his eyes. His left hand was stretched out as though he were balancing on an imaginary surfboard, his knees slightly bent, and turned a little to the right, his body twisted slightly at the waist. When he took up this pose, the audience knew they could soon expect a powerfully explosive mouth-organ solo, and the girls began to scream and the boys to shout.

It was a night at Dingwalls writ large. Steve Hanson wrote of the event in his autobiography.

At Dingwalls with Big Walter and the Stand, there had always been a moment when we would find some direct connection with the audience. They would as often as not be half-drunk and, if our set had been long, they would be tired. But when Walter adopted his famous 'stand', the atmosphere would transform into one of complete anticipation and wonderment. It was as though we were all waiting for an orgasm to complete, one that had begun, but stalled for a moment.

At some of the stadium shows in the eighties and nineties with Hero Ground Zero, there would be a similar moment. Patty would stand poised, her tambourine fluttering rapidly in the air, the music silent, the breeze blowing her dress. The tambourine sounded like a rattling hiss. The audience were hanging. Patty was like a sparrow-hawk that had spotted a field mouse. And when she finally brought it down to her side, and the rest of us in the band took off, the energy and tension in the audience would be released in what felt like a spiritual ascendance.

Really, you have to be a musician in a big band at a huge concert to know how that feels.

And when the four of us were together again at Hyde Park, performing Walter and Harry Watts's soundscapes, when we were done there was nowhere else to go. Floss's lost daughter Molly had been found. She had been in our midst all along. Walter took up his position and when he finally began to wail his heart-wrenching harmonica solo, we all ascended.

This time when the music ended there was applause, and it was gratefully acknowledged.

We heard the band walk off.

We heard the technicians leave their posts.

Soon the audience was gone, and the cordoned area in Hyde Park began to clear.

An hour later it was all over.

This time the silence was appropriate, delightful, and free of tension and expectation.

The show was over.

Selena looked at me with love and a little lust in her amazing blue-green eyes; was it possible she really saw me as an attractive older man? Was this extraordinary young woman really going to take me on?

I lowered my head and she seemed intuitively to know what I was thinking. Shame flitted over my face.

Selena hugged my arm and gave me one of her knowing looks. I knew then that if she didn't betray me, if she stayed with me, I knew there was no doubt that I would love her until the day I died. She laughed at me in a relaxed, natural way. Was the psychic in her off duty for now?

I am Louis Doxtader. Dealer in Outsider Art. After the wonderful concert we all gathered backstage in the hospitality tent. I didn't tell Selena what Floss had told Walter before the show, the rape, the drugs, the mystery of who the father might have been.

Of course the last thing I wanted to do was encourage any more discussion of what might have happened at that wedding.

But I was aware that Walter was giving Selena very dirty looks.

Maud was standing with her arm around Molly, who really did have many of Floss's features. Could Molly really be MY daughter? I had always thought at the height of my heroin use that I probably had no sperm. I could hardly get an erection back then.

Around the tent, laughter was breaking out as it does on such occasions after a performance. It always feels too loud, too raucous, the sound of people who want to let go at last and have fun; the sound of musicians and technicians, managers and agents who are relieved the show is over, everyone is safe, and the ship may sail again. Glasses clinked, corks popped. From somewhere in the marquee the smell of very strong marijuana wafted over. It was now my turn to keep a firm grip on Selena. I wanted to kill her as much as I wanted to fuck her. Then suddenly she pulled herself free of me and began jumping up and down in very small leaps, fists clenched.

'I have to tell them,' she said.

'Tell them what?' I was starting to panic all over again.

'What you did,' she said, looking at me with her brow furrowed.

I looked her directly in the eyes in order to plead with her, my hands gripping her forearms so tightly she grimaced.

'Everything that's wrong with you now,' she spluttered, 'is all because of this. Set yourself free.'

I was terrified. I could feel the urgency of the moment in her, see it rising in her eyes. I knew if I didn't stop her, she would move quickly. She had to win. I had always been a manipulator and had interfered in the lives of others, but I knew by now I had met my match. Selena was the arch-manipulator.

I protested: 'I'm Walter's godfather. It was years ago. For fuck's sake,' I snapped, 'it sounds to me as though you were the only one who was conscious!'

But this threw Selena into a fit of rage. 'No, Louis!' she cried and everyone in the tent looked over at us.

I tried to pull her closer to me, so she would speak more quietly. She hissed, 'I saw you and Floss together. I saw her pull you down on to her. I saw her kissing you hungrily. She was not innocent.'

As Floss and Walter looked at each other wondering exactly what was going on, Selena grabbed my hair angrily, pulling my head from side to side. She started sobbing.

'Please' – my voice sounded pleading now, pathetic and whining – 'if you know, you've known for so long. Why must you break the news now, when everyone has been through so much? Let this be our secret.'

Selena seemed to quieten down for a few beats. Then she smiled that slightly crazy, conspiratorial grin of hers; her blue-green Irish eyes shone, her all-seeing third eye blinked at me, and her angelic witchery caught fire.

'But it's no secret, Louis,' she whispered, laughing. 'Soon after the wedding I told Siobhan. And there are other secrets you should know, secrets about your wife and daughter.'

'I'm not ashamed,' I said loudly, 'that Rain lived with Siobhan. I don't mind that they were lovers.'

She laughed. 'Siobhan was fucking your *wife*,' she said in a piercing tone. 'Not your daughter. That's why you could never track her down, never find her.'

Everyone within earshot at the party was looking at us again. Could they hear? I thought probably not. Siobhan was standing with Pamela and Rain by a long table at the far end of the room. Its white tablecloth was covered with bottles, glasses and buckets of ice. I felt like the clumsy, possibly evil, fool I knew I was in

Selena's eyes. I realised how stupid the notion had been: Pamela, the ginger-headed sex machine, would never have survived for a month as a nun. For some reason, this made me smile: good old Pamela. As I grinned, the guests who had been watching me all turned back to their conversations, assuming that whatever had blown up had blown away.

Perhaps aware of the attention we had been attracting, Selena suddenly broke away and bolted towards the toilets; as she ran she looked as if she were trying to wave invisible mosquitoes out of her hair.

She left me standing alone in the throng. Walter, I saw, was talking to Molly and she was obviously thrilled to have him in her family, even as a stepfather. There was an older couple with her, and from their uneasiness I guessed they must be her adoptive parents.

It took me a few minutes to work through the questions to which I needed answers. Had Pamela really told Rain that I was a rapist? Was that conceivable? If so how could she have left me to look after Rain?

Had Rain ever told Floss?

Floss had never given any hint of knowing . . .

I stood there, still alone in the middle of the room. Selena reappeared and stood at some distance looking at me sternly, a bright lamp shining up to the roof framing her hair in a halo. Dreams were converging again in my head. Again I thought I might go mad.

Selena must have seen my terror, and moved to my side and impulsively wound her arm through my own. She locked me down.

'I saw you carry her to the sofa,' she said. 'We were all tucked away in that arbour in the garden.'

An icy hand grasped my heart. She was simply picking up where she left off. I could hardly breathe.

'I heard Floss say you were a very attractive older man, then she pulled you down to kiss her. Not entirely your fault given the circumstances. I didn't want to watch. I left you both to get on with it.'

I was shaking, overcome with a mixture of nausea and anxiety so powerful that I knew if heroin had been available to me at that instant I would have taken it.

'Attractive older man!' She was scoffing now, teasing me, but held my arm tightly to her bosom even so.

'You got it up all right, Louis,' she whispered closely in my ear. 'You made her pregnant.'

It wasn't possible. That's all I could think. I couldn't speak. I felt lost in a deluge of shame and misery. Then the atmosphere was broken. Walter was about to make a speech.

'Friends!' He shouted at first, then one of the crew gave him a microphone. The rabble in the tent all calmed down and focused. He continued.

'Many wonderful things happened to me tonight. I have been back on stage with my old friends from the Stand.'

There was a loud cheer.

'Together we have performed the most difficult piece of music, something none of us ever thought we could ever do. And the images and inspiration came directly from the audience, my soundscapes, that you all – and especially my dad, Harry – brought to life.'

Another huge cheer. Harry and Sally were holding on to each other as though they were on a sinking ship but still smiling. Sally kept looking at me, and I thought I saw her shaking her head slightly.

Walter went on: 'And then Floss and I had the most incredible piece of luck when the daughter she gave away for adoption when she was nineteen years old turned out to be our Molly from Dingwalls!'

There was then an immense roar of delight from all the assembled VIP fans who had attended as special guests, and the friends, family and crew members in particular joined in. Molly had always been popular.

Frank Lovelace gave Molly a hug, no doubt taking credit for starting her career as a lighting engineer. Walter and Floss brought Molly in between them as their friends all started to take pictures.

Then there was a shout.

'So who *was* the father, Floss?' It was Selena.

She had stepped forward, towards the centre of the tent. So perhaps her machinations, her subterfuges, were not all about me? Did she still hate the idea of Floss having married Walter, the man who had always been her number one?

'Do you even know?' Selena demanded furiously.

Everyone in the marquee went quiet. I froze with fear. There was a ripple of muttered outrage; everyone was clearly bitterly angry with Selena. Some people started to berate her loudly.

'Selena!' Siobhan shouted. 'Just stop! Stop this now!'

Frank rushed over and started to manhandle her out of the tent. I interceded.

'No, Frank,' I insisted. 'Let me handle this.'

I put my hand in the air and walked over to Walter and took the microphone from him.

I was about to confess. I hadn't really thought it through, but the impulse to say something was very powerful. As I took a deep breath, and the people in the tent began to turn to me, I noticed Ronnie approaching me. Usually so handsome and powerful-looking, he seemed shrivelled, his skin pallid, his gait uneven, his skin not bronzed but yellow. Did he have AIDS? Cancer? What could possibly be wrong with him? He reached me, gently took the microphone from my hand, and turned to the audience.

'I am this young woman's father, I believe.' Ronnie was laughing now. He looked relieved and happy, tottering on his high heels, his face covered in thick make-up; he wore black mascara, blusher on his cheeks, bright red lipstick and his hair was clipped up with a pink clasp. He pulled Molly to his side, and stood next to her. 'Look at her. She's totally beautiful. And she's probably gay, bless her. *I'm* her father.'

I almost collapsed. I was literally seeing stars, my vision was flashing and I felt unsteady. Had I been saved?

Molly was a tomboy. Ronnie had recently emerged as a cross-dresser. Man, woman, woman, man. Both of them looking exactly as they felt they should, as they felt they were deep inside. Ronnie took it all with aplomb. They met somewhere in the middle. Their faces were almost identical. Was Ronnie right? A DNA test might prove it. A frisson of latent violence suddenly gripped the room, as Walter advanced towards Ronnie. Crow went to stop him but Walter turned on Crow and made to throw a punch. Frank stepped in and, to everyone's astonishment, held Crow and Walter apart by their collars like squabbling kids in a playground. Walter tore himself away abruptly and lunged at Ronnie, throwing a meaty punch that knocked his victim to his knees.

This time Frank and Crow leapt in together to contain Walter, but Ronnie was actually laughing, blood pouring from a cut on his lip. Now two huge gymed-up security guards stepped in, and tried to take control. They pulled everyone apart.

Molly seemed moved to have Floss for a mother and maybe gay Ronnie for a father. She was beaming like one of her own follow-spots and light was streaming around the two of them, mother and daughter.

Despite the post-concert gaiety that had prevailed earlier, despite the aura of light surrounding Molly, poor pale-faced Ronnie, bruised and battered, was being circled by some of the guests, chiding him. Some were still very angry. But Molly put herself between them and the fighting was over. I could see Floss was clearly not happy about what Ronnie was admitting; Walter still looked edgy, still ready to fight. He brushed himself down after the fracas. He had recently been disabused of his notion that his wife and her business partner had been conducting a relationship for years, and now here was Ronnie – that very partner – almost bragging about having impregnated Floss when they were both using hard drugs laid on by me, his godfather. Albeit many years before, it was not something he felt deserved such an outburst of flip levity among the backstage guests. As for a violent outburst, if anyone should be angry, and get out of line, it should be him.

'Oh darling,' said Ronnie. He was lying in a heap on the floor and holding his face. 'Forgive me, sweetheart. Really.' He turned to Walter. 'And Walter, I'm sorry, my friend. I'm all carried away.'

From his position on the floor, Ronnie put his arms out to Floss; he looked like a spurned child reaching out to his mother after some minor misdemeanour. Maud took pity on him, and knelt by his side.

'Darling Floss,' Ronnie croaked. 'You won't remember us having sex. It was rape. I'm so sorry. You were completely out of it, but you did enjoy it, I'm sure of that. Not sure I did.'

He started cackling again, like a music-hall queen. He tried to get to his feet, but was clearly still dizzy. Then he lay back gracefully into Maud's arms like La Dame aux Camélias. No one in the room seemed to want to listen to him. Everyone turned away.

Ronnie addressed Walter. 'Dammit, Walter,' he said, shifting his sore jaw from side to side and managing to rise on to one elbow. 'I'm such a dork. I should have kept this back until a quieter time, but I'm so excited to be a daddy.'

He laughed again, and Walter attempted to laugh with him, but he still looked angry.

'Walter,' pleaded Ronnie, 'forgive me, will you? Floss was the only girl I ever had sex with. We love each other. We always have since school, but we have only ever touched each other that once. And that shit Louis gave us was so powerful I really don't think it should count.'

This justification energised him, and he got to his feet.

He turned to Floss. 'You!' He threw up his hands, and with his high heels he must have been at least six feet four inches in height. Wobbling slightly, he said:

'Floss, you never told me you had become pregnant.' He was trying to look downcast, but he couldn't hide his joy for very long. He turned to Molly and hugged her. 'I would have been glad to be a father to this beautiful young woman.'

'Ronnie,' chided Floss, 'I couldn't have told you. I didn't know who had had sex with me. I swear. I wasn't even sure I'd had sex until I realised I was pregnant.'

I didn't feel much like staying with the festivities. It was time for me to leave.

Looking back, I can only say that Selena must have cast some kind of spell over me. Every time I looked at her, she behaved as though she had simply been playing some kind of mad, mischievous game. The truth is probably that the pheromones were pouring from her all over again. All I could think about was that my life hadn't been destroyed and instead this eccentric and extraordinary woman was still by my side.

We were moving to leave, and no one tried to persuade us to stay. The fraudulent spell Selena had attempted to cast had failed, and she took my arm, held her head high, and with her free hand made little waves to anyone who caught her eye before walking out in a stately way, like a deposed French princess being led to the guillotine.

We walked through the park with some stragglers from the audience. When we got to the gates at Hyde Park Corner, we hailed a black taxi, and snuggled into the seat. My head was still reeling. I was relieved but didn't know whether to be angry or happy. As Selena sat back, her belly seemed swollen; she'd either eaten too many cakes or drunk too much bubbly or was again carrying too many angelic spirits. Now she embraced her tummy, and looked sideways at me. Fuck, she was so lovely. I hated her then, but she was still so lovely. She saw me looking at her belly.

'I have an angel here, that's what I am pregnant with – a beautiful angelic force. I will protect you.'

'Protect me!' I practically spat the retort. 'You've attempted to destroy me.'

'The entities occupying your body are already leaving,' she said. 'Can't you feel that?'

I thought about what she was saying. I had to admit that something was indeed happening to me, something strange. I felt in that instant as if the waking dreams I had been experiencing for the past few months were beginning to recede. My body felt calmer. I started to get a warm feeling. Not the 'Little Mother' of heroin, but something almost as good.

'Yes,' I admitted. 'I know you have healing powers, Selena. I just wish you weren't so fucking wicked.'

Chapter 23

Selena truly was a healer, the real thing. It was then that Selena properly captured me, ensnaring me, and she would hold me for ever.

The wine I had been drinking in the tent may also have contributed to what made me feel better, but she had been right. The whole time she'd been speaking to me, bringing me down, now building me up, she had held my right arm close to her bosom.

I could feel the swell of her breasts and the hardening of the nipple closest to me. She was seducing me. She had accused me of a rape only she had witnessed, then been outed as a fantasist if not an outright liar, and now she was seducing me. It was bizarre, but to be honest it was also a wonderful feeling. I can't say I felt normal again, but the anxiety and nausea receded to be replaced by a sense of something solid and reassuring in the pit of my stomach. I only ever feel that when I know for certain that the woman I am with is going to have sex with me.

So, I defend myself. I had never known, perhaps since the act itself, that I had tried to impose myself on Floss, if I had – or had she pulled me down on to her? Those two girls had been hard cases, even when they were younger. Spiritual twins, that's what they thought they were. But they were wild, intoxicating girls – no, they had been women. Truly they were. Worldly and fabulous is how they had seemed at Siobhan and Walter's wedding.

Playing at being bridesmaids. Stunning. But I had been so drugged, so insane, and so had they; and now here I am covering my arse again.

I had either lived for years in denial, or been unconscious of what I had done to Floss, Selena and Ronnie with my stupid drug-sharing. Either way, if it happened the way it seemed, it was the worst thing I had ever done to any human being, even if my godson's wife, this young woman I had groped and tried to kiss in drugged insanity, might never remember it.

I felt at least Selena knew the worst of me, and was forgiving me. Selena, who had stabbed her brute of a father to death, was forgiving me for what she had taken to be a terrible sexual assault against her best friend. I had to forgive her in return, otherwise the scales would collapse.

And so it must be clear now why this narrator felt the need to tell this story. It must also be obvious why I have struggled to keep Walter at the heart of it, and to bring the heroine of my tale – the beautiful Floss who it seems I so brutally abused one way or another – to the finale in all her glory as a mother reunited with her lost daughter. For I knew that as Walter and Floss moved on to their next chapter, my entire relationship with both of them would probably end. I hope readers of this story will understand even if they cannot forgive. This story is my penance to Floss, to Walter, to Pamela, to Rain, and to all the angels, entities and bed-head ghosts and drug-induced apparitions that had haunted my relationships with my most precious friends and family.

Yet all this insanity swirling around in my world had made me rich. The premiere of Walter K. Watts' Apocalyptic Soundscapes in Hyde Park was dedicated to the memory of Walter's mentor, and the founder of Hero Ground Zero, Nikolai Andréevich. It would help sell many pictures.

I come to the end of my story. Bingo is getting restless. Selena is calling from downstairs; she has made some lunch for us both. This house of ours in Grasse, that she looks after so beautifully, is a wonderful place. It has sunshine, breezes and in the distance a view of the sea. From the hills comes the smell of fir trees and pine cones. I suppose I am hiding here. Selena's version of what happened at the wedding will certainly become widely known. One day the police may turn up. Floss may visit to gaze into my eyes and try to see the truth. Or Walter will come to beat me up. Or Molly will want to meet the man who for a moment – before Ronnie interceded – was apparently willing to put his hand up to being her long-lost father and perhaps still could be a good godfather to her. The waiting is the worst part, not knowing. But I am not hiding from Walter or Floss, or from anyone else in my story. Neither am I hiding from angels or faces in the clouds or the bedhead. Not any more. Remember what I said at the beginning? *I don't want to be forgiven; I want to sense some balance. I can't change the past, but* neither can I allow a misunderstanding of the past to change the future. *After you've heard my story, you will be able to make up your own mind.*

You will now make up your mind, and I am afraid. Before we set off to come home to Grasse, Walter sent me a copy of the completed lyric he wrote before the show, the one I had found him writing. It seems to fit this moment.

A few more hours
And these lights go dark
For me
If not for you

I'll get no flowers
A fading spark
I see
Nothing I can do

And as you sit in judgement
I wait to disembark
This tale,
This trail
Goes dark . . .

A few more hours
Post your remark
It's free
Post your review

You're the superpowers
No question mark
Agree
And you are guilty too

And now you make your mind up
For you, it's all a lark
This tale,
This trail
Goes dark . . . so dark . . .

A few more hours
And the lights go dark

Today I am hiding from normal people like you, who will read my account of the life and career of my godson Walter Karel Watts, and his second wife Florence Agatha Spritzler, and you will judge me. You, who constantly feel fear and apocalyptic anxiety that cannot be described; you, who need Nik and Walter – indeed me as their narrator – to foretell your future.

You must learn to wait. The moment will come. Waiting is the black art of creativity, not inspiration. Be ready. Be alert. Always. And then when the moment comes, you will be waiting, and you will have nothing else to do, nothing better to do than to fall in love all over again. As I once was, you are the mirror of everyone around you. You are their conscience and their voice. Look to the future, whatever you see will come about, good and bad, it is inevitable. Look to the light.

Nikolai Andréevich. AKA Paul Jackson.

His advice to Walter

Chapter 24

I am Selena Collins. Dealer in angelic miracles. I bring you the Epilogue. Yes, yes, yes, Louis. Yours could have been a very nice ending. Very neat. Very high-toned. But let me complete the book. I remind everyone: without me none of this would ever have taken place. After the concert, which I admit was a wonderful event, and the chaos I caused at the after-show party, I was left with you. Sweet Louis. Rich Louis. Stupid Louis. I love you so much.

Louis, you drip, the police will never come. Floss will never come. Molly may indeed come. We have to wait for the DNA test after all. Walter may knock your teeth in one day, but it will do you good. You men can preen. See the 'Harvest'. Hear music. Make great art. Sell it. Sell your very souls if you wish. It is we witches who know the truth. We see what we see, and we see everything. What I can see, and know, and do, is beyond your understanding. You men.

The police will never come, the drug story is already old news; but even if the DNA test proves Ronnie is her father, one day Molly might come, and may want you – my beloved Louis – to be a godfather again. Because poor sick Ronnie won't be able to do what you, who are so rich and influential, could do for her. Did I lie? I saw what I saw. Yes, I saw you try to have sex with Floss at the wedding, and she would have done it, she was so smashed. Ronnie says you fell in a heap and he took your place. I believe you couldn't have fucked an inflatable doll let alone a real woman. Apparently Ronnie believes that too, that you could never even have got it up. But perhaps you could have done it. I don't know for sure, and you certainly don't know. The question of whether you fathered a child is less important than the fact you plied us with your drugs, and lost your mind and your moral compass. I still hold so many cards.

So you see this is my story, not yours, Louis. Floss is more my creation than yours. Floss was my ghostly twin; I was inside her all the way.

Why would I do all this? At the end of it all, surrounded by a hundred thousand angels that only Old Nik could ever see, I wanted to hold at least one good mortal man. I couldn't hold Walter, or Frank, or Crow, but I could hold the man called Louis Doxtader – and my darling I have held you. Louis, you addled your brain; Nik, you saw the Harvest; Crow, you listened to just six vinyl albums; Walter, you heard the anxiety of your peers.

I have dangled you all on strings.

Author's Postscript

This book was finally finished in May of 2013. I am sixty-eight years old. The world wobbles slightly on its axis, and even the most cavalier of us are a little anxious. I hope that this tortuous tale will one day form the basis for an opera, as Selena promised me. In the future, opera may look more like art-installation, or *Son et Lumière*, all wired into a global network of feedback and evolution. In that case – once the play is finished, the music ended and the racket is quiet – I hope that the appeal planted here for optimism, hope and appeasement among all the people of this fragile planet will begin to take root. The story is ended, but the idea behind it will continue to unfold and grow and hopefully conclude. We should not be afraid; we can have faith in our species.

We do not need to burn witches.